"DID YOU SEE IT?
DID YOU SEE THAT THING?!"

McCoy nodded. "I saw it."

Breath gusted out in an explosive sigh that shook her entire willow-thin frame. "Thank God! At least it wasn't my imagination." Her eyes searched his face. "Though I don't know which is worse— having it be my imagination or having it real. What *was* that thing, Dr. McCoy?"

He shook his head. "I don't know, Hallie. I thought I'd seen or read about nearly every strange thing in the galaxy, and I can't even make an educated guess."

"But it was real? You weren't just saying that to make me feel better?"

He managed to find a chuckle somewhere deep inside and draw it to the surface. "I almost wish I were, Ensign, but no. It was real."

Her eyes challenged him. "You said there were no ghosts, Dr. McCoy, but I think you're wrong. I think we both just saw our first. . . ."

Look for STAR TREK Fiction from Pocket Books

Star Trek: The Original Series

Star Trek: The Next Generation

Star Trek: Deep Space Nine

A VECES GANAR
TIENES QUE
CEDER.

STAR TREK®

SHELL GAME

MELISSA CRANDALL

POCKET BOOKS

New York London Toronto Sydney Tokyo Singapore

An *Original* Publication of POCKET BOOKS

POCKET BOOKS, a division of Simon & Schuster Inc. 1230 Avenue of the Americas, New York, NY 10020

Copyright © 1993 by Paramount Pictures. All Rights Reserved.

STAR TREK is a Registered Trademark of Paramount Pictures.

This book is published by Pocket Books, a division of Simon & Schuster Inc., under exclusive license from Paramount Pictures.

ISBN: 0-671-79572-4

First Pocket Books printing February 1993

10 9 8 7 6 5 4 3 2 1

Printed in the U.S.A.

This book has a two-fold dedication:

First, it's for my niece Leslie Danielle Cootware (1964–1989), who, with her life and death, taught me everything I'll ever need to know about dignity. Carpe diem, kid.

Secondly (but no less sincerely), it's for those who have helped along the way, whether or not they know it:

JoAnn and Bruce Baasch—for saving my life.

Keith Birdsong—for his *BAD* jokes.

Eric Halter, the Jessup Family, Barbara Maxwell, Rise Shamansky, and Pam Spurlock—for their encouragement.

Anna, Brian, Connor, Debbie, Uncle Gunnar, Jim, Jon, Jorik, Maeve, Michael, and Scott—new friends, all.

Bob Greenberger—for being the best dip in the world.

Michael Henigan—for keeping me humble.

DeForest Kelley—for bringing life to my favorite physician.

Howard and Virginia Limbacher—for 35 years of vested interest.

Kevin MacKrell—for his friendship and music.

Paul and Antoinette O'Donnell—for their friendship and occasional employment.

The Parting Glass—everyone's home away from home.

Michelle and Tim Perkins—for bringing me home.

JoAnn Quinones—for returning that which was lost.

Kristin Rooke—for 26 years and counting.

Kevin Ryan—my editor at Pocket, for challenging me, improving me, and encouraging me.

Scott Shannon, Kevin's assistant—for answering every

Melissa Crandall

question with grace and humor, and for putting up with my changing this dedication a billion times.

Arne Starr—for being my best friend.

Howard Weinstein—for helping to make my first professional convention so much fun.

SHELL GAME

Prologue

WAITING HIS TURN in the *Elizsen's* transporter room, Rinagh suddenly felt his legs grow shaky. He locked back his knees, willing the tremors away. The last thing he needed was to collapse like some swooning character in a melodrama. Nonchalantly, his eyes flicked briefly around the room, checking to see if any of the other Romulans crowding the area had noticed.

It didn't appear they had, and it wasn't likely they would in any case. They, like he, had more important things on their minds. Rinagh read their body language as easily as he read a medical reference manual. He recognized the shifting, the clenched hands, and the tight, short bursts of nervous laughter as company to his own swirl of emotions. What they began here this day would sing through the annals of Romulan history for all time and make the rest of the galaxy finally sit up and take notice.

It seemed almost impossible that this well-tended

Melissa Crandall

and long-nurtured dream had finally borne fruit only a few days earlier. . . .

He was in the clinic when the news came. Though largely retired from active medical practice, Rinagh still enjoyed maintaining a small clientele by tending to the needs of patient families he'd administered to throughout the years. He was too much of a doctor to retire outright. The itch to keep active was pervasive, like an incurable skin disorder.

So he was doing just that, tending to the grandson of a longtime patient, when his wife, Elani, poked her head around the doorjamb.

"Rinagh? I'm sorry to interrupt, but there's a call for you."

He didn't look up, just kept winding the bandage around Aifor's forearm and talking quietly to the youngster. "This is going to keep happening if you continue to persist in playing near knifeweed." When he answered her, his voice did not break its gentle cadence. "Elani, please tell whoever it is to hold on. I'll be right with them in a minute."

"I don't think it can wait."

He looked up at her then, his attention completely caught. Elani had been his nurse before she was his wife, and he knew and respected her judgment better than anyone's. She would never have used that particular phrase unless she felt it was completely warranted. He read her expression and paused in his ministrations, his hand wavering uncertainly over the half-wrapped bandage. There was a particular look in her eyes he'd learned to appreciate.

"I see." He nodded. "All right, then." Nervousness abruptly fluttered in his stomach, like an insect beating its wings between his hands. Rinagh covered it by patting the boy's shoulder. "I need to take an impor-

2

tant call, Aifor. Elani will finish wrapping this for you."

"Yes sir."

"Good boy." He waved an admonishing forefinger under the boy's nose. "But no more playing near knifeweed." Rinagh smiled reassuringly and tried not to hurry too quickly out of the examining room. He crossed the hall to his office, closed the door behind him, and sat down behind the communications console on his desk.

Nervousness sprang into full bloom when Kashi's handsome face appeared on the screen. The first thing Rinagh noticed was the excitement in the dark eyes of the young Romulan officer. The second was the brand-new insignia pinned over the left breast of Kashi's black uniform. It shone like a newly minted coin, and Rinagh could hardly tear his eyes away. "Kashi! By all the Hells—! You *got* it, didn't you? You got the commission!"

One hand swept gently over the golden polyhedron bars, and Kashi's head dipped in a brief nod. "I just came from the proconsul's office." Sheer emotion drew a joyous laugh from the usually staid Romulan. "Rinagh, you're looking at the commander of the new Romulan space station *Reltah!*"

The doctor leaned back in his chair and stared in amazement. *"Excellent,* Kashi! Congratulations!"

"Thank you." Kashi couldn't hold back an expectant grin, even if he'd been inclined to try, which Rinagh doubted. "And *I'm* looking at the station's newly appointed chief physician."

It was one of those moments in time when the entire world around one comes to a standstill. It was a moment before Rinagh remembered to breathe. "You— You're joking." He shook his head. "You *must* be joking. There are other men, *younger* men—"

"But none with your background and abilities," Kashi avowed. "The proconsul and the Senate confirmed it for me after my appointment. Our Lady seems very pleased that you're going to be a part of this endeavor. She expressed the greatest confidence in your contribution to the success of the project. She made it quite clear that she's expecting great things from this venture." He winked somberly, only half joking, for the proconsul's wishes and expectations were never to be taken lightly. "Let's make certain we don't disappoint her."

"I'll endeavor to do my best," Rinagh promised breathlessly.

"I don't doubt that for a moment, my friend." Kashi glanced away and nodded at someone off-screen, then looked back. "I have a lot to do and my time is short, so I'll make this quick and speak to you in more detail later. Now that the proconsul has assigned personnel to the station, she wants us aboard *Reltah* as soon as possible. A transport will pick you up this evening—"

"This evening!?"

Kashi pretended not to notice the physician's discomfort. "—and convey you to the capital city, where we will be shuttled to the *Elizsen,* the ship that will take us to the station." He held up a hand apologetically, forestalling any interruptions. "I know this is abrupt, Rinagh, but we must move swiftly if we hope to gain any upper hand over the hold the Federation and its cursed Starfleet have on the galaxy." Kashi's eyes were serious now, brooking no argument. He had been made commander of the space station and their mission, and commander he would be, starting now. "The majority of your possessions will be shipped

4

later, when Elani comes to join you. Bring only those personal effects you want or need. I'll see you in a few hours." He cut the connection without saying goodbye.

And that was that. Rinagh stared at the blank screen, shaky hands splayed atop his thighs, his mind fighting the desire to run in six different directions at once. On the one hand, he wanted to laugh with excitement. At the same instant, he wanted to hide under the couch like one of Elani's pets and forget that he ever had the temerity to apply for a coveted position at his advanced age. In the space of a few heartbeats, he had gone from being a contented, semiretired doctor with a tiny practice to fill his declining years, to the chief physician of a project the likes of which the Romulan Empire had never before undertaken.

And here he stood now, with the others who would make the proconsul's and the Senate's dreams come true. What in the name of all the Blue Hells had possessed him to apply for this job, it was far too late to back down now, whatever his personal fears. He knew he could do whatever the job required. He had the experience and the knowledge, and he'd been fortunate enough to have one of the more distinguished medical careers on Romulus.

But I'm an old man, he thought fleetingly. *Certainly too old to be picking up my entire life and heading for the stars.*

The stars. Until Kashi's call, they were the stuff of nursery chants to his grandchildren. Since coming aboard *Elizsen,* they had become a daily, wondrous vista a hand's breadth beyond the ship's lounge. No, he'd trade his place with no one, Romulan or alien, fears or no fears.

His foot tapped against the small carryall on the

floor between his feet. Kashi had said to bring only what he felt he needed, and inside were the few baubles of personal sentimental value in which he allowed himself to indulge: a hand-sized painting of his family, two medical awards conferred upon him by his peers several years earlier, and a carefully preserved book of real paper, page after page filled with his tiny, cramped penmanship.

The diary was an affectation he allowed himself and shared with no one. Not even Elani, whom he trusted in all things, knew of its existence, chiefly because he found it slightly embarrassing. Logs and diaries were meant for computers, for the daily roll of life and duty. This small book was something entirely different, something he would have been hard put to explain to anyone. Rinagh was not even altogether certain himself why he felt such a deep desire to put his feelings, thoughts, and dreams into written words, only that doing so gave him a sense of peace and completion that nothing else ever had, not even his pursuit of medicine.

"Next group, please." The transporter technician's voice brought Rinagh out of his reverie as those ahead shouldered their packs and stepped onto the transporter platform. Two more groups and it would be his turn.

His eyes sought the large screen over the transporter console. *Reltah* looked like a jewel flung against a patina of stars. The big station reflected the brilliant starlight, glowing like a star itself and champion of those lesser lights.

The first of her kind, the station was a radical step forward for a race so long imbued in tradition and form, and so much more conservative compared to the galaxy's other conquering races. In ages past, Romulans were content to use their home worlds as a common base of operations. But with the continued advance of Humanity into the galaxy, the Romulans found themselves forced to readjust their way of thinking. They could no longer remain blindly content with one center, one hub. They must endeavor to be as rapacious as the growing hoard of infesting Humans, or never hope to survive as a people.

Hence, they followed the Humans' unwitting lead and built what they had every confidence would be the first of many such space stations throughout Romulan territory. In ages to come, how far might they venture? Perhaps the Humans, and the Klingons too, would one day know of reckoning and destruction, servitude and death.

In anticipation of that grand event, they now stood on the brink of taking control of the station for the very first time. In the ensuing weeks, these administrative officers and their crews would bring *Reltah* up to running trim and prepare for the arrival of those others who would pump further life into the station's arterial corridors. After that would come the ships, glorious vessels of Romulan pride that would dock here and clarion to the rest of the galaxy the bright power and promise of the Romulan Empire! Then the others would come, every race eager to partake of what the Romulans could offer in their bid for supremacy. The thought made Rinagh's skin tingle, and his heart grew tight in his chest with an upswelling of pride and satisfaction.

"Doctor?" Rinagh brought his eyes down, and the transporter chief gave him a tiny smile. "Your turn, sir."

"Thank you." He picked up his pack and joined the others of his group on the transporter platform. Eyes forward, he waited in the rising hum from the pad beneath his feet. There was a slight sense of disorientation and a moment's deprivation of the senses, then, abruptly, Rinagh found himself blinking at an unfamiliar wall and knew they'd made a successful transport to the space station.

He followed the others off the transporter pad, joining the excited exodus out the door and along the corridors in dispersal to duty stations. When the doctor's feet hit the decking for the first time, a thrill of anticipation shuddered up his legs, and he grinned with excitement. Oh, they were going to do wonderful things here, and the Federation be damned!

Chapter One

"THE CREW OF THE *St. Brendan* cautiously followed Captain Loughran over the railing and onto the derelict vessel they had discovered. The *Stephanie Emilia*'s sails hung unfurled overhead, the wide sheets of heavy canvas motionless in the still air. Ropes lay neatly coiled on deck, and everything appeared to be in order, but the wheel was unattended and there wasn't a crewman to be seen.

"Captain Loughran's men shifted nervously. An empty ship hadn't been what they'd expected to find when they spied the *Stephanie Emilia* moving as though a drunk were at the helm, and their hands tightened nervously around the truncheons they carried. The captain was likewise unnerved, but, being a sailor of long history, he did not intend to show fear to his men when there was likely a reasonable explanation for the *Emilia*'s abandonment.

"Pirates might have been at the vessel, he thought, but there were no signs of struggle. Perhaps the crew

9

had been overturned and were confined below, locked in the hold, or been made to walk the plank. Maybe they'd mutinied and left the ship altogether. Standing out on deck wouldn't discover the truth, so Loughran raised his chin bravely and called out in a strong voice, 'Is anyone here?' The heavy air swallowed his words like muffling cloth, and there was no reply."

Chief Engineer Montgomery Scott paused to run a calculating eye over his audience. The Scotsman looked as though he were thoroughly enjoying himself. Certainly, his audience was having fun—every available chair in the *Enterprise*'s rec room was taken. The crew had also found other perches on counters and gaming tables, or sat cross-legged on the floor.

Seated at a corner table, his chair tipped back on two legs against the wall, Doctor Leonard McCoy basked in a warm and lazy sense of complete contentment brought on by the fact that he'd beaten Jim Kirk three games out of four in Riseaway. The antigrav game was hard and strenuous, and Kirk was a worthy opponent, but McCoy had gained the upper hand this evening and put a spin on his ball that pleasantly trounced the captain right down to his boot tops. It wasn't often he got one over on Kirk, and the doctor smiled with satisfaction as his gaze drifted over the assembled crew.

Most of those present he recognized from the pictures in their med files, particularly those who had just recently come aboard, as he had only that day finished reading all the profiles. Some he knew by name from frequent encounters in the big ship's corridors, and there were the special few he felt comfortable calling his friends. Everyone was caught up in the chief engineer's tale, their eyes glued to the Scotsman, and more than one sat with mouth hung slightly open, raptly awaiting the rest of the tale. Their expressions reminded McCoy of those of little children at bedtime, and he smiled at the special memory evoked.

"Nervous sweat stuck Captain Loughran's shirt to his back like a second skin," Scotty resumed. "The heat was oppressive, and with it came the rising stink of fear from his men. He drew a long cutlass from his belt and held it at the ready. 'You men'—he pointed to several of his crew. 'Stand watch here. The rest come with me.' He crossed the deck with his unhappy followers close behind. Their footfalls sounded hollowly on the boards of the sunbleached deck, and they stepped into the darkened stairway leading below to a stygian darkness.

"Loughran waited quietly a moment, listening, every sense alert. At a gesture, one of the crew struck flint and tinder, lit an oil lamp, and passed it forward. The captain's fingers closed tightly around the thin metal handle, and he held the lamp aloft as he slowly descended the steep stairway into the hold.

"The darkness seemed to fight the advance of light, but Loughran would not be defeated. He pressed forward, his crew close behind. The flickering lamplight lit the planes of Loughran's rough face with amber, highlighting the deep creases around his eyes and the lurid scar across one cheek.

"The corridor belowdecks was empty in the circle of light thrown by the lamp. Loughran tried to swallow and found he couldn't. Silently cursing his fear, he moved forward and called out again. 'Is anyone here? Is there anyone below?' Silence. He continued down the long, dark passage and called out once more. Still he received no reply. It was eerily quiet in the hold. No creaking of the rigging reached them deep within the ship's belly. They could not hear the sigh of ocean waves caressing the outer hull, and even the ever-present rats were quiet, staring with reddish, hateful eyes as the crew passed by.

"A roughly carved sign over a broad door identified the room beyond as Captain Beppe's quarters. It was a name they all recognized, for Marco Beppe was reputed to be the fiercest pirate ever to plunder Italy's coastline. Rumor had it he'd scuttled his last ship, drowning half his crew in the process, rather than have her spoils taken. What his new vessel was doing, adrift and unmanned off the coast of Scotland, was anybody's guess.

"Loughran pounded against the door with the cutlass's heavy hilt. 'Captain Beppe? Are you there?' A sudden scream tore the silence beyond the closed door. Without thought of his own safety, Captain Loughran slammed his shoulder against the door and brought it crashing down. He rushed inside and stopped, frozen by what he saw."

The quintessential storyteller, Scotty paused here. McCoy bit back a grin and made himself resist the nearly unbearable temptation to yell *Boo!* and send better than a dozen crewmen flying into the air.

"A single whale-oil lamp lit the room. The chamber well befitted a pirate captain, with its heavy furniture and the walls hung with thick tapestries. Books bound in leather and a king's ransom in jewels lay strewn across the floor. An ornate wooden table occupied the center of the room, its surface covered with plates of hot food, and seated with his back to the door was a curly-headed giant of a man.

"Captain Loughran approached him. 'Captain Beppe?' When there was no reply, he reached out and gingerly touched the man's shoulder. It was as hard and cold as rock. Rounding the table to face him, Loughran's heart hammered. It was Captain Beppe or, rather, it had been, for the pirate was dead. His fingers were hooked like claws and had driven deep yellow furrows into the tabletop. His wide eyes showed white all around and stared out of his head in terror at whatever had been his last sight. His mouth gaped in a silent scream, the tendons in his neck stretched beyond endurance. They covered him with a sheet from the bed and continued on, but the rest of their exploration revealed nary another soul aboard that ship, and never a sign of whatever or whoever killed Captain Beppe."

Scotty's bright eyes gauged his audience carefully, and his voice lowered confidentially before he continued. "They buried Beppe at sea. But during the voyage home, as the *St. Brendan* towed the hapless *Stephanie Emilia* toward safe harbor in Scotland, insane laughter was often heard from her vacant deck. The laughter of the damned."

After a moment of silence, a shuddering sigh rippled through the assembled crowd. Several people rubbed their arms hard and exchanged nervous laughter. Uhura and Sulu grinned appreciatively at their friend's story.

Seated across from McCoy, Jim Kirk glanced at the doctor with a tired smile and winked. "Commander Scott, do you enjoy giving my crew the heebie-jeebies?"

The chief engineer smirked at his captain, and his cheeks dimpled until he looked like a Scottish kewpie doll. His eyes danced with delight. "T'was only a wee ghost story, sir," he replied innocently.

"Wee?" Ensign Hallie's voice raised in objection from the next table over, but her tone and look were both teasing. "I don't know about the rest of you, but here's *one* security guard"—she stuck a thumb

against her chest—"who's sleeping with a night-light on!" Several other personnel laughed with enthusiastic agreement and applauded.

"Wonderful, Scotty," McCoy drawled. "Now I'll have to prescribe sleep inducers to half the crew and psychological counseling for night frights to the other half. I guess there's no rest for the wicked." He had thoroughly enjoyed the story. It recalled fondly remembered nights around a campfire at his uncle's place in the Adirondack Mountains of northern New York State, nights he'd spent buried deep inside his sleeping bag with a flashlight as comfort against the dark and the frightening sounds of night-prowling creatures.

Kirk joined in the friendly laughter generated by the doctor's remark. "All this time, Scotty, I thought you spent every evening holed up in your quarters with a good technical manual," the captain teased. "Now I discover you while away your time giving the crew the willies."

Commander Scott's expression was the picture of injured pride, and McCoy thought, not for the first time, that the stage had lost a great actor when Montgomery Scott took up his chosen field of engineering. "I don't want you to think I'm neglecting my duties, Captain Kirk," he said forthrightly. "I keep abreast of all the current engineering literature." Humor twinkled in the depths of his eyes. "I only scare the crew for recreational purposes."

This comment elicited more robust laughter and incited Uhura to lob a wadded napkin in the chief engineer's general direction.

"At least I'm assured you're getting your proper exercise," McCoy countered dryly. He grinned and stretched, shifted sideways, and crossed his legs. "Is that a true story, Scotty?"

"About the *Stephanie Emilia?* Aye, Dr. McCoy, that it is, though I'm not surprised you've not heard of her. She wasn't around a very long time, and she's more of a Scots legend than a tale for the history books." He sat back and crossed his legs, ready to begin another tale. "She was an Italian vessel of Spanish make back in the sixteen hundreds. Captain Beppe was her sole master for her short life, and in his time didn't he create quite a stir along the Italian seaboard with one ship and another!" Scott leaned forward, warming to his lecture. "I saw a painting of him once, in a museum in Edinburgh. He was the very picture of a storybook brigand, with his size and curly dark hair and beard, but there was no touch of romance in the reality of him. He's said to have had the soul of a heartless monster, and by all accounts that's true.

"Be that as it may, shortly after the *St. Brendan* towed the *Stephanie Emilia* into the Firth of Tay in Scotland, Beppe's ship caught fire and burned to the waterline. As you can well imagine, there was all sorts of speculation on the cause of the blaze. Some accounts say the townsfolk considered the ship cursed and wanted her gone, so they fired her. Some say an unknown owner burned her for insurance money. Still others told stories as to how a large, shadowy figure was seen floating across her deck shortly before the fire began." Scott shrugged philosophically. "Whatever caused it, the *Stephanie Emilia* was certainly an unlucky vessel her entire short life."

"Reminiscent of the *Mary Celeste,*" Kirk commented.

Ensign Markson turned in his seat beside Hallie, round features alight with interest. "The *what,* sir?"

McCoy caught the tiny sigh that escaped his friend, and smiled slightly with sympathetic understanding. Maybe Starfleet cadets these days only dreamed of starships and planets to steer them by. Kirk was proud of his vessel and prouder still to be her master, but McCoy knew that deep in Kirk's heart there would always be the desire for salt-scented air and the sting of spray, tall ships, billowing sail, and the creak of tight rigging. McCoy had lost count of how often during their long friendship Kirk had admitted to a yearning for the bittersweet tang of the open sea and the roll and surge of breakers beneath his feet as the ship leapt from the crest of one wave to another.

Kirk turned to Markson. "The *Mary Celeste,* Ensign. She was a seagoing vessel on Earth, built in 1868 and captained by Benjamin Spooner Briggs. She left Staten Island on November 7, 1872. Aboard were Captain Briggs, his wife and two-year-old daughter, and several crewmen. Just short of one month later, on December 4, the ship was sighted by the *Dei Gratia.* Captain David Reed Morehouse reported finding the *Mary Celeste* under short sail and moving erratically. Upon receiving no reply to their hailing, he and his men went aboard to investigate, just as Captain Loughran did with the *Stephanie Emilia.* Not a single passenger was found."

"What happened to them, Captain?" Hallie asked, leaning around Markson, her eyes wide.

Kirk shrugged his broad shoulders in a manner that caught the attention of several of the women present. McCoy snorted and rolled his eyes. "No one knows for certain, Ensign, though there was certainly a lot of speculation at the time."

"Wait a minute," McCoy interrupted. He leaned forward, and his chair legs hit the floor. "Wasn't the *Mary Celeste* that ship where they found the captain's pipe still burning, food warm on the table, and the ship's cat sound asleep? That sounds a lot like Scotty's story."

"And it's a good story," Kirk agreed with a smile. "But that's exactly what it is, a story. The worst sort of yellow journalism to come out of that era. The final consensus in the investigation that followed the *Mary Celeste*'s return to port was that the load of alcohol the ship carried in her hold gave off enough fumes to cause an explosion. There were indications that at least one of the hold doors exploded outward off its hinges, and several feet of water was taken on in various areas of the ship. The general belief is that Captain Briggs, his family, and the crew feared a greater explosion would occur and sink the vessel, so they took to one of the lifeboats and abandoned the *Mary Celeste* to her fate. She put out in November off New England, remember. That isn't exactly the best of times in which to trust any boat to the vagaries of weather. No evidence of the missing lifeboat was ever found, and it is generally assumed that it capsized and all hands perished at sea."

"That's so sad," Uhura commented, and several people concurred.

Kirk glanced back at his communications officer and nodded in agreement. "It *is* sad, Commander, but it was the risk everyone took when putting out to sea at that time in history. Things weren't as safe as they are now, and those who chanced it knew they might not make it back. Whatever was their goal, they evidently thought it worth the risk. In many respects, it's the same risk you make in taking an active part in life, rather than just letting it happen to you." The corner of his mouth twitched upward in a half-smile. "Or in becoming a Starfleet officer."

"That's it!" Hallie vowed. "I knew I should have read that fine print more carefully."

"You and me both, Ensign," McCoy called out in agreement. He grinned at Kirk over the others' laughter. "See there, Commander Scott? There's a perfectly logical explanation for what happened to the *Mary Celeste,* so I'll bet the same is true of the *Stephanie Emilia.*"

"Dr. McCoy!" The chief engineer's tone spoke of grave wounds inflicted. His dark, silver-shot brows beetled together in an admonishing frown of utter disappointment. "There are more things in heaven and earth than are dreamt of in your philosophy. I'll grant you that it's anybody's guess what happened aboard the *Stephanie Emilia* to cause Captain Beppe's horrible death, but it's common knowledge among the Scots that every derelict vessel carries its haunt. It's practically a cosmic law. I can't believe you'd think I'd waste the crew's time telling them something that wasn't true!"

McCoy tipped his head with mock solemnity and raised his empty hand as though it held a glass. "My apologies, Commander Scott, if I inadvertently cast aspersions on the storytelling abilities of your regal, ancestral bloodline or your fine *true* tale." He feigned draining the drink, making the toast final.

Scott returned the salute and favored the doctor with a friendly wink.

"What about the drone we're going to retrieve, sir?" Ensign Markson queried of Kirk. "Lieutenant Chekov told me that it's been superfluous for a long time now and hasn't sent any data back to Earth for decades. Do you think that could be haunted, too?"

McCoy eyed the new ensign consideringly. Markson wasn't from Earth. According to his medical profile, he was born of Earth parents and raised on Vindali 5, whose natives had a very active belief in the supernatural. Even so, four years of the Academy's particular brand of pragmatism could practically knock the belief in *pon far* out of a Vulcan, and

Markson didn't look like he was about to go into trance or anything. His psyche scores had been particularly high.

"Right, Dan." Hallie jibed and poked her friend, then wiggled her fingers in front of his face, her eyes huge and her face contorted. "And all the little creepies and gobblies are going to come out and take control of the ship when we get the drone aboard!"

Markson grinned, slapping her spidery hands away, and McCoy spoke over the wave of laughter that greeted her ghost impersonation. "If what Commander Scott says is true, Ensign Markson, then the derelict shipyard in Tau Ceti should be jam-packed with more ghosts than you can shake a stick at, but I've never heard of any being reported."

"Maybe you can get reassigned to go out there and take a look, Dan," someone called from the back.

Markson glanced in Kirk's direction and, McCoy guessed, modified what he was going to reply to a simple, "No, thanks. I'll let you have the honor."

Further conversation was precluded by an interruption from the wall speaker. "Bridge to Captain Kirk."

Kirk leaned across the table and pressed the stud on the intercom with his thumb. "Kirk here."

"Captain, you wanted to be notified when we reached the drone. We are now within range."

"Understood. I'll be right there. Have Mr. Spock join me on the bridge. Kirk out." He shoved back his chair and stood, tugging his uniform straight. "Ladies and gentlemen—" He smiled, hands out apologetically. "It's been fun, but duty calls. Would you like to join me, Doctor?"

"Certainly, Captain." McCoy didn't even consider not accepting. His ex-wife had once observed that he liked sticking his nose into other people's business. He had retorted that he merely liked to be informed.

Kirk paused in the doorway with McCoy behind him and looked back at the gathering. "Commander Scott, let's see if you can find a more soothing sort of bedtime story for the crew, all right?"

Scott obediently looked abashed and nodded soberly. "Aye, sir. You have my word on it."

"I'll hold you to that, Mr. Scott," Kirk replied. "Come on, Bones."

McCoy followed him out of the room, the door closing on Scott's voice saying, "Now, then, children. Once upon a time . . ." Exchanging smiles, the two friends walked down the corridor to the nearest turbolift. Once inside, Kirk commanded, "Bridge," and the doctor felt a faint vibration as the lift began to move.

McCoy glanced at Kirk out of the corner of his eye, and one eyebrow rose marginally. The doctor quelled the desire to slap a hand across his forehead. He hadn't even been aware that his eyebrow arched until Uhura laughingly pointed it out to him one day. It was just what he needed—a personal quirk to remind him of Spock! "You look tired."

Kirk's eyes slid toward him. "I ought to, staying up half the night playing Riseaway with you, you old horse thief! What have you been doing, practicing on the sly?"

The doctor buffed his nails on the front of his uniform. "Some of us are just born with an innate talent."

Kirk snorted. "Oh, I won't deny that, but I don't think it's Riseaway you have an innate talent for. You're not a good influence, Doctor," he said sternly. "I was supposed to be getting some sleep, not floating around in zero-gee getting my socks knocked off by a con man. Are you sure there aren't any riverboat gamblers in your bloodline?"

"I make no promises as to that, Captain. But don't go blaming me for your poor judgment," McCoy teased.

"How's that?" Kirk raised his eyebrows.

"I didn't twist your arm to come out and play. You could always have said no."

"And miss Scotty's story afterward?" Kirk huffed. "Not likely."

"I didn't think so." McCoy laughed and shook his head. "You know, he's probably better for the psychological well-being of the crew than anything else I know."

"How do you figure that?" Kirk asked curiously.

McCoy folded his arms and leaned against the wall. "Mankind has been telling ghost stories to itself practically since we crawled out of the primordial ooze and gathered around the first campfire to let the mud flake off. Scaring the bejesus out of ourselves serves a real purpose, not the least of which is drawing us together as a community against the unknown. It hasn't hurt us and, in a lot of ways, it's helped us. It's part of the culture that's made us what we are. The ones who were brave enough to test the tales are the ones who got us onto the high seas and into space." McCoy eyed him. "I'll bet your grandfather told you ghost stories."

"Now that you mention it"—Kirk smiled—"he did."

"Thought so," McCoy retorted.

The turbolift doors opened and they exited onto the bridge. Spock was already there and at his station. He looked up as they entered, and nodded fractionally. "Captain. Doctor."

"Spock." Kirk nodded distractedly to the rest of the night-watch bridge crew. His eyes sought the viewscreen even before he lowered himself into his seat at the conn, with McCoy taking his customary place behind him. Kirk pointed to a small irregularity, unfamiliar against the pattern of well-known constellations. "Is that the drone?"

"Yes, sir," answered the ensign at helm.

"Magnify."

The image on the screen immediately grew in size and was unmistakably the gawky, antiquated piece of scientific equipment. It looked like a mechanical eggplant. An antenna lay skewed against one side, and from another side protruded a stump where most of another antenna had been sheared away in some ancient accident. The drone looked dead and lifeless and totally outmoded.

"Well, that's it," Kirk said. "It's hard to believe that something that archaic helped get us where we are today."

"See any ghosts, Mr. Spock?" McCoy queried brightly, glancing over his shoulder at the first officer.

Spock's eyebrow rose. "Doctor?" he questioned.

Kirk waved a hand without turning around. "Ignore him, Spock. He's only trying to cause trouble."

"I see." Spock inclined his head politely. "There is something to be said for the steadfastness of certain archaic structures."

McCoy felt confused. "Is he talking about the drone or have I just been insulted?" he asked.

Kirk suppressed a smile. "You've got me. Ensign Devin, commence drone retrieval procedure. Lock on tractor beam. I want that thing safely stowed in cargo bay twelve."

"Aye, sir."

Kirk watched confidently as the drone was slowly drawn closer by the tractor beam.

"Ugly sucker, isn't it?" McCoy commented. "Nothing like our *Enterprise.*"

"Not much, Bones, no. But in some respects, that outdated mechanism is our ship's ancestor."

"I guess it's true what they say. You can't pick your relatives."

Point of view switched as other hull cameras came into play, following the drone as it passed out of their direct line of sight and down around the ship. In a few moments Ensign Devin turned, clearly proud of his job. "Drone safely on board, Captain. Pressure is stabilized and crew are securing it in bay twelve."

"Well done, Ensign. Lay in a course for—"

"Captain." Spock's voice interrupted him. "I am picking up a reading on a large object just entering sensor range, bearing mark 0703.54."

"Identification?"

"Unknown."

The line of Kirk's shoulders tensed beneath the ruddy burgundy of his uniform jacket. "We're damned close to the Romulan Neutral Zone," he murmured. "Go to yellow alert and let's have a look at it."

The annoying klaxon began its familiar cry. The strident shrilling set McCoy's teeth on edge, and he stepped closer to the conn, resting one hand on the back of the chair.

Kirk glanced fleetingly at his friend, then the captain's eyes narrowed speculatively as the image came onto the screen. At this distance, it didn't look like much. "Magnify."

The bridge crew stared silently at the unexpected image now on the screen. Even Spock seemed to be momentarily struck dumb, trying to comprehend what it was they were looking at.

McCoy had no such handicap. He leaned over Kirk, his arm brushing the captain's shoulder, and thrust one finger at the viewscreen. "What the hell is *that?*"

Chapter Two

McCoy DIDN'T REALLY expect an answer to his question, so he wasn't disappointed when one wasn't immediately forthcoming. Like the others, he stared at the viewscreen and tried to puzzle out this enigma facing the *Enterprise*.

The enormous structure dwarfed the starship. There was a certain strange attractiveness to the alien creation despite all the unusual lines and angles, in the same way that some babies are so ugly they can only be termed cute. In spite of its appearance of having been put together by someone with absolutely no sense of aesthetics, it exuded a frightening feeling of functional purpose.

Lights glowed a dull, sickly red against the gray-green outer hull. The vessel resembled nothing so much as a sprawling, metallic plant like those McCoy remembered from his grandmother's garden and the swamps of the far South. Runners and their offshoots sprang off a central trunk at intermittent levels with no evident rhyme or reason to their design and placement, and with no obvious avenues of connection between them. The old phrase 'You can't get there from here' wafted briefly through the physician's mind, and he smiled grimly. Given the right tender loving care, the damned thing looked as if it might sprout and grow and take over the entire galaxy the way kudzu had taken over and choked out Grandmother McCoy's garden. The comparison made him uncomfortable.

McCoy looked down at Kirk. The captain sat forward at the conn, eyes narrowed in a calculating squint. The doctor fancied he smelled gray matter burning.

"I don't know what it is," Kirk finally responded to the doctor's question. His voice held a touch of caution, as though he weren't quite ready to commit himself to a definition without more information. "I know what it looks like, maybe, but I don't recall hearing—" He shook his head wonderingly. "Turn off that damned alarm, but stay on yellow alert," he ordered. His voice was clear in the sudden silence that resulted. "Any ideas, Spock?" he asked.

The Vulcan bent intently over his equipment, then straightened and turned his sharp, scrutinizing gaze toward the front viewscreen and its unanticipated vision. "This is most intriguing, Captain," he replied with what McCoy took to be the understatement of the century. "All indications point to this being a space station." Whatever emotion lurked behind the simple statement was betrayed only by the slight elevation of one peaked eyebrow.

Spock's pronouncement was greeted by a quiet murmuring and shifting that coursed fleetingly through the late-shift bridge crew and was gone. McCoy quelled the desire to rub gooseflesh from his arms.

"A space station." Kirk parroted the Vulcan's calm words and pursed his lips ruminatively. He leaned forward, elbow cocked on one knee, chin resting against his fisted hand. With his proud profile, he looked like "The Thinker" brought to sudden, fleshly life. "And this close to the Romulan Neutral Zone . . ." He pondered, then sat up straight. "Spock, I don't recall hearing anything from Starfleet about any Federation stations being under construction in this part of the galaxy."

"Indeed, Captain," the Vulcan readily agreed, hands clasped loosely behind his back. "According to a computer scan of Starfleet communiqués for the past five years, there is no corroborative evidence to place this, or any other construction, in this area of Federation territory. In any event—"

"Well, sir, someone's been building *something* out here, and I don't think it's a birthday present for the Federation council president." Arms folded stiffly across his chest, McCoy stared at the viewscreen.

"May I proceed, Doctor?" Spock queried politely.

McCoy flapped one hand. "Oh, be my guest."

"Thank you. As I was about to state, Captain, in any event, this construct's layout adheres to no current Federation parameters. In fact, its design structure, while being markedly dissimilar to those presently in use by any of the Federation's member worlds, bears a striking resemblance to early Klingon prototype stations. Given our close proximity to the Romulan Neutral Zone, however, I can only postulate that it is of their making."

The bridge crew's silent uneasiness at this remark was like a condensation against the skin, chilling and slick. "If that's a Romulan station," noted Ensign Nyssa, seated at the communications console, "what's it doing in Federation space?" Her soft voice was tinged with suspicion with which McCoy could readily sympathize, and her blue eyes were full of pensive speculation. One hand drew into a tight fist in her lap.

"That's a good question, Ensign." McCoy studied the viewscreen closely and didn't like the way the hair rose along the nape of his neck.

"It's a very good question," Kirk concurred. "Are there any identifying markings on that thing? I want to know what we're dealing with."

"Captain, I believe if Ensign Devin magnifies the station's center quadrant, we may be able to make a positive identification."

At Kirk's nod, the helmsman did as Spock bade. A close-up portion of the space station came into sudden, sharp focus. The outer hull was pocked and scratched—evidence of collision with space debris—but was otherwise in excellent condition. A slanted, blocky line of script decorated a series of panels directly across the center of the viewscreen, just below a wide section of covered viewports.

"That's Romulan writing, all right," Kirk said.

"Correct," Spock confirmed. "We are in the presence of the *Reltah.*"

The name slipped about the bridge on a susurrus of sound like the wind through dry leaves. The space station had appeared as unexpectedly as a white rabbit out of a magician's hat, and one almost expected it to disappear just as abruptly and with as little fanfare or explanation.

McCoy uncrossed his arms and leaned against the back of Kirk's chair. He jerked his chin at the mystery. "I thought the Romulans didn't build space stations," he commented.

"Until this moment, they didn't, Bones," Kirk replied. His intent hazel eyes studied the visible hull critically. "Though I suppose it was only a matter of time. It's not like they're exactly new to space travel." He thoughtfully tugged his bottom lip. A gentle sigh, so light that only McCoy heard it, was the only indication of the captain's bafflement and concern. "She doesn't seem very lively, though, does she? No signs they're even aware we're here."

"Scanning further." Spock bent over his console once more, then looked up. "Life signs are negative, Captain."

"Are you sure?" McCoy asked.

The unemotional first officer quirked an eyebrow at the remark. McCoy figured it was the closest the Vulcan would come to claiming insult at such an absurd suggestion, and it gave a warming sense of normalcy to all this weirdness. "Affirmative, Doctor. Scanners indicate minimal power only. The station is adrift at nearly impulse speed."

"You think it's just garbage that got away from them, Jim?"

"Not by a long shot, Bones." McCoy practically heard the gears turning in Kirk's head as he decided how to proceed. "The Romulans wouldn't let something like this just drift away." He shook his head. "Something else is going on here." He motioned with one hand. "Ensign Nyssa, send a hail. Life signs or no life signs, I want to keep to procedure." He tipped a look at McCoy. "We don't want anyone saying we don't know how to play by the rules, do we?"

"Good point."

"Aye, sir." Slender fingers flew over the communications control board, and Nyssa's voice reached out to the darkened hulk before them. "Space station *Reltah*, this is the Federation Starship *Enterprise*.

Respond, please." She waited a moment, listening intently, with her head tilted fractionally to one side, her brow furrowed with concentration. "Romulan space station *Reltah,* this is the Federation Starship *Enterprise.* You have passed out of Romulan territory and into Federation space. Respond, please." Nyssa paused again, then continued. "Space station *Reltah,* are you in need of assistance? Respond, please." The ensign looked over her shoulder and shook her head at Kirk. "No response, sir. I'm not even certain they're receiving us."

"That's fine, Ensign, just so long as it's all on record." He tapped an index finger against the side of his nose. Fine lines creased the skin at the outer corners of his eyes as he pondered his next move.

Kirk's voice was so quiet that McCoy wasn't certain he'd heard him at all. "Did you say something, Jim?"

"I said, what are the Romulans up to?" Kirk shook his head, but without any real evident meaning behind the gesture. "They've been very quiet lately, Bones, and now this." He waved a hand at the screen. "They're getting too cocky if they think they can just traipse over into Federation space without repercussions. That's a direct violation of the Neutral Zone Treaty they're so fond of invoking every time they think we're going to stick a toe over the line."

Spock spoke up. "Have you considered the possibility, Captain, that this could be a ruse?"

"To draw our attention away from their antics elsewhere? The thought *did* cross my mind, Mr. Spock." Kirk shifted in his chair. "Ensign, send to Starfleet Command, Admiral Cartwright's attention. Let them know we've encountered an apparently unmanned Romulan space station in Federation territory, are proceeding with caution, and will inform them of our findings. Recommend watch points along the Neutral Zone be notified to keep an eye out for unexpected activity. Better safe than sorry, after all."

"Aye, sir." She turned away.

"I don't suppose we could just call them and tell them to come pick up their trash?" McCoy asked dryly.

"Are you suggesting, Dr. McCoy, that we turn the station back over to the Romulans without first investigating it?" Spock asked.

Kirk allowed himself a small, lopsided grin. "I'm with Spock, Bones. As they say in the beachcombing business, finders keepers. I want a closer look at that thing myself."

"Surprise, surprise." McCoy's eyes glinted. "Was that an outbreak of *curiosity*, Spock? Sounded pretty close to an emotion to me."

"Hardly, Doctor," the Vulcan replied coolly, and his eyebrow twitched. "I merely feel it would be in our best interests to gain as much information on this vessel as we possibly can in the time afforded us."

"Of course," McCoy agreed readily. "And your own personal desires didn't come into play at all."

"I assure you, Dr. McCoy, as I have in the past, that I am without—"

"Right, right, sure." McCoy gave the first officer a long, appraising look just to let him know he had him right where he wanted him, then turned away with a Cheshire Cat smile. His hands gently kneaded the back of Kirk's chair. "Checking out the damned thing sounds good to me, and I don't mean to be a Nosy Peter, here, but . . ."

"I'm open to suggestions, Bones."

"Well, what if it doesn't belong to the Romulans?"

Kirk canted his head back in interest. "I beg your pardon?"

McCoy shrugged. "If it *is* a ruse, it might be more than just a Romulan ruse. Maybe someone else is involved, either trying to put one over on the Romulans by getting them in trouble, or working in tandem with them."

"Like the Klingons, you mean?"

"Sure, like the Klingons, or any of the other less savory types we've encountered. But I'd put my money on the Klingons if it came to a bet. They've been in cahoots with the Romulans before." The doctor leaned down. "Think about it, Jim. While the Federation is busy trying to figure all this out, and possibly being put in a position of antagonizing the Romulans in the process, what's to stop the Klingons from blithely cruising their cloaked ships across the Neutral Zone and wreaking their own special brand of havoc? I'm not saying that's the case, but I think we ought to consider the possibility that more than one group is involved. Hell, neither group has much loyalty except to themselves. For all we know, they could have started out as partners and ended up with a space station full of dead Romulans killed off by the Klingons." He pointed at the viewscreen. "That's one damned huge unknown quantity out there, Captain. I think we need to look at it from as many angles as possible, just so we don't get our tails caught in the screen door."

Kirk nodded and slouched back in his chair, almost pinning McCoy's hastily removed hands. "I'll keep that all in mind, Bones, even though I think you're being just a tad paranoid. Much as it might rankle, we have to give the Romulans and the Klingons the benefit of the doubt until we have more concrete evidence. Maybe the Romulans don't know their new toy has wandered away from home. If not, they'll owe us a big favor for finding it, and maybe several if someone else is trying to pull something and put the blame on them."

That drew a slight smile from McCoy. "Now that you put it that way, it would be kind of nice having something to hold over their heads for a change."

"And if there's something else going on, whether or not they admit to it or we catch them in it, they'll know we're not sleeping at our posts." Kirk looked around. "Spock, do we need to be concerned about any of the energy readings off the station? Could the *Enterprise* be in danger if we stay in this area?"

"I speculate no need for concern," the first officer replied. "Output is minimal, as I stated earlier, and I note no undue fluctuations in the readings to cause concern."

"Good. Ensign Devin, are there any other ships in the immediate vicinity?"

The ensign shook his head after consulting his instruments. "The nearest Starfleet vessel is the *Tandarich,* Captain, and she's docked in at Homeaway Station. I detect no alien vessels present."

"So, if they're out there, they're cloaked, and there's nothing we can do about it until they decide to show themselves."

"That's a comforting thought," McCoy remarked.

Kirk shot him a sardonic look. "Any danger in sending a team aboard to investigate, Spock?"

"None that I can foresee, Captain. Though power is low, the ambient temperature poses no threat, though I would recommend wearing field jackets as a precaution. In addition, might I recommend taking handlamps and a portable generator with us? With systems low, there may be areas we wish to explore that are not illuminated. As for the generator, it may be useful should we desire access to the station's computers as an avenue of exploration."

"Good idea, Spock. Make a note to Lieutenant Chekov's station." Kirk touched a button on the arm console of his chair. "Lieutenant Commander Sulu and Commander Uhura to the bridge. Lieutenant Commander Sulu has the conn in my absence." He touched another button. "Kirk to Lieutenant Chekov."

The security chief's voice sounded muzzy over the intercom, his thick Russian accent fuzzed with interrupted sleep but rapidly clearing. "Lieutenant Pavel Chekov here, Captain."

A faint smile curled the corners of Kirk's mouth. "Sorry to interrupt your off hours, Lieutenant, but I need your expertise. We've encountered what appears to be a Romulan space station, apparently unmanned and adrift. Assemble a security team and meet us in the transporter room in twenty minutes, Lieutenant."

"Aye, sir!" Chekov replied sharply, all vestiges of sleep gone. "Chekov out!"

The captain's fingers again sought the intercom. "Bridge to Commander Scott."

"Scott here, sir."

"Scotty, I want you down in the transporter room in twenty minutes. We've encountered a derelict space station and I want a tight fix on the away team. If something unforeseen *does* occur, I want beam-out immediately."

"Aye, sir. I'll keep as tight an eye on them as my sainted granny did me. Scott out."

Kirk stood. "Care to take a walk, gentlemen, and have a look at our find?"

"I thought you'd never ask." McCoy followed Kirk and Spock into the turbolift. When they were moving toward the transporter room, the doctor cleared his throat. "Not that I mind, of course, but why are you sending me along onto a space station with no crew?"

"A precaution, Bones. Someone might get hurt. Besides," Kirk added, "All we know for certain is that Spock's sensors didn't pick up any life signs. That doesn't necessarily mean there's no one aboard."

The faint smile touching McCoy's features drifted away like a vagrant cloud of smoke, and his face settled into its more familiar, somber lines. "I *hate* it when you say things like that."

Chapter Three

THUMBING OFF the communicator switch on the wall by his head, Security Chief Pavel Chekov sat up and swung his legs off the bed. He stretched, arms high above his head, and banished any remaining vestiges of sleepiness with a huge, jaw-gaping yawn.

He had been dreaming of the Russian countryside and his Uncle Vanya's small farm outside Velikiye. Kirk's call had shattered the rest of the dream, sending it spinning into fragments. Chekov *thought* it had been nice. Had the Captain really said it was a *Romulan* space station?!

Chekov glanced at the time on his computer console as he stood. He had fifteen minutes to get himself ready, assemble a security team, gather the necessary provisions, and meet in the transporter room. Anticipation made him grin expectantly. Close deadlines and little time for preparation were the meat of his life and one of the reasons he had gravitated toward Security in the first place. He liked the fine-line tension and living "on the edge," and felt it helped keep him always on his toes, ready for anything, mentally and physically.

Mind racing, calculating how long it would take to prepare his team, he dropped to the floor.

Two dozen fast one-arm pushups got his blood pumping. Rising, he again touched the wall control for the in-ship communicator just before stepping into the shower, and cleared his throat. "This is Security Chief Pavel Chekov. Ensigns Hallie, Markson, and Leno, assemble in the main transporter room in ten minutes in preparation for landing party duty." He paused. A derelict station might mean lower temperatures. Better to be safe than sorry. "Bring your field jackets. Chekov out." He grinned with only a slight trace of malicious intent. Looked like he wasn't going to be the only one rudely awakened. Well, it was as he so often told his team . . . being part of the security forces aboard a starship was a dirty job, but someone had to do it.

The master of the short shower, Chekov was in and out practically before the stall tiles had a chance to become moist. Toweling his dark hair into spikes, he glanced at the time and saw with satisfaction that he had a whole eight minutes to go. He put on pants and pulled a uniform shirt on over his head. Straddling the chair before his computer console, he called up the necessary programs. First out was a short memo transmitted to the personal computers of each member of the ship's security force, the ship's log, and his own duty log, notifying the team of their chief's absence during the mission away from the ship, and putting Ensign Estano in charge until Chekov's return.

Next came a request to the quartermaster of stores, which was immediately flagged by a notation from

Mr. Spock. Chekov read the brief message and nodded with satisfaction, grateful for any additional information the Vulcan could provide on the situation and happy to see that his guess on field jackets had been correct.

Communicators and handlamps, then, issued to each person on the mission, and phasers as well, of course, just in case the station wasn't as unmanned as the captain had been led to believe. Chekov was both annoyed and glad to see the recommendation for a portable generator. Though it was an unwieldy piece of equipment, Chekov had been in too many situations without one, when one would have been very handy, to complain about its addition. Besides, as Mr. Spock's note indicated, it might be their only way of accessing the Romulan computer banks.

He tucked his shirt into his pants and slipped on his field jacket. Five minutes gave him plenty of time for boots, a quick trip to Stores, and the short hike to the transporter room. He only hoped for their sakes that his chosen team was equally as punctual.

Running his fingers through his damp hair, he smoothed it to rights as he left his quarters and hurried down the corridor to the turbolift and the quick descent one level to the Quartermaster's Stores. His mind clicked over like a well-oiled machine. What were the Romulans up to *this* time?

Out of career-long habit and a strong vein of ingrained Scottish common sense, which left little to chance, Chief Engineer Scott ran a quick diagnostic test through the transporter console while awaiting the arrival of the away team Kirk had chosen to be beamed into the space station.

His eyes flicked over the various readouts, and dark brows bunched as thick-fingered hands maneuvered deftly across the console so much like the ones he'd known for better than half his life, and knew so well now that it was little more than an extension of his body rather than a separate unit.

The Scotsman's brow furrowed as he worked, but not out of any real concern for the machinery he tended. The transporter gave him no cause for anxiety. The equipment checked all clear, as he had known it would.

A derelict space station, the captain had said. Scott had shipped with Kirk enough years to be able to read subtle nuance in his commander's voice. If he was any judge, the tone in the captain's voice had hinted that this wasn't just your run-of-the-mill derelict space station, nor necessarily any derelict *Human*-built space station.

That line of reasoning led to contemplation of all sorts of interesting possibilities, and for a moment, Scotty was jealous that Kirk hadn't ordered him to participate in the exploration. The opportunity to investigate a heretofore unknown piece of hardware, particularly something as large and mysterious as a space station, awoke in the chief engineer a desire strong enough to make his back teeth ache.

But his job was here, tending the transporter module. Kirk wanted him here, to see the crew safely gone and safely home, and here he'd stay until Kirk told him otherwise, no matter how badly he wanted to get his hands on the space station and take it apart bit by bit.

The transporter room door slid open and Scott looked up from the console, suppressing a quick smile. Doing their chief proud with four minutes of their allotted time to spare, Chekov's security officers assembled before the transporter pad.

Suzanna Hallie, her petite frame misleadingly

dwarfed by the height and overt power of her two companions, smiled and nodded hello to the chief engineer. "I didn't think I'd see you again so soon, Mr. Scott," she said, closing the front tab of her red field jacket.

"Never underestimate the power of Lieutenant Chekov, lass," Scott replied sagely.

"Oh, I *don't!*" she agreed strongly, and her grin widened when he chuckled. "I learned that lesson early on."

"I guess we all did." Daniel Markson spoke like he knew what he was talking about.

Christina Leno made up the third side of this Security triangle. She crossed the room with a restless grace, a pale-skinned, violet-eyed amazon. Nodding her greeting to the others, she cocked an elbow on the transporter console and leaned sideways, the picture of utterly feigned relaxation.

"What's going on, Commander Scott?" Markson asked suddenly. It occurred to Scotty that poor Markson had one of those faces that for years would make him appear too young even to be aboard a starship, let alone be part of its security team. He should probably grow a moustache or beard. "What's happened?"

"I'm not altogether sure myself, laddie. Even if I knew, though, it's not my place to say. That's for your commander to do."

As though Scott's somewhat stern words had invoked his presence, the door slid open again and Chekov strode in, arms laden with equipment. The security team rushed forward to relieve him of his burdens, placing the things on a nearby counter, and then snapped to immediate attention, heads high and eyes forward, backs as rigid as cabers about to be tossed at the Highland Games.

Scott grinned broadly at the lieutenant from behind the transporter console, bright eyes alight with humor as he gestured with his chin toward the security team. "They've been here awhile, Lieutenant Chekov. What do you do to them, then? Put rockets in their boots?"

"Ejector mattresses in their beds, Mr. Scott." The young Russian allowed himself the briefest smile, then turned and faced his team. "At ease." Hands behind their backs, they took the traditional open-legged stance, Markson flanked by the women on either side. Chekov swiftly, critically scanned each of them in turn. His gaze lingered longest and most sternly on Markson until the young ensign ran a hand quickly through his hair to smooth it and tugged the crease back into his pants.

Satisfied, Chekov proceeded. "Captain Kirk reports that we've intercepted a Romulan space station." His back to the transporter console, the lieutenant didn't see Scott's eyes widen with surprise nor the contemplative purse of the Scotsman's lips. However, both officers clearly saw the startlement register on the faces of the three security guards. A thousand questions brimmed in their eager eyes, and tension suddenly blossomed in the room, like dogs hot on a particularly fruitful scent, straining against confining leashes.

"The station is apparently unmanned," Chekov continued. "But we're going along in the event that doesn't prove to be the case. Ensign Estano will be in command in my absence. I'm issuing each of you a handlamp, a phaser, and a communicator." He spent the next few moments doing just that. Each security guard immediately checked the energy readings on the equipment they were given before securing the units onto their belts.

"Keep your phasers on stun," Chekov cautioned.

"Mr. Spock informs me that the station is adrift and under minimal power only, so in addition to our standard equipment, I'm bringing along a portable generator in the event we need help accessing the station's computer. Unless otherwise ordered, we will stay in one group during the exploration, and you will each have a senior officer in your charge. Markson, you're assigned to Mr. Spock, Hallie will accompany Dr. McCoy, and Leno and I will stay with the captain."

"Aye, sir," they responded in precise unison.

"Are there any questions?"

"Does the captain know what the station is doing here, sir?" Markson asked curiously.

"If he does, Ensign, he hasn't decided it's something I need to know at this time. My guess is we'll find out all that and probably more once we get aboard. Anything else?" There were no further questions. Chekov nodded. "All right. Now—"

The transporter room door slid open again, interrupting anything further Chekov might have had to say. Kirk entered, followed by McCoy with his medical equipment, and Spock bringing up the rear with a tricorder. The security chief and his crew immediately came to attention. "Security personnel assembled and prepared for transport, sir!" Chekov reported smartly. He stepped forward. "I have communicators, phasers, and handlamps for the rest of you."

"Very good, Lieutenant Chekov," Kirk responded. "At ease, the rest of you."

"Captain, may I have a word with you?" Spock asked.

Kirk looked over. "What's on your mind, Spock?"

"In private, if you please." The Vulcan took several steps away from the group.

Kirk's eyes flicked toward McCoy, but the doctor

shrugged with lack of understanding. "Does this have something to do with the mission, Spock?"

"Yes, sir, it does."

"Well, then, out with it. We don't need to have any secrets between team members, especially when going into unknown territory."

Spock looked about as discomfited as he ever let himself get. "I would rather—"

"Out with it, Spock," Kirk ordered and waited.

Scott got the impression that the Vulcan wanted to do nothing more than heave a sigh. His expression was almost painful when he began. "Captain, I do not think the captain will be joining us on this mission."

"What?" Kirk and McCoy chorused. Kirk looked at his first officer as though he'd grown another set of ears, and a tail to boot. "Spock, what's that suppose to mean? Of course I'm going."

"I think it would be ill advised, Captain."

Kirk started to say something, then stopped. "This isn't about that communiqué we received last week, is it?"

"It is precisely that."

"Oh!" Kirk held up his hands, evidently relieved. "Well, we don't have to worry about that. It was only—"

"Captain," Spock interrupted patiently. "It was on recommendation from Starfleet Command."

"What's he talking about?" McCoy asked, curiously.

Kirk didn't look as though he wanted to answer at first. He did as much squirming as a person could do without moving, then turned toward the doctor. "Oh, it's just this message we received from Starfleet Command. They're recommending that captains should avoid routinely going out with landing parties, leaving the brunt of these duties to their first officers and the security teams."

"Well, it's about time!"

Kirk stared at McCoy. "Et tu, Bones? What do you mean, 'it's about time'?"

The doctor folded his arms and cocked a hip to one side. "Well, I always thought it was damned foolish of them to allow all the flag officers to participate in landing parties. What if some catastrophe took place and left the ship and crew without command personnel?" McCoy grinned to soften his words. "Sorry, Jim. Much as I thought I'd never say it, I'm on Spock's side."

"Thank you, Dr. McCoy."

"Sorry, my—! I'm not going to adhere to it, Bones!" Kirk vowed stubbornly. "And I won't be breaking protocol. It's not policy yet."

"No, Captain," Spock agreed. "It is not policy at this time. However, it did come as a strong suggestion from Starfleet that we begin implementing the idea in order to see how well it works."

"I'll consider it. Perhaps next time," Kirk cozened.

McCoy's hands dropped to his hips. "What next time, Captain? You know as well as I do that you'll always find a way to push 'next time' back unless we make you stick to it, just because you always want to be at the forefront of everything. What's the matter, don't you trust us to do a good job? Come on, Jim, let the rest of us go off and have a little fun on our own, why don't you?" He leaned forward and softly added, "Captain, you're not being a very good example to these impressionable young ensigns on the importance of following Starfleet's procedures—"

"It's not a—"

"—*and* recommendations."

Kirk was stymied. He pursed his lips, quietly fuming for a brief moment, before nodding sharply. "You're right, Bones. That's *exactly* what I'd do. All right, have it your way."

"Good boy," McCoy praised. "It pays to listen to your doctor now and then." He held out his hand. "Lieutenant, if you please."

Kirk refrained from further comment, watching while the doctor and the first officer readied the equipment Chekov handed them. "Now, no loitering over there," he jokingly admonished the away team when they turned toward him in readiness. "See what there is to see, then get back here and report your findings. We'll leave it to Starfleet to decide whether or not there's to be further examination at a later date. Who knows," he mused, gaze momentarily distant, focused beyond them at something only he could see. "Maybe they'll decide we need to give this find a thorough going-over." He glanced over his shoulder. "What do you say to that, Mr. Scott?"

The chief engineer's chin elevated slightly. "If Starfleet *does* decide to explore the station further, sir, do you not think you might find it in your heart to recommend a certain chief engineer to oversee taking her apart?" He smiled engagingly.

"You, Scotty? Take a vacation from the *Enterprise?* You know what they say about curiosity." Kirk smiled. "If that comes to pass, I'll see what I can do, Mr. Scott."

"Thank you, sir."

Kirk turned back and held a hand toward the transporter. "Much as it galls me to be left behind . . . ladies and gentlemen, if you please?"

The landing party stepped up the riser to the transporter platform and each took their place over a disc. Each member of the security team placed a hand at the ready over the butt of their phaser.

"Now, remember what I said," Kirk repeated sternly. "No hanging around sightseeing. Energize, Mr. Scott."

McCoy's mouth dropped open. "Sightseeing—" was as far as he got. The transporter hum rose to a whine, and the six travelers vanished in a scintilla of spectrumed light.

Scott's eyes flicked toward his commander, reading the expression on his face. "It's hard being left behind, isn't it, sir?"

Kirk nodded. "That it is, Mr. Scott." He turned and raised a forefinger in the air. "But mark my words, Scotty, having the captain stay behind while a landing party takes risks is an idea that is *never* going to pan out."

Chapter Four

McCOY KNEW THE OLD ADAGE "Hours can seem like days." In his personal experience, it was more like "Microseconds can seem like years," especially when the blasted transporter was involved.

As the mechanism kicked in, he was cut off in the middle of what he felt would have been an utterly brilliant riposte to Kirk's snide, sour-grapes remark about sightseeing. A tremor of disorientation started at the tips of his extremities and thrummed inward through his discorporeating body, making him feel profoundly nauseous. His vision swam sickeningly and darkened to black as sensory input cut off entirely, as if he had suddenly been confined to a deprivation tank.

No one McCoy had ever compared notes with seemed to have the same reaction as he did to using the transporter. Jim had told him more than once that the intense response was probably rooted entirely in the doctor's well-known dislike for the machine.

While McCoy was grateful for his friend's concern, he didn't appreciate Kirk playing junior psychologist with him, even if there probably was some very sound basis to the diagnosis. The rational, medically- and psychologically-educated part of McCoy's mind knew beyond a shadow of a doubt that the transporter procedure was rated safer than any other mode of transportation ever known to mankind, including walking, and that the entire process lasted only as long as it takes the human heart to pulse three beats. Even knowing all this, the rest of his psyche was screamingly confident not only that the trip took an eternity and was fraught with dangers he couldn't even see, but that it also gave him the closest thing to an out-of-body experience he could ever have without actually dropping dead. No one, not even Kirk, was ever going to convince him otherwise. For McCoy, stepping onto the transporter was almost as bad as stepping into deep water.

But three heartbeats later, his senses returned as promised, and he blinked rapidly, focusing on the shades and contours of a dimly lit, unfamiliar room. His skin crawled with a transporter aftereffect shiver, which Kirk had tried to convince him didn't exist except in his own mind.

"You were saying, Doctor?" Spock questioned politely.

McCoy turned around. The eerie lighting from the emergency lamps overhead cast a most peculiar aspect to the Vulcan's saturnine features, suggesting that Scotty had erred and transported them to Hades instead of the space station. The doctor fought down a strong desire to ask Spock to display his pointed tail and pitchfork—he was afraid Spock might just do it. "What, Spock?" he asked guardedly, his breath condensing in the air. The temperature felt about as cool as a brisk, autumn afternoon, chilly but not unpleasantly cold.

"You were in the process of saying something when Commander Scott initiated the transporter procedure. I merely thought you might wish to complete your statement."

"Yeah, I'll just bet you did." McCoy shook his head and waggled a finger at the Vulcan. "Nice try, Spock, but you can just forget it. You're not going to goad me into making a fool of myself this time."

One eyebrow did a slow rise. "I wasn't aware you required goading, Doctor," the Vulcan remarked calmly.

McCoy wished that just once his angry glare would make somebody, preferably Spock, burst into flames. He turned his back on the first officer. "Spock's in rare form. Did everyone else make the trip in one piece? No extra appendages? Nothing important missing?"

They were all fine and, at Chekov's nod, spread out in a perimeter guard around the senior officers.

Spock flipped open his communicator with a deft flick of the wrist. "Spock to *Enterprise.*"

"*Enterprise* here." Kirk's strong voice sounded clearly over the tiny speaker, affording a measure of comfort. Clarity meant no undetected or unexpected interference and a clear passage back home, even if it was via the transporter.

"All personnel have arrived safely, Captain, and we are about to initiate exploration."

"Affirmative, Spock. Keep me apprised of your situation. Mr. Scott is locked onto your team's coordinates. If there's any sign of trouble, I want you all back aboard the *Enterprise* immediately. That's an order. I don't want heroics. Lieutenant Chekov?"

The security chief raised his voice. "Here, sir."

"That goes double for you and your squad."

There was no arguing with that tone of voice, even had Chekov been so inclined. "Aye, sir," he replied.

"That's all then. Good luck. Kirk out."

Spock shut the communicator, snugged it back onto his belt, and stepped forward. He said nothing, but quirked an eyebrow when Markson stepped up beside him. For his part, McCoy was grateful for Hallie's diminutive but staunch presence at his side. He'd seen her work out in the gymnasium and knew what kind of damage she could inflict upon an adversary when she chose to. Hell, he'd repaired her opponents more than once in the short time she'd been aboard the *Enterprise.* Chekov and Leno covered the rear.

It took them only a moment to realize that Scotty had set them down in the *Reltah*'s own transporter room. It was darker than the one aboard the *Enterprise,* and it didn't help that only the emergency lights shone, throwing everything into a murky, reddish relief.

Ten elliptical transporter pads covered the deck, which was set flush into the floor. Unlike Scotty's streamlined station, the operator's console was a massive, bulky contraption set behind a transparent protective wall. The room was utterly austere and functional in appearance, with no overt signs of having been recently used.

Leno wrinkled her nose. "It smells funny in here."

"That's no surprise if systems are down to minimal." Chekov inhaled deeply through his nose and shook his head. "I can't place it. Can anyone else?"

Markson and Hallie were equally confused. Even Spock was unable to suggest a possibility. McCoy inhaled deeply, held it a moment to savor the scent, exhaled, and repeated the process. A faint, not-quite-unpleasant odor tickled his nostrils and coated the back of his tongue.

"Peaches?" he wondered aloud. The others stared at him as though he were crazy, but there was no help for it. He nodded. "Yes, that's it. That's exactly what the smell reminds me of. Rotten peaches in my grandfather's orchard."

"What would peaches be doing aboard a Romulan space station?" Hallie queried confusedly.

"Not a damn thing," McCoy agreed. "I don't think there are any, but that's what it smells like."

"Is there something else that would cause that same smell, Doctor?" Chekov asked.

"You've got me, Lieutenant. The only thing I know of that smells like rotten fruit is rotten fruit. Any thoughts, Spock?"

"No, Doctor. Perhaps further investigation will provide a solution." Spock unslung the tricorder from around his shoulders and clicked it on with his thumb. "Scanning produces the same results we garnered aboard the *Enterprise*—low power, support systems on minimal, and no life signs. Let us proceed." Markson at his side, the Vulcan stepped behind the partition separating the transporter module from the rest of the room. He scanned the console with his penetrating gaze and ran his hands above, but not on, the controls. "It appears this unit has gone into some type of standby mode, probably due to the drop in power. It is impossible to determine when the last transport took place."

"You weren't planning on using it, anyway, were you, Spock?" McCoy asked uneasily. He wasn't relishing another trip by transporter, particularly one of alien make, and in any case, where would they go?

"Hardly, Dr. McCoy. But I *was* hoping to learn how long ago this station had been unmanned, and the transporter might have been able to provide such information. In addition, I was hoping my inspection would produce computer access." Spock's eyebrows dipped—the closest he ever came to a frown. "Unfortunately, there seems to be no linkup of any kind at this terminal. Most unusual. I find that hard to accept at such an inherently integral portion of the station."

"Integral to *us,* Spock, but this is the Romulans, remember? Go figure them. Maybe it's their idea of security." McCoy leaned his shoulder against the partition. "Remember what this thing looked like from the outside? I haven't seen anything so plug-ugly in all my life. Maybe the haphazard layout is their idea of security, too."

"Perhaps. In any event, we will not be able to extract any information on the station or its crew from this point. I suggest we proceed in our exploration and find a computer relay access."

McCoy waved a hand. "Ready when you are, Gridley." He stepped aside and let Spock and Markson past, then he and Hallie took up their places in the center of the line, with Leno and Chekov again bringing up the rear.

Fortunately, the low power to systems did not impede their exit from the transporter room. The wide double doors were fully open and afforded them access to the rest of the station.

One hand raised in a cautionary gesture, Markson peered around the doorjamb and looked back and forth. "All clear," he reported and stepped into the corridor, motioning for the others to follow. "Which way, sir?"

The question was directed toward Spock, who stood in the center of the hallway, head pivoting to take in a 180-degree view. There were no marks on the walls to give them any clue as to where they were within the immense station, or to where they might best proceed to get answers to their questions.

"The most common figure found in nature is the spiral," Spock said, "moving from left to right in a sunward, or clockwise, direction. It seems to be a universal, though largely unconscious, truth from race to race. I suggest, then, that we proceed down the left-hand corridor." He started off. Markson had to hurry to catch up and overtake him, whereupon the Vulcan fell in at the security guard's heels, a tall, cranelike figure in the subdued lighting.

McCoy trotted to keep up with the long-legged Vulcan, Hallie padding along at his heels. "You know," he said quietly when he once again walked at the first officer's elbow. "You're making quite a leap of faith in assuming the Romulans have adhered to the same rules that have guided so many cultures. Who's to say they didn't do just the opposite just to be contrary?"

"You make a valid point, Dr. McCoy," Spock concurred, his eyes flicking briefly toward the physician. "Indeed, at this time, I have nothing on which to base my conjectures except my knowledge of the Romulan people from their relation to the Vulcans. However, I must base my theories upon something, even if it is just the observation of other cultures, if we are to proceed at all. Rest assured, I will modify my speculations as soon as I am presented with concrete evidence to the contrary. Until then, I must proceed as best I can."

"Hmmm." McCoy lessened his stride, letting Spock draw ahead, and looked over at Chekov. "Pragmatists irritate the hell out of me," he commented, voice pitched low so as not to reach the Vulcan's supersensitive ears.

The corners of the Russian's eyes crinkled with amusement. "Pragmatists have their place in the world, Dr. McCoy," he replied magnanimously.

"So do body lice, but I wouldn't want to share my office with them."

Hallie bit her bottom lip to keep from laughing, and Leno grinned. "Better pragmatism in a situation like this, sir, than screaming hysteria," Leno said.

"Now, that paints an interesting picture, Ensign," McCoy drawled. "I always thought there was a place in this world for a good, old-fashioned, screaming hysteric." He attempted to look annoyed. "And did I ever tell you that pragmatic security personnel annoy the hell out of me, too?"

Chekov's expression was irritatingly innocent. "You have very good taste in your irritants, Dr. McCoy."

Leno bobbed her head. "Thanks, Chief."

McCoy shot a look at the Russian. "You worry me, Lieutenant," he said gravely.

"How so, sir?"

McCoy made a face, as though a bad taste were taking a crawl up his throat. "You're starting to behave more and more like Spock every day. Come see me in sickbay when we get back to the ship. I think you need a thorough going-over."

"Yes, sir," the security chief agreed seriously, but his eyes shone with humor.

"Lieutenant Chekov! Dr. McCoy!" Spock's voice hailed them from far ahead. "If you would join us, please."

"Coming!" The others hurried ahead, nearly colliding with Spock and Markson where they waited beyond a turn in the corridor.

"What is it, Spock?" McCoy asked.

"Nothing specific, Doctor, beyond my desire that we keep together during the exploration. I do not think it would be to our advantage to split up at this time."

"Well, if you hadn't run off like one of those guides on a 'See Eleven Planets in Three Days' tours, we could have!"

Spock didn't bat an eye at the doctor's habitual rancor. "I am merely trying to facilitate the exploration process, per Captain Kirk's orders."

McCoy couldn't argue with that. Much as he liked to bait the stoic Vulcan, even he knew when it wasn't the correct time and place. "You're absolutely right, Spock, and I apologize if I contributed to detaining us in any way. Lead on."

If he hadn't known Spock better, the doctor could have sworn he saw surprise flash through those unbreachable, dark eyes. He felt a tingle of delight. Could it be that the best way to irritate and annoy the Vulcan was to do the unexpected? That was a theory he would have to test more thoroughly once they were back aboard the *Enterprise*.

Together, the six companions traversed the empty, featureless corridors. Not a single door broke the blank expanse of wall. Spock's tricorder continued to emit the same readings. There were several cross-corridors, and at each one the company turned to the left. Sometimes this proved to be to their advantage, letting them progress further on. More often than not, though, it would lead to an unexpected dead end and they would have to backtrack to their point of departure and go forward from there. Spock briefly contacted Kirk once more to report nothing new. The signal between the station and the *Enterprise* continued to be strong and clear.

The landing party progressed along the empty passageways. After yet another dead end in a blank corridor with no doors, McCoy came to the decision that the station was the most oddly put together structure he'd ever been in. Maybe it was just him (and he didn't think so, if the frustrated sighs of his companions were any indication), but the layout seemed singularly inefficient, with no rhyme or reason to many of the corridors. It was as though they branched out because someone thought it would be a good place to put a corridor, without an eye to the overall productivity of the station as a whole, like hive insects on some sort of hallucinogenic drug.

"Mr. Spock!" Chekov's voice hailed them from a little way ahead. He and Leno had split up, he taking point and she riding shotgun at the rear of the group.

"Yes, Lieutenant?" Spock called, leading the others forward.

The Russian sounded relieved. "I've found a door!"

"At last!" McCoy enthused. "I was beginning to get the uncomfortable feeling that we were nothing more than rats in a maze," he said to Hallie.

She rolled her eyes. "I know *exactly* what you mean, sir."

Chekov stepped to one side when the others arrived, and indicated the partially open entryway with a wave of his hand. "It appears to have been forced."

The door and frame were bent as though with a pry bar or some other such object. The first officer wedged his lean body into the dark, narrow opening before Markson beat him to it. He flicked on his handlamp and flashed it around the interior of the room in precise, rapid movements.

Standing on his toes to peek over Spock's shoulder, McCoy was unable to pick up any clear images at all. "What is it?" he questioned.

In lieu of a reply, Spock placed his hands against the edge of the door and pushed hard. His Vulcan strength, so much greater than that of his human companions, stood him in good stead. The door grated a little further into its wall slot with a sound of protesting metal that set McCoy's teeth on edge. Spock took one step and paused as Markson's arm blocked his way.

"This is my job, sir," he said firmly and with a confidence that earned him extra points in McCoy's book. "The chief's orders. I have to go in first."

If Spock considered arguing the point, he gave no indication. "Correct, Ensign." He moved out of Markson's way.

Moving carefully, the security guard wheeled around the door frame with a modicum of movement and disappeared into the protective shadows against the inner wall. His light flashed about the interior in a pattern understandable only by someone versed in the mysteries of working security. A moment later, his hand emerged and motioned the others inside.

No emergency lights pierced the darkness before the combined illumination of the six handlamps, which lit the interior like day. The small room was obviously an office of some kind. The walls were bare of decoration. Cabinets along one wall were empty when Leno opened one door to peer inside. A harsh-angled desk and a chair that looked almost impossibly uncomfortable to sit in were stationed directly opposite the door. The furniture was in keeping with what little McCoy knew about Romulan psychology. They were fierce and unyielding with themselves when it came to work.

Spock stepped further into the room and flashed his light behind the desk. "Most intriguing . . ."

McCoy crowded at his shoulder, eager to see, and was aware of Ensign Hallie beside him trying to put herself in a position of defense should whatever Spock had discovered turn out to be less than friendly.

It was far from life-threatening. The desk drawers were flung open, some halfway, some overturned with their contents spilled across the floor. The random collection of effects showed nothing noteworthy. They had evidently been gone through quickly, but by whom and for what purpose? Were these the remnants of thievery or expediency?

Spock's light held steady on something of even greater interest, a computer terminal. "Lieutenant Chekov, please bring the generator." He swung around the desk and settled into the chair. Chekov set the generator on the desk beside the terminal and waited while the Vulcan tried several different ways to access the computer system. "Just as I surmised," Spock finally said. "We shall need to use the generator to boost power in order to enter the system." For the next few moments, he and Chekov conversed quietly, determining how to best set things up. Then they started hooking the generator into the terminal. Finally, Spock turned, once more placed his hands on the computer keyboard, and set to work.

Nothing happened. There was no sound, no run of lights across the computer's face. Nothing. Spock kept working, without results.

"It's dead, isn't it?" Hallie asked dismally.

Spock shook his head. "I don't think 'dead' is the proper phraseology, Ensign. The terminal is receiving low power from the station, but I cannot seem to access the correct programming to allow me to boost the power with the generator. This terminal behaves much as the transporter did, as though a fail-safe of some kind has been thrown."

"Well, that's just wonderful," McCoy groused. He stuffed his hands into his pockets to warm them. "Any recommendations, Spock?"

"We need to find another computer outlet. If we discover that auxiliary computer stations cannot be accessed, our only alternative is to find the bridge and attempt log-on from there. In any event, locating the bridge would no doubt help our investigation of why this station is in Federation space. In all likelihood, much of the information we need will be there."

"Well, it's too bad we couldn't have had Scotty beam us right onto what passes for a bridge around here."

"I endeavored to do just that, Doctor. I theorized that the station's central command area would be located at the centermost juncture of the station, to facilitate access by all personnel. That seemed the most logical locale."

"I agree. It's worked on our space stations. So?"

"Evidently, that was not the case, since Mr. Scott beamed us into the transporter room."

"I wonder where the bridge *is,* then?" Chekov shook his head. He looked around the room. "You know, Mr. Spock, I've been thinking about something Doctor McCoy said earlier. Maybe the weird layout of this place *does* have something to do with security measures. Perhaps it's a way to lead unfriendlies astray and shut off specific areas. Not knowing what the Romulans planned to do with this thing, it might have been to their advantage to be able to isolate specific areas of the station at will. Like the bridge, maybe?" He turned in a circle. "For all we know, the bridge is stuck out on the end of one of the arms, just so no one can find it."

"Or so it breaks away if there's fighting," Hallie added.

"An interesting theory, Ensign," Spock concurred. "But until we are able to access a computer terminal and find a map or schematic for this station, we cannot turn in any direction with specific surety." He disengaged the generator, packed it back into its sling, and stepped into the corridor with the others behind him.

A vague uneasiness crawled around McCoy's insides, and he gestured back toward the vacant office. "Shouldn't we close the door again?"

"What for?" Hallie asked, genuinely confused.

The doctor shrugged. "I don't know. I guess I feel like I'm leaving the door open on a tomb." He knew by her expression that it was no explanation at all. She had no clue to what he was getting at.

"It can hardly be called a tomb when the body, if there was one, is no longer here," Spock pointed out.

"Tell that to the Egyptians," McCoy said edgily. "Look, forget I said anything. Let's just get this show on the road. I want to get back to the ship." They fell into formation again and continued down the corridor. Around them, the station remained silent and devoid of life.

As time passed, they began finding more and more rooms, all of them offices of a spare, utilitarian nature. Spock made two more attempts at accessing a computer, without success. Both rooms appeared locked into the standby mode he had discovered in the transporter room, and he came to the conclusion that auxiliary systems were, indeed, inaccessible, and that their best chance of getting into the system was from the bridge. *If* they could find it.

Each of the offices showed signs of having once been occupied. A black jacket hung over the back of one chair. In another, computer discs lay scattered in a random spray across the floor. In a third, a small meal sat untouched and molding on the edge of the desk.

McCoy ran a sensor over the food. "This is several weeks old."

Hallie nudged Markson sharply in the ribs. "Just

like the *Mary Celeste,* huh, Dan?" she said with a wicked grin.

He wasn't happy with the comparison. "That's not funny, Suze."

"That's enough, Ensign Hallie," the doctor ordered. "We don't need bogey-men on our minds. Thanks all the same."

She had the good grace to look abashed. "Yes, sir. Sorry, sir."

"Mr. Spock!" Chekov's voice was strident, and it was only then that McCoy realized he and Leno had moved out of the room and down the corridor. "Dr. McCoy!"

Several yards farther on, before a half-seen corridor juncture made murky by shadows, Chekov and Leno knelt on the floor. Between them, lit by Chekov's handlamp, was a spill of oddments—a cloak, some type of hand tools, a blanket, and several trinkets that had no meaning to the visitors from the *Enterprise.*

"What's all this?" McCoy bent to look more closely.

Spock stooped and sorted gently through the detritus of someone's passage. "Merely more fuel to the mystery, Doctor. Let us proceed."

"Wait!" Leno held up her hand and inhaled. "What's that *smell?*"

Hallie made a face. "Ugh! That doesn't smell like rotten peaches."

"I don't know—" Chekov turned, still on his heels. The beam of his handlamp played haphazardly across the corridor, illuminating the floor and walls in an abrupt spray of light. Unexpected movement caught their eyes as something startled in the sudden brightness and flashed out of sight around the distant corridor juncture.

Like a hound upon the scent, Chekov was on his

feet, phaser at the ready, and led the rush down the long corridor and around the corner.

The smell hit them hard here, rancid and randy. Chekov plowed to a stop so abruptly that the others almost careened into him. He played his light over the floor.

A figure sprawled halfway down the hall, slender limbs akimbo, its head cocked oddly against the juncture of wall and floor. Hallie held a hand over her nose and made a sick noise. "I thought there were no life signs aboard," she whispered.

"There are no signs, if no one's alive," McCoy said grimly. He slowly approached the decomposing body and knelt on one knee, staring down at the scanner he'd slipped into his hand. "Romulan female. Young." He'd smelled worse. *Just keep telling yourself that, Leonard.* He ran the unit in a slow sweeping motion over the corpse's entire length, interpreting the sounds emitted by the equipment. When he was done, he stood, returned the scanner to the medipouch, and turned, wondering if he looked as gray as he felt. "She's been dead several weeks, Spock."

"Cause of death?" the first officer inquired.

McCoy reached out with one boot and gently toggled the corpse's head back and forth. "Spinal fracture and concussion. What they call a hangman's fracture."

"What do you think happened, Dr. McCoy?" Leno asked quietly. In this lighting, her eyes appeared almost black. "Did someone murder her?"

He shrugged. "Let's not jump to any conclusions, Ensign. I don't know what happened here. She could have just fal—"

"Wait a minute," Markson interrupted, staring

down at the corpse with an odd expression in his eyes. "If she's been dead several weeks, what did we just see moving?"

"Good point," Chekov agreed with his team member, voice low. As though commandeered by a single thought, every handlamp in the group flicked on and played around the corridor. The hallway ran arrow-straight for several meters, apparently unbroken by door or hallway juncture. There was nowhere for anyone to hide, nowhere anyone could have escaped to where they wouldn't be seen.

"There *was* something there," Leno stated firmly. "I *saw* it. I don't know what it was, but I *know* it was there." She turned toward Chekov, her eyes almost pleading. "You saw it, too, Chief, didn't you?"

The Russian's dark brows furrowed over his eyes. "I saw *something,* Ensign," he acknowledged. "But I don't—"

"I believe I know what you saw, Lieutenant. Please extinguish your lights, everyone." When they did as he asked, Spock waved the single beam of his handlamp around the corridor. The walls caught a sheen of light, a strip of metal meant for decoration or direction, and flashed it in their eyes as the light traced its length and disappeared into the darker reaches of the corridor.

Leno sighed with disgust. "I guess your eyes can really play tricks on you." Chekov nodded but didn't look so convinced.

"Yes, they can, Ensign, especially when you're keyed up," McCoy said soothingly. "This place is eerie enough in its own right without *this.*" He gestured at the dead Romulan.

"Are you *sure* there wasn't anything there, Doctor?"

Markson asked hollowly. "Light or no light, something killed this Romulan."

"Now, Ensign, we don't know—"

Before McCoy could say anything more, the emergency lights and Spock's handlamp went dead without a warning flicker and plunged them into total darkness.

Chapter Five

THE CHANNEL CLICKED SHUT on the landing party's signal, and Kirk leaned back in his seat at the conn. He sighed deeply but quietly, his chest rising and falling in a tightly controlled movement too small for the bridge crew to notice. He didn't want the others to hear, didn't want them sensing his concern or picking up on the brooding uneasiness that had settled over him as soon as the landing party was out of his reach.

Unidentifiable apprehension lay against his skin like the ghostly touch of the finest Pantazian silk. Unlike the rare, rich material, this sensation gave him absolutely no pleasure at all. He felt edgy, certain that something was happening somewhere of which he should be cognizant but wasn't. He had a feeling of . . . well, the only phrase he could think of was the overly melodramatic one of "impending power," but that wasn't quite it. More accurately, it felt like he remembered the air feeling on a swollen summer's day when a thunderstorm threatened across an Iowa cornfield. He recalled sitting on the back porch, watching thunderheads build on the horizon, dark cones of cloud piling higher and higher, scattershot with lightning and grumbling with ominous power and the threat of rain that might, or might not, become a promise. Yes, this was *exactly* the same sort of feeling, and it annoyed Kirk because he couldn't find a logical reason for his apprehension. He'd just spoken with Spock and everything was fine. So why the worry?

Kirk's left index finger traced mindless circles around the call button on the arm of the chair. His eyes focused on the small movement, flicking in tiny, sharp motions to hypnotically follow the circular pattern of his fingertip but not really registering the gesture. His lips pursed pensively as he settled more deeply into thought, probing down into the level of sixth sense he called hunches, upon which he had learned to rely so keenly in the years he'd been with Starfleet.

What had him riled? There was no indication from the scanners or the landing party of trouble aboard the Romulan station, despite its unheralded and utterly mystifying appearance. Helm reported no other ships in the area, though that reading could only be trusted halfway. It was all too easy to imagine a Romulan vessel standing hard by but cloaked and hidden from the *Enterprise*'s instruments, just waiting for Kirk and his crew to become lazy and complacent before the Romulans uncloaked and dove in for the kill.

Kirk shook his head slightly. If he let it, his propensity for speculation would gladly take the bit in its metaphorical teeth and run like hell with it. If he was going to start doing that, Bones may as well just lock him up in the Home for Old Spacers and throw away the key.

That thought lightened some of his concern. If he could find humor in this situation, it couldn't be nearly as black as he was trying to make it out to be. There was *nothing* to worry about.

Besides, *if* by some chance a problem did raise its ugly head aboard the station, Scotty had the reflexes and the wherewithal to beam the team home and prod the *Enterprise* to warp nine before anything adverse could occur.

Fine. So, given all that, why did he still have the unscratchable itch under his skin?

Kirk sighed again, this time with genuine irritation at himself and his overanxious sixth sense. There was no answer for it. He'd been a captain long enough to know that there might *never* be a satisfying explanation for his unrest. He'd also been in command long enough to know that there was something not right going on and that, sooner or later, he and the *Enterprise* would be in the thick of things.

With that less-than-comforting thought as his companion, he pushed himself to his feet and tugged his jacket into place. "Well," he said dryly, in an attempt at joviality. "If they're going to get to have all the fun and I have to miss out, I guess I'll go work off some of this excess energy." He smiled at the beautiful Bantu woman who was at the communications station. "Commander Uhura, I'll be in the gymnasium, perfecting my Riseaway game. Contact me there or in my quarters if you need me or when you hear from the landing party."

She nodded briskly, eyes smiling. "Yes, sir."

"Commander Sulu, you have the conn."

"Aye, sir." The lanky helmsman nodded once sharply and rose gracefully to take the seat Kirk vacated.

Once inside the turbolift, he voiced a request for

Deck 7 and the gymnasium. Now was a perfect time to get a leg up on McCoy's unexpected proficiency at Riseaway. If Kirk had anything to say about it, the good doctor would have a surprise coming when he returned to the ship.

He felt the almost subliminal vibration of the floor through his boot soles as the grav plate kicked in. As the turbolift began moving, he folded his arms across his chest and sighed.

Annoyed, Jim? he wondered silently, and decided that, yes, he was, just a little. Being the captain of a starship was by no stretch of the imagination an easy job. Oh, the perks were many, for rank *did* have its privileges, but the responsibility had its share of frustrations, too. Like right now.

The turbolift slowed, the indicator light glowing a hearty 7, and the doors opened. Kirk immediately turned toward the gym.

It was hard for someone with Kirk's sense of adventure and consuming curiosity about the universe to be captain and get left behind while the landing party went out to explore! He knew which admiral had appended his name to the preliminary order "recommending" that captains begin turning the majority of the away-team supervisions over to the executive officers. The man was a good friend of long standing, but Kirk felt as though he'd been betrayed, if only just a little. He'd even scoffed at the memorandum when it first appeared, chiefly intending to ignore it until it was made official policy or someone shoved it down his throat. Unfortunately, that someone had been his own first officer, and Kirk had learned a long time ago not even to attempt debating semantics with Spock, particularly if McCoy was in the room. Bones got too damned much pleasure out of it.

Kirk would have preferred to say that he didn't

begrudge Bones or Spock their exploration of the Romulan space station, but that wouldn't be truthful. He was envious as hell and itched furiously to get a look for himself at what the Romulans had produced so furtively.

The gymnasium doors parted at his approach and he entered. The big room was largely empty, except for two off-duty crewmen practicing tumbling falls on thick mats in one corner. However, the individual cubicles along the periphery of the main room were more fully occupied—the orange lights over their doors glowing warmly to indicate occupancy. From where he stood, Kirk saw a lone handball player sweating heavily and whacking the daylights out of her ball, and two other people, gender hidden by thick, protective clothing, sparring with the brilliantly lit quarterstaves used in playing Littlejon.

Kirk crossed to the locker room and spent a few minutes shedding his uniform and skinning into the tight white suit used in Riseaway. He adjusted the material carefully, making sure it lay smoothly against all the lines of his body. Unnecessary ridges in the material influenced play. He'd discovered that the hard way. Pulling up the cowl, he fitted it snugly around his face, and lowered the protective goggles over his eyes. Taking his racquet from his locker, he left the room and crossed the gym.

Cubicle nine was empty and Kirk entered. He flicked the switch beside the door, engaging the occupancy light and the opaque controls for the windows. He didn't want his workout to be a spectator sport, particularly when he was endeavoring to get in some extra practice time on the sly to surprise McCoy. Bones had gotten pretty cocky after beating Jim so soundly. Kirk would enjoy giving the doctor some of his own medicine. That thought made Kirk smile, and he felt an immediate corresponding lift of spirits. The black cloud was dispersing. Perhaps the unsettled feeling wasn't due so much to an impending doom hanging over them as it was to feeling left out of the exploration with his friends.

"My God, you *are* jealous." He shook his head with a feeling of mild amusement. Grinning, he touched a third control, and gravity in the room abruptly ceased. He felt himself begin to rise gently, and kicked very slightly against the floor. The small impetus was enough to give him a great deal of momentum halfway up the wall to a series of rest handles. He snagged one with his gloved hand and paused for a moment, surveying the room below.

The rules of Riseaway were comparatively easy, unlike those for some of the card games Bones had tried to teach him in the past (like the thoroughly incomprehensible Sheepshead). It was a cross between handball and cricket, with the logic of chess and the addition of zero-gee. The "ball" was a sphere of colored light, different colors denoting different point values, which a player had to deflect off a paddle and strike against a goal pin to score a direct hit and gain points. Added to that was the complication of having to scale the walls at the same time, in a prescribed order known only by the game computer generating the balls. Buzzers would sound when scaling was inaccurate, and a corresponding loss of points would result, with the turn going to your opponent.

Kirk had fallen in love with the game the first time he played it, and it had been he who introduced McCoy to it, figuring the physician could use the exercise and confident of a long string of wins until Bones hit his stride. Now Kirk realized that he needed to practice to compete with the doctor, if only to gain that particular spin McCoy put on his ball so well.

"Computer, begin," Kirk said and ducked reflexively when the first ball of light shot out of the slot on the far side of the room and came straight at his head. Maybe he was worse at this than he thought. "Beginners level one, please," he appended. "Just as a warmup." The next ball came more slowly and he was off.

Quite some time later he was soaked with sweat but had risen in the ranks of play quite admirably. He put a spin on his last ball that would leave McCoy with his mouth open, centering onto the score pad with perfect accuracy, and glanced at the tally. Not bad. Not bad at all. Next time around, McCoy wouldn't know what hit him.

He pushed away from the wall toward the floor and the catch ring beside the door. Any further speculation on Bones's spectacular downfall as the *Enterprise* Riseaway champion was thrown to the four winds when the antigrav unexpectedly cut off. Fortunately, Kirk was not that high off the floor, so he didn't have very far to fall. Even so, it took him by surprise, and he landed hard, twisting at the last moment to take the brunt of the fall across his shoulders. Pain bloomed and he clamped one hand along the left side of his rib cage, eyes squeezed shut.

After a minute or two, he opened his eyes and gingerly sat up, testing his side with carefully probing fingertips. Nothing broken, but he'd probably have one hell of a bruise in a few hours. "Face it," he muttered, all good feeling from the game rapidly evaporating. "You're getting too old for this sort of thing." Standing slowly, he powered down the rest of the switches and left the room.

Everyone else had gone from the gym, so there was no one he could ask to see if any of the other rooms had been similarly affected as his own. He touched the communicator in the locker room. "Kirk to Commander Scott."

"Scott here, Captain."

Kirk pushed back the cowl and ran one hand through his sweaty hair. "Scotty, the antigrav in gym room nine just cut out on me."

"Are you all right, sir?" the chief engineer asked concernedly. "Should I send for Dr. Chapel?"

"That won't be necessary, Scotty. I'm fine. But have one of your engineers check into it, would you? I don't want to run the risk of someone getting seriously injured."

"Aye, sir," came Scott's voice over the intercom. "I'll do that right away. And I'll post a note to crew to not use the rooms until they get my all-clear."

"Very good, Mr. Scott. Kirk out." He peeled the wet suit down around his waist and stepped up to a mirror to inspect his side more closely. No doubt about it, he was going to have a bruise to beat all bruises. Muttering dire imprecations against a certain simple country doctor who should have known better than to get so good at such a stupid game, Kirk stepped the rest of the way out of the suit and immediately into the showers. The hot water felt good on his battered body, but he didn't give himself the luxury of time to enjoy it. He was out again in a matter of moments and, shortly thereafter, emerged from the gymnasium and headed toward the turbolift to go to his quarters.

A very perplexed-looking crewman stood outside the turbolift, her fingers tapping an agitated cadence on the wall. "Problem, Lieutenant?" Kirk asked pleasantly.

She glanced over her shoulder, a disgusted look on her face, then, seeing who it was, immediately came to attention.

Kirk waved her at ease. "What seems to be the matter?"

"It's this turbolift. There's no response."

Kirk frowned. "That's peculiar." And after a few moments, he became impatient himself. "Well, this is nonsense," Kirk murmured in annoyance, hands planted firmly on his hips. He raised his voice. "Computer!" he demanded.

"Working," the androgynous voice responded promptly.

"Define cause of malfunction of starboard turbolift."

There was a minuscule pause, then the computer's neutral tones returned. "The starboard turbolift is functioning normally in all parameters."

Kirk raised his eyebrows at the lieutenant. "The hell it is," he swore.

"Please restate request."

Kirk rolled his eyes. What he wouldn't have given for the good old days, when you had a computer that did what you asked, instead of trying to pass the time of day with you. He leaned on the button again and was a little startled when the doors opened immediately. *"Finally,"* Kirk breathed with satisfaction. "That's more like it. Could have been heavy use, Lieutenant. After you."

"Thank you, sir." She smiled and Kirk was a hero one more time.

He vacated the car on Deck 5 and moved down the hall past McCoy's and Spock's quarters to his own. Once inside, he shed his jacket, wincing at the movement, then settled into the chair pulled up before his personal communications station. With one knuckle, he flicked a switch. "Kirk to Uhura."

"Here, sir." Her melodic voice was soothing to his ears.

"Have we heard anything from the landing party?"

"Negative, Captain."

Kirk glanced at the clock and pursed his lips. "They're overdue, Commander. See if you can raise them."

"Aye, sir." She paused, and he could hear the open channel. "Captain, I have a message coming in from Starfleet Command. It's Admiral Cartwright."

Kirk settled more comfortably into his chair. He debated putting his jacket back on, but he and Cartwright were old friends and he thought the Admiral wouldn't begrudge him this one slight drop in protocol. "Put him through, Uhura, and get Spock or McCoy on the line."

"Aye, aye, sir. Starfleet Command, this is *Enterprise*. Go ahead, please." Uhura's channel closed. The communications station screen momentarily flared with brilliant light, then cleared to show Admiral Cartwright's dark features. The handsome Starfleet officer nodded pleasantly. "Hello, Jim."

"Admiral."

"I just got your message. Are you certain it's a Romulan space station?"

"Reasonably certain. I won't know any details until the landing party has returned to the ship. Mr. Spock and Dr. McCoy are there now with a security crew."

"Very good."

Kirk leaned forward, arms folded on the desk top. "Admiral, has there been any word of activity along the Neutral Zone? Is there anything we should be on the lookout for?"

Cartwright's expression was serious. "We haven't received any reports that give us concern. Nothing to make us wary. But that doesn't mean the Romulans aren't out there cooking something up. Just so you know, on your recommendation I've notified Zone checkpoints to keep their eyes peeled for activity of any kind. Has there been anything on your end?"

"Negative, Admiral. Sensors indicate no alien or unidentified ships in the area."

Cartwright nodded, though he didn't look particularly happy. "I don't like this. If it is a Romulan station, it represents a huge threat. Jim, I'm going to send you some backup. I can have the *Kongo* there in thirty-six hours and the *Lexington* there in three days. I hope we don't need them, but we can't take any chances. Let me know if there are any developments or if you hear at all from your landing party."

"I'll keep you notified, Admiral. As soon as I hear something, so will you."

Cartwright smiled then. "I know I will, Jim. Good luck. Starfleet out." The screen went dark.

Kirk leaned back in his chair and stared at the wall. It was good knowing that Starfleet was apprised of the situation and taking steps to keep a sharper eye on the Romulan situation, if there was one. And the reinforcements would help deter anyone with hostile intent. Should he have voiced McCoy's earlier speculation that it might not be the Romulans at all? That was a hard call. He didn't want to light too many fires under Starfleet Command's collective rumps, and there were some members who would jump at the slightest spark and suggestion of heat. Better to wait and see what happened. Speaking of happening . . .

He toggled a switch again. "Uhura, did you get hold of Spock?"

She sounded perplexed when she replied. "Still

trying, Captain. There's minor interference on the channel, and I can't seem to—"

Montgomery Scott's rough brogue broke into the channel and overrode her, stopping Kirk's breath in his throat and sending an icy chill spreading out from his heart. "Captain! I've lost the landing party's coordinates!"

Chapter Six

A SMALL, FIRM, and utterly adamant hand came down hard upon McCoy's shoulder and drove him painfully to the cold floor. He gasped sharply when his knees protested the harsh action, and felt the other members of the landing party draw around him in a huddle in the sudden darkness. As close as they were, he could see nothing, not even the glint of insignia. Their breathing sounded light and rapid in his ears. His own heart trip-hammered against his rib cage like a native drummer gone berserk, and he fought down the adrenaline-shot desire to flee. Panicked retreat in blind darkness would only spell disaster for him, if not for the entire party. Ensign Hallie's flash-encumbered hand stayed firmly in place on his shoulder, and he was grateful for the physical contact. It gave him a point of reference in the disorientation of utter sightlessness.

"Spock—" McCoy's whispered voice sounded raspy with stress and overly loud. Hallie's fingers tightened on his shoulder, bidding him be silent. He was probably breaking some important rule by speaking out, but he had to know—

"Silence, Doctor," the Vulcan ordered sharply. The hushed command, delivered in an inarguable tone, came from McCoy's right and above his head. Evidently Ensign Markson hadn't had as much success as Ensign Hallie in getting his charge to crouch at floor level. Spock was still standing.

"What are you doing?" McCoy demanded hoarsely, ignoring Spock's command. He wanted so badly to know if something was creeping up on them, though if there were, it was probably as hindered by the darkness as they. *Right,* he snorted to himself. *With my luck, it's wearing infrared glasses.*

The first officer's next words were short, his speech clipped in the closest approximation he ever had to genuine irritation. "Endeavoring to listen, Dr. McCoy, if you would be so kind as to cease your unnecessary chatter."

That shut up the brash physician and heated his face with a sudden, well-justified blush. He stayed silent, crouched where he was with one hand against the cool floor between his knees for balance and the other wrapped securely around the butt of his phaser, for all the good it would do. He wasn't about to start shooting in the dark, even if one of Commander Scott's shipboard bogeymen *was* coming at them. He wasn't going to risk killing one of his crewmates on the unlikely off-chance that he *might* hit whatever was out there. If there *was* anything out there.

He looked down toward his phaser and was startled to find he couldn't see the power indicator light. What the hell was going on here?

Someone's shoulder bumped his lightly, startling him and rocking him slightly off-balance for a moment. A whispered voice that sounded a little like Leno's, murmured, "Sorry," and the contact was immediately broken. He missed it as soon as it was gone. The brief touch was immeasurably reassuring. It was nice knowing he wasn't alone in this, even if he couldn't see the other person's face.

Wait a minute . . . yes, he could! The corridor's murky emergency lights flickered and grew steady. The unanticipated illumination was comforting, for all that the reddish hue lent a sepulchral, other-worldly cast to everything. *Welcome to Hell Dr. McCoy,* the doctor thought sourly.

The doctor looked up. Spock stood over them, his lean form tensed. The Vulcan's head turned slowly from side to side as he attempted to catch any vagrant sound with those superior ears of his. The weird lighting edged the sharp contours of his face and drove skeletal hollows into his cheeks and around both eyes until he looked more like a Vulcan corpse than a flesh-and-blood entity.

"Can we get up now?"

When the first officer nodded once in response to his question, the doctor and the others climbed to their feet. Almost without conscious thought, they stood nearly back-to-back, at least one pair of eyes trained in each direction.

"Did you hear anything, Mr. Spock?" Chekov inquired.

"No." The Vulcan seemed disappointed. His dark eyes searched the empty corridor.

"Is everyone all right?" McCoy asked the others. They all nodded assent, and Hallie blew a stray lock of hair out of her eyes. Leno's eyes flicked in rapid movements as she checked every angle for something that wasn't right.

McCoy drew a deep breath. *All the more power to her,* he thought. *I don't think there's* anything *here that's quite right.* "Well," he said, "What the hell was that all about?"

"Uncertain, Doctor." Spock said evenly. His eyes continued to hunt the shadowy corridor, though there was obviously nothing to see. "My shipboard sensors indicated systems on bare maintenance with no draw of power. Even were systems to fail entirely, such failure should under no circumstances affect our personal handlamps."

"That's not all it affected," Hallie spoke up. She raised her phaser. "The power's up now, but during the blackout even this went dead. At least, the indicator light did," she amended. "I don't know if we would have had power if we needed it."

McCoy nodded. "Hallie's right. I know my light was out."

"Not good," Leno muttered, and shared a look with Chekov.

"This is most curious," was Spock's response to the news.

"'Most curious'?" McCoy parroted, irritated by the first officer's calmness. "Is *that* all you can say? 'Most curious'?" Hands on his hips, he quelled a desire to shake the Vulcan.

"I fail to understand what it is you desire me *to* say," Spock replied. He swung his tricorder around front and thumbed the controls. "My tricorder is functioning along normal parameters." He turned in a slow circle and stopped, facing in the direction they had been heading. "However, there is no indication of a power drain." He held up the instrument for all to see. "Fascinating. I suggest we proceed with our search."

"Wait a minute!" McCoy's voice brought the Vulcan up short. "What are we going to do if our lights fail again?"

Spock turned and gave the doctor an appraising once-over. "We will have to deal with that when, and if, it occurs," he replied pragmatically.

"Terrific," McCoy sneered and turned away.

"I would prefer to submit almost any other positive alternative course of action, Dr. McCoy, but our options seem to be singularly limited in that regard at this time, until we gain further information."

Was that testiness edging the Vulcan's firm tones like ice forming along the shore of a lake? McCoy turned back and peered closely at Spock's emotionless face, zeroing in on the dark orbs beneath the peaked and shadowed brows. Spock could swear on all his Vulcan ancestors that he harbored not one whit of emotion in his soul, but McCoy knew differently. Just as he now knew, clear as day, the message Spock silently broadcast via those dark, bottomless eyes: *We are the senior officers on this mission. We need to be together in this, if in nothing else.*

McCoy felt a stab of shame for his behavior. He was well deserving of Spock's chastening. This station and everything in it was an enormous unknown quantity. Spock would do everything in his power to keep their group safe and together, but he was obviously bothered by the situation, whether or not he'd admit it. The fact that all this had spooked the unflappable Vulcan was enough to make McCoy sit up and take notice. "Don't you think we should contact the ship?" he asked quietly and far more appropriately. "The captain might want to reconsider an exploration if we don't have any assurance of lights."

Spock paused, deep in thought. "While I do not

wish us to be caught at a disadvantage should our lights fail us again," he concluded after several moments of silence, "neither do I necessarily think that abandoning our exploration is our best course of action. Your recommendation is sound, Doctor. We shall let Captain Kirk advise us on how to proceed. He may, indeed, prefer that we return to the ship at this time."

"Sounds good to me," the doctor agreed readily. Chekov and Leno looked slightly disappointed by the decision, but they had the notorious reputation for being two of the more adventuresome spirits aboard the *Enterprise*. Hallie seemed ambivalent, her eyes on her chief. For his part, Markson looked enormously relieved.

Spock unhooked his communicator and flipped it open. "Spock to *Enterprise*." When there was no immediate response, he glanced briefly at his companions and toyed with the dials on the mechanism's face before he tried again. "This is Mr. Spock. *Enterprise*, do you read me?"

The responding silence made McCoy's stomach try to climb up the inside of his throat. "What's the matter, Spock?"

The Vulcan stared thoughtfully at the communicator a moment before folding it shut. He looked up. "We appear to have lost contact with the ship," he said simply.

An icy chill trickled along Kirk's stomach lining at the chief engineer's dire words. He inhaled sharply and hunched over the desk in his quarters. "What's happened, Scotty?"

Despair colored the chief engineer's rich tones even over the shipboard communicator's tiny speakers.

"That's just it, sir! I don't know! One minute they were there, safe as a bairn in a basket. The next minute they were gone, like they'd never even been there!"

"Did you have a clear reading on them the entire time?"

"Aye, sir, that I did!" came the Scotsman's vehement reply. "It was a strong, solid signal, all but for an instant."

"An instant?" Kirk repeated, jumping on the chief engineer's words. He leaned farther forward, as though he could squeeze himself through the linkup and appear at Scott's side in the transporter room. "An instant, you said, Scotty?"

"Aye, sir. For no reason I can fathom, the signal fluctuated a wee bit." Scott's voice grew mournful. "The next thing I knew, they were gone."

Kirk slumped back, mind racing. "The antigrav failed in the gym," he murmured to himself. "And the turbolift . . ."

"Sir?" Mr. Scott questioned. "What was that about the turbolift?"

"I'm not certain, Scotty, except that it was behaving oddly a little while ago. I just thought there were a lot of people using it at once, but now I think that may not have been the case. I want you to check on it and compare your findings with whatever caused the antigrav to kick out in the gym. And stay on the transporter. Keep trying to find the landing party, and when you do, beam them back immediately."

"Aye, sir!" The line closed.

Kirk stabbed a button on the console, his reflection cast back waveringly from the dark screen. "Uhura!" he barked. "Have you got a fix on that channel to Spock?"

"I'm sorry, Captain." The communications officer sounded angry with herself or her equipment. "I've tried everything, but I can't access the channel."

"Is something jamming us?" Dammit, *was* this a Romulan plot and were they about to attacked?

"I don't know, sir. It's not like any jamming I've ever come across. It's more like . . . well, like *leaching,* sir. As though the signal's just evaporating."

Kirk's mind leapt like water across a hot griddle as a wash of adrenaline set his heart thudding rapidly against his ribs and painfully reminded him of his bruised side. "All right, Uhura." He kept his voice calm, reassuring. "I know you're doing your best. Keep trying to raise them. I'm on my way to the bridge."

"Aye, sir."

Kirk leaned forward, "And, Uhura, I want reports from all sections regarding any malfunctions, power drop-offs, or unusual energy drains or fluctuations of any kind in the past couple of hours. I don't care how minor they might appear."

"Yes, sir. I'll have the information waiting for you." Uhura dropped out of the connection.

There has to be a correlation, Kirk thought as he started for the door. This couldn't be just coincidental. Besides which, he didn't happen to believe in coincidence. Too many close brushes with death had instilled in the captain a firm philosophy that everything happened for a reason, no matter how obscure. You might never know or understand the reason, but it was there.

He hit the corridor almost running and strode quickly toward the turbolift. The doors silently opened as he reached them. Good. At least they were back to working normally. He stepped inside without hesitation, and the doors closed quietly as his back. "Bridge."

The grav plate beneath his feet hummed quietly as the turbolift accelerated, moving with a smooth, upward sensation, the readout over the door glowing. Deck 3 . . . Deck 2 . . . Next would be the bridge.

The turbolift ground to a halt with a sound that set Kirk's teeth on edge. The door panel stolidly read 2, and the doors did not open.

Kirk's sigh was an explosion of frustration. "Dammit, I don't have time for this!" He had an away team missing, at least so far as the transporter console was concerned, and he needed to find a way to reach them. What he did *not* need was a malfunctioning ship!

The turbolift car suddenly dropped away beneath him, leaving Kirk's stomach hanging in his throat. He lunged toward the manual override but was knocked off his feet as the car unexpectedly jerked sideways on Deck 5. Kirk lost his balance, spun around, and hit the floor hard, knocking the air from his lungs. His formerly bruised side exploded with a flare of brilliant pain as two ribs snapped. Fighting for breath, he hitched gasps against the rush of agony and fought the encroaching dark that threatened to leave him unconscious on the floor. The deck indicator over the door glowed a steady 5 as the turbolift hurtled the length of the saucer section.

There was a roaring in his ears and, despite his efforts, his vision was going gray. Kirk blindly shambled to his knees, one hand pressed firmly against the white heat in his rib cage, and tried to remember through the haze of pain and disorientation in which direction lay the manual override. With his free hand, he clawed sightlessly for the handrail and pulled himself up, forcing himself to stand on knees watery with shock and pain.

The turbolift abruptly paused. There was the briefest, most horrible moment of silence . . . then the car fell. Utterly out of control, it plummeted in free-fall in a destructive destination to the shaft bottom.

Chapter Seven

"WHAT DO YOU MEAN, we *appear* to have lost contact with the ship?" McCoy's voice broke the profound silence following Spock's terrible pronouncement. "Have we or haven't we?"

The Vulcan's one eyebrow twitched slightly. "Yes, Doctor, we have." He glanced curiously at the communicator still cupped in his hand, then returned it to his belt.

"Well, that's just terrific!" McCoy crossed his arms tightly over his chest, not because he was annoyed or angry (though he was both), but because his hands were suddenly colder than they had any right to be, even considering the cooler temperatures of the derelict space station. He crammed his hands into his armpits and tried to ignore the shivering sensation that sprang to life somewhere deep in his solar plexus. He unhappily eyed Spock's stoic features. "Now what do we do?"

"I recommend that we carry on our investigation of this vessel as planned," Spock said simply, and with more calmness than McCoy felt he had any right to display. "We are still under orders from the captain to try and discover why this station is here. I think it likely that whatever caused our power outage may also have contributed to the station's present condition. We will attempt to reestablish contact with the *Enterprise* at routine intervals during our search."

"And hope for the best?" McCoy asked sourly.

"And find an alternative system of communication, if necessary, Doctor," Spock replied.

"Where, sir?" asked Markson.

Spock turned toward the young security guard. "Despite the fact that auxiliary systems are inaccessible, Ensign, I believe our chances of success are greater on the station bridge."

"Mr. Spock," Leno spoke up. "Do you think that the same thing that drained your hand lamp is interfering with our ability to contact the ship?"

"And yet the lights didn't go out again," Chekov pointed out to her.

"Even so, Lieutenant," Spock replied. "Which makes these circumstances even more curious. It may mean that the *Enterprise* is affected as well and is unable to receive my signal or respond if they *are* receiving."

"I was afraid you'd say that," McCoy grumbled.

"Mr. Spock, what happens if we get to this bridge and you're wrong? That the generator can't access the computer?" Markson's dark eyes looked huge in the odd light. "What if we can't reach the *Enterprise* to let them know what's happened? What if she can't reach us? What do we do then?"

Spock stared down at the younger man and was

quiet for longer than McCoy liked. "I do not know, Ensign," he replied evenly. "That line of speculation is useless until it becomes a necessity."

"He's right," McCoy added more gently, and laid a careful hand on Markson's arm. "In psychology it's called fortune telling. You predict that things will turn out badly before waiting to see what's the reality of the situation. That produces stress and makes the current situation just that much more difficult to deal with. We're going to be okay."

"If you say so, sir," Markson said gamely. His Adam's apple bobbed twice. "It's just that, well, something might have killed that Romulan." His hand waved out in an unhappy gesture at the sprawled corpse. "What do we do if it's still aboard?"

"You're doing it again, Dan," Hallie warned.

"What do you suggest we do, Markson?" Leno asked tersely. *"Walk* back to the ship?"

"Easy, you two," Chekov said quietly. His voice brought their eyes to his face and they visibly relaxed after some silent, secret message passed between them and their chief. Leno nodded an apology at Markson, and he smiled slightly.

"Maybe something killed her," McCoy added. "And maybe something happened so that she fell and landed wrong and fractured her neck that way. It's been known to happen."

Markson nodded. "Yes, sir. Thank you, sir."

Hallie patted her friend's shoulder. "Take it easy, Dan. Everything's going to be all right. We're not out of this yet." She grinned gamely at Chekov. "I'll bet the lieutenant's been in worse scrapes than this in his career, right, sir?" McCoy didn't need a degree in linguistics to read her body language. She wanted her friend reassured, and maybe herself, too.

Chekov rolled his expressive eyes and nodded.

"There are a number that come to mind, Hallie. Dr. McCoy can attest to that?"

"Right, Lieutenant," McCoy agreed enthusiastically. "Why, Ensign Hallie, I could bore you for hours recounting some of the stuff we've been through."

She smiled and nodded. "I'll take you up on that sometime, sir, if I may."

McCoy put a reassuring hand on Markson's shoulder and squeezed, then turned his attention to Spock. "Well? If we're going to find that bridge, or anything else, we'd better get a move on."

"I agree. Doubtless, the captain is as concerned by our silence as we are by theirs."

"Concerned? Jim's probably pulling out his hair." Just talking about his friend, and reminding himself that Kirk was out there, made McCoy feel better. He swung one arm in a broad arc. "After you."

They fell into a close file. Chekov led, phaser in one hand, light in the other, with Markson and Spock behind him. McCoy followed with Hallie protectively at his heels, while Leno brought up the rear.

The corridor seemed a dead end until they drew closer and discovered a slight turn. There they found a door set into the wall at such an angle that it had been impossible to see it before, even when their handlamps lit the corridor. When Chekov tried the door, it opened easily. Beyond him, stairs rose and descended into red-hued darkness.

The discovery made McCoy uneasy. He'd done a fair job explaining away the Romulan woman's death, and he believed Spock's explanation for the flash of movement they had seen. Mostly. But being the devil's advocate that he was, there was an annoying trait of speculation in his soul that made him wonder if, indeed, there had been something in the hallway that had escaped into this stairwell. If so, was there any guarantee that it wouldn't conceal itself farther along to do them mischief later?

"Well, Spock? Which way should we go?"

The first officer stepped into the stairwell and shone his handlamp above and below. The tricorder in his hand gave off no pertinent readings, and he put it away after brief consideration. "I recommend we go up."

McCoy shrugged. "Suits me. Let's go." He followed the others inside.

The stairs were open-worked metal and clanged gently at each step they took. After two turns, McCoy expected to find a landing for the next level, but that was not the case. The stairwell extended on above them into darkness and he sighed, resigned to a long climb on calf muscles not used to such exercise. He'd have to stop playing Riseaway so often and concentrate on leg weights for awhile, unless he wanted his lower body to turn into a sponge.

Hallie's low voice in his ear was so unexpected that McCoy started slightly, only then noticing that she was pacing him, rather than following behind. "Is he going to be okay, sir?" Her chin jerked. "Dan, I mean. I've never seen him get edgy like this before."

"How much do you know about Ensign Markson?" he caged.

She shrugged one shoulder, her eyes following the motion of her feet. "We were pretty good friends at the Academy, and it was nice being assigned together, especially to the *Enterprise*. I know he's from Vindali 5, if that's what you mean."

McCoy nodded. "Has he told you much about Vindali 5? About the culture?"

"A few things, now and then. We've talked about our families and stuff, and a little bit about growing up, but Dan's not a great one for talking about his past. He's not secretive or anything, it just doesn't seem to him that anyone would be interested."

The doctor paused, thinking, then decided that, while personnel records were confidential, he wasn't exactly breaking the doctor-patient code of silence to discuss the religious habits of a rim world. "Vindalins are devout believers in the supernatural, Ensign. Ghosts figure very strongly in their daily lives, whether it's an ancestor you hope will guard you or an enemy you want to be guarded against. The belief is an integral part of their society and their daily lives."

"So Dan's afraid of ghosts?" She looked vaguely disgusted, vaguely disquieted, and she studied her friend's broad back where he walked ahead of Spock. "But, he's not even really a Vindalin, except by birth. His folks are originally from Earth."

"In some ways, he's Vindalin in *all* but bloodline," McCoy continued. "He was raised with Vindalin children, educated in Vindalin schools. I'm sure his parents taught him about Earth and our beliefs, but kids are an impressionable lot, especially if their peers are radically different. Without a doubt, he internalized a lot of that culture. And we don't have any idea what kinds of things he's seen." McCoy pursed his lips, pondering, suddenly sorry there hadn't been more detail in Markson's file. "And I don't know if 'afraid' is the correct word to describe what he's feeling, Hallie, but I think he's bothered by all this creepiness. Hearing Mr. Scott's story about the *Stephanie Emilia* just before this assignment probably didn't help any."

She nodded. "You know, I tried talking about that a little after we left the rec room, because I thought it was such a neat story, but Dan wouldn't join in, so I dropped it."

"There you go. We don't know what Dan was

exposed to as a kid, what he saw while he was growing up. But I'll tell you something . . . I've been trained by Starfleet and I'm about as down-to-earth as you can get without becoming a Vulcan, but I've seen a few things in *my* life that, were I inclined to believe in spirits or influenced by a culture that does, all the Starfleet training in the world wouldn't get me to change my mind. There's some spooky stuff out there in the universe, Ensign."

"I know," she agreed. Her eyes shone. "I want to see it all."

McCoy laughed quietly. "Spoken like a true Starfleet graduate!" He patted her arm. "Markson's feeling nervous, Hallie, that's all. His past is coming out of the closet, so to speak. Most of us deal well with fear until our own personal bogey-man comes along. You never know how you'll react under those circumstances, so maybe we all should show him some understanding. Hell, we may all be more than a little frightened by the time this mission is over." He didn't like saying that, but it was a way to let her know to expect the unexpected.

She nodded and he saw that she understood and appreciated not only his words but the underlying message as well. "Thank you, sir. I'll keep that all in mind."

"Good."

They followed the others, progressing up the stairs, turn after turn, until McCoy began to wonder just where the hell they were headed. Spock periodically attempted to raise the *Enterprise,* but with no success. The communicator remained resolutely silent, as though the universe had ceased to exist beyond the tiny sphere of what was readily observable by the landing party. *That* thought made McCoy's skin crawl, and he hurried to make certain very little distance opened up between him and the long-legged Vulcan ahead of him. He wasn't about to be left behind in this Romulan excuse for a funhouse.

"Here's another door, Mr. Spock," Chekov announced from the front. "And it's open."

"Great!" McCoy exclaimed. "Let's get the hell out of here, even for a few minutes." He followed the others out of the stairwell and stopped dead, his mouth hanging open.

It had never really occurred to him how much this station might incorporate, how much it might resemble other stations he had visited in his travels around the universe, despite its odd appearance from the outside. What he saw now left him as speechless as Dorothy Gale suddenly plopped down in the center of Munchkinland.

The area they had stepped into was enormous, stretching away in all directions with a spiderwebbing of access corridors going every which way. McCoy couldn't see the ceiling in the encroaching gloom, but there was an impression of distance. All around them were shops and storefronts, and—he guessed—the Romulan equivalent of bars and such. The transporter room might have been at the center of the station's mass, but this was the hub, the life of the place. Or, rather, it was meant to be, for every establishment was dark and silent, empty of any sign of life, past or present.

"It's like a ghost town," McCoy noted quietly. One look at Ensign Markson immediately made him regret his choice of words. "Just a figure of speech," he amended.

"It looks so . . . *innocent,*" Chekov said, sounding surprised. "I expected to find something more—" He sought for a word. "*—sinister* on a Romulan space station."

"There *is* nothing more sinister than a Romulan bar, Lieutenant, or so I've been told." McCoy rubbed his hands together and tipped a look at Spock. "What do you say we do a little looking around?"

"That's what we are here for, Doctor. While you and the security team explore, I shall endeavor to locate a computer terminal access junction and patch into the mainframe of the station to contact the *Enterprise.*"

McCoy nodded and waved an arm. "Come on, Ensign Hallie. You can be my shadow. You wanted to see everything in the universe? Let's start here."

"Do not wander off too far, Doctor," Spock cautioned. "We should stay within earshot."

"Whatever you say, Spock." McCoy started away, the security guard close behind him. He unslung his medical tricorder as they walked and took a quick reading that showed him nothing worth mentioning to anyone. The place might as well have been filled with dust mice and tumbling tumbleweeds, for all the indications of life it showed.

He looked around as they walked up the wide avenue, staring upward at the structures that disappeared into the gloom. Some seemed unfinished, or perhaps that was just the way they were intended to look, with skeletal projections of metal reaching toward the unseen ceiling or across the gaping street at the buildings standing opposite. McCoy stopped to peer into one building, wiping his sleeve across the window, then moved on.

"It's like an amusement park at night, isn't it?" Hallie asked wonderingly.

He looked over. The security guard was standing still, staring upward. "Beg pardon?"

She looked embarrassed. "I've never seen one, of course, but it looks like the pictures on the vid. All metal and spidery-looking. Not when it's running, but afterward, when everyone has gone home and all the lights are turned off."

The doctor followed her gaze. He'd seen tapes of Coney Island, before it had disappeared into the sea so many years ago. He knew what she meant. "Yes, Ensign, I guess you're right."

They kept walking. Most of the buildings were barred to their entrance and neither of them thought it prudent at this time to force way in. They peered through windows when they could, remarking on the wares within. Bolts of brilliant cloth caught the illumination from their handlamp when the beams were trained inside, the light catching and running along metallic threads woven into the sumptuous material. Food was molding in the window of another shop they hurried past. Farther along, plants lay brown and dead. In a fourth were displayed items that made Hallie blush and look away and made McCoy chuckle.

"Well, they didn't close up for lack of variety, that's for sure," McCoy remarked. He stopped to stare at the next shopfront. It was low and long and seemed to go back for quite a distance. "Now, this looks interesting." He gestured at the sign overhead. "Can you read Romulan, Ensign?"

"No, sir. It wasn't one of my languages." She tilted her head, studying the front of the building. "Maybe it's a bar."

"Too big." McCoy furrowed his brow, considering. "Could be a theater of some kind." He reached out and jiggled the catch on the door, and it moved under his hand. His eyes lit. "Hey! This one's open! What do you say we—"

Spock's voice cut him off, hailing them from the far end of the street where he stood with Chekov, Leno, and Markson. "Dr. McCoy! Ensign Hallie!"

"He always finds a way to spoil my fun," McCoy muttered. "What is it, Spock?" he called.

"I have managed a partial access into the computer system."

"Great! What have you found out?"

"Relatively little before the system shut down. However, I did gain a map of the station in the process, so we can now proceed to the bridge."

"All right!" McCoy called. "We'll be right with you. I just want to check this one—" He depressed the catch even as he spoke and hip-shoved the door open.

The smell that assailed them turned Hallie around in her tracks, gagging, one hand pressed tightly over her mouth. Breathing deeply through his mouth, McCoy shoved her back with one arm as he stepped farther into the room and clicked on his handlamp.

The building was an amphitheater or something along those lines, with a high, vaulted ceiling that vanished into shadows. Whoever had been performing had played to a packed house. Now the room was filled with Romulans who had been dead some weeks.

"I don't need this," McCoy said quietly. An undefinable sadness swept through him as he swallowed a roil of sickness and removed the mediscanner from his pouch. "I don't need this at all."

Chapter Eight

THROUGH THE ENCROACHING snowy gray haze of his vision, Kirk crabbed blindly for the turbolift's manual control. His brain raced, fighting against the throbbing pulse of pain in his side, striving to retain consciousness, striving to regain equilibrium. He felt, rather than saw, the latch under the groping fingers of his fumbling hands spring open at his touch. Ribs shrieking, he used both hands to grasp the handle within, and hauled on the manual override like a sailor at the rudder of a storm-tossed vessel. The emergency couplers locked in with a clang and squeal of metal, slowing the turbolift's runaway descent and leaving Kirk's heart in his throat.

Gasping, he looked up at the readout over the door. The gray haze vanished from his vision, and his tight grip on the manual control lever was the only thing that kept him on his feet as shock kicked in. It had been close, too damned close! Another few moments

97

and it would have all been over for James T. Kirk. Bones would have had to scrape him off the shaft floor and ship his remains home in a mason jar.

Kirk felt a white-hot flash of pain from his broken ribs every time he took a breath. He watched the readout through the thatch of hair across his dazed eyes as the turbolift car began to rise: Deck 14 . . . Deck 13 . . . Deck 12 . . . and still it rose at its normal speed, as sedate as a coach and four out for a turn around the park. When it reached Deck 7, a mellow tone sounded. The turbolift stopped its ascent without any impetus from Kirk, and the doors slid open silently.

Scotty, and the two engineering techs with him, blinked with astonishment at the sight of their captain slumped against the turbolift wall. "Captain Kirk! What in the name of all that's ho—"

"Get me out of here!" Kirk rasped and lunged for the door, not wanting to remain inside the ill-behaved contraption one moment longer. Their hands caught him and pulled him free. Kirk's legs gave out, and he sagged to the floor with Scott's supporting arms around his shoulders. Chest heaving with aftershock, the captain watched as one of the techs deactivated the turbolift, locked the doors open, and applied a bright orange strip that said No Access. Kirk's eyes tracked to Scotty's concerned face. "How did you know I was in there?"

"I didn't, sir. These lads called me in the transporter room and said the computer had flagged a malfunction on the starboard turbolift, that it was in free-fall. They threw an immediate coupler, but by that time one had already been thrown manually from within the turbolift, so we knew someone was inside. I had it routed here so I could take a look for myself."

"You're supposed to be in the transporter room tracking the away team."

Scott met his captain's accusatory glare without batting an eye or flinching. "Aye, sir. I've got Lieutenant Rand on it. She's as good as they come, with none better. If the landing party's signal comes back on line, she'll fetch them home as quickly and neatly as I could." Scott's expression was serious. "I was needed here as well, sir, to assure the safety of the crew. And speaking of which, you've cut your forehead, Captain."

Kirk probed his brow with gentle fingers and winced. A goose-egg swelling rose over his left eye, though he couldn't remember having hit his head. The center of the contusion was damp, and his fingers came away spotted with red. Blood had trickled into his eyebrow and caked there in a sticky patch.

"You should have that looked at, Captain," Scott suggested.

"Later, Mr. Scott." Kirk wiped his sticky fingers on his pant leg and held out his arm. "Help me up." The jolt of pain as he rose was so severe that Kirk's teeth snapped together, clacking like an Arn dreamtalker's divining bones, and he hissed sharply. His knees turned to mud, and his vision momentarily grew cloudy again and faded at the edges.

"Captain!" Scott snugged a firm arm around Kirk's waist, and the captain fought back a desire to scream. "You're hurt!"

"You could say that, Mr. Scott," Kirk grated through clenched teeth. With the chief engineer's help, he staggered to the intercom console on the wall beside the turbolift. An unsteady finger depressed the speaker button. "This is Captain Kirk." He closed his eyes, hating how weak and reedy his voice sounded.

He felt as though all the blood had drained out of his body. "The turbolifts are off-limits to all personnel. Repeat, *all* personnel. Use of the turbolifts may be a risk to your life. Until further notice, you are ordered to use the main stairwell and access ladders only. Kirk out." He forced his eyes open.

Scotty was staring at him, obviously perplexed. "Captain, there's no reason to shut down the entire system. These lads and I can take care of it in a jiffy. T'was only a wee malfunction."

"I don't think so, Mr. Scott," Kirk said grimly. "I think it was a whole lot more than that." He hitched a deep breath, wincing. "I have to get to the bridge."

"Aye, sir," Scott agreed readily. "As soon as you've been to sickbay."

"Scotty—"

"This isn't the first time this old pub crawler has seen a man suffering from broken ribs, Captain," Scott said sternly. "You'll never make it the seven levels to the bridge on your own without that being tended to. Sickbay is only down the hall, right on the way to the stairs. Can you not take a few minutes to have Dr. Chapel take a look at you?"

"I don't have time for that." Stubbornly, Kirk pulled himself out of the chief engineer's supporting embrace and turned away. One hand pressed tightly against his side, he took a single limping step down the corridor toward the stairwell and felt the recently regained color drain out of his face.

Scotty was at his side in an instant, lending a strong arm for Kirk to lean on. "Aye, but you're an obstinate man, sir. Do I have to carry you to sickbay?"

Kirk stared back, dumbfounded. "You wouldn't dare." He watched the chief engineer for a moment, then silently acquiesced with a weary sigh. "You would, too, wouldn't you?"

"Aye, sir." Scott glanced back over his shoulder. "You lads run a diagnostic on that turbolift and send the findings to my station on the bridge."

"Yes, sir, Commander." They turned away and began to work.

"Shall we, then, Mr. Scott?" Kirk held out an arm for Scotty's support and, quite happily, Scott slid in under the offered arm as they started toward sickbay.

It didn't take long for Christine Chapel to minister to Kirk's injuries and send him on his way with a strict order not to overdo. Two of his ribs were cracked, though fortunately not broken through. Chapel agreed to wait to repair them until the end of the present crisis, contenting herself with dressing the cut on his forehead.

Now he gusted a heavy sigh as he and Scotty reached the main stairwell leading upward through the *Enterprise*'s inner workings to the emergency hatch on the bridge, located just forward of the helm console. "I'm not looking forward to this, Mr. Scott."

"I know," Scott replied with feeling. "I can't say as I am, either." He stared up the long stairwell, and his head cocked sideways. "If need be, sir," he offered generously, "I can always take you piggy-back".

"Be careful what you offer, Mr. Scott," Kirk warned. "I may just take you up on it." He batted the chief engineer's arm. "Let's go."

It galled Kirk to have no real strength or stamina for this climb, no ability to draw the deep breaths necessary for such exertion. The painkiller dosage Dr. Chapel had given him was light, because he needed to remain sharp, but he was paying the price for the stitch of pain tracing along his side. His initial speed, an attempt not to give in to the injury, fell off after two flights, his breath catching in his chest and his lungs laboring like captives behind the prison of his rib cage.

The cut over his eyebrow, butterflied shut by Dr. Chapel's efficient hands, throbbed like a second heart, keeping juxtaposed rhythm with his labored breathing.

Kirk held up a hand, calling for a momentary halt, and hating to have to do it. His sight was fraught with pinpoints of light. If he didn't stop and rest, he'd pitch over and Scott *would* have to carry him. "Have we heard anything from the landing party?" he gasped.

"Not that I know of, sir," Scott panted, out of breath but not nearly as badly as Kirk. "And no sign of their signal on the transporter."

"Damn." Kirk ran a hand through his sweaty hair. "Can we send someone else over?"

Scotty looked dubious. "I suppose I could try, Captain, but I'd really rather not unless I have to. The transporter's been acting a bit queer since I lost the signal. I'd hate to transport someone into the bulkhead."

It wasn't a pleasant image. "How about sending over a shuttlecraft?"

The chief engineer thought a moment, then nodded. "Aye, it might be tricky with the fluctuations, but we could try that. Send a security crew over with another generator to patch into an airlock."

"Good. We'll do that." Frustration itched at Kirk like a rash. He needed to act. He needed to know what had happened to his landing party and what he could do to retrieve them, and he wanted to find out what the hell was wrong with his ship.

"Captain?" Scott asked as they resumed their climb. "What *did* happen on the turbolift?"

Briefly, Kirk outlined the story. Then he said, "Remember, I called you and told you about the antigrav cutting out on me in the gym?"

"Yes, sir."

"Well, the turbolift was acting odd earlier, too. Didn't come when the call button was depressed. And the transporter is out and Uhura can't raise the away team." His eyebrows rose. "Does that produce any theories, Mr. Scott?"

"Sounds like it may be an energy drain from somewhere, Captain, but I can't imagine from where. I'll check on it as soon as we reach the bridge."

In four million years . . ., Kirk thought. "Uhura's compiling a list"—Kirk paused to catch his breath—"to see if there have been other aberrations aboard the ship. If there are, we need to know where they're located, how widespread they are, and just how they are manifesting themselves." His sharp eyes sought Scott's. "And we need to find out what's causing them."

"If it's the *Enterprise* herself," Scotty vowed, "I'll know it."

"I appreciate your assurance, Mr. Scott, but I don't think it *is* the ship."

"Sir?"

"Our problems didn't start until we found that space station, Scotty. And we can't just assume that the reason we haven't heard from the landing party is because of our own problems with power. For all we know, they may be experiencing their own difficulties."

"That's not a pleasant thought, sir."

"No, Mr. Scott, it's not. But I don't know as much about that station as I'd like." He continued to climb.

As the levels approached and passed, Kirk leaned more and more heavily on the metal banister, relying on that and Scotty's staunch presence at his side to get him up the next flight.

Chest heaving and sending a jolt of pain into his side with each labored breath, Kirk leaned against the railing as Scott loosened the toggles securing the hatch cover. When it was loose, he pushed past the chief engineer, lifted the hatch, and climbed onto the bridge.

He grimaced as he climbed forth, grateful for Scotty's assistance from below. "Status report, Uhura!" he barked as evenly as he could, hauling himself out of the way so the chief engineer could climb past and head for his station.

"No contact with the landing party, Captain. Several decks reporting a variety of malfunctions," she announced briskly, "with more reports coming in."

Kirk all but fell into the command chair. He swallowed a groan and, for a moment, wished for another of Chapel's painkillers. He took the computer pad a yeoman offered, and his heart fell. Though the majority of problems were relatively minor, the list was much longer than he had anticipated. And had Uhura really said something about more reports coming in?

A profound tiredness stole over him, threatening to wash him away in a darkening tide, but there was no time for weariness, not with an away team missing aboard a space station that shouldn't even be there, and a starship that was falling to pieces around him.

"Scotty, I want you to see this." Kirk passed the list across to the bridge's engineering console. The captain didn't know the exact English translation of the Gaelic words that escaped Mr. Scott's lips in a vitriolic rush, but he could extrapolate very well, because the same general thought had crossed his own mind moments before.

Scott shook his head in disbelief. "I don't understand this at all, sir." He waved a hand at the readout. "Systems are falling off at different times. There's no pattern to the fluctuations nor where they're occurring. It's like we're a main course at a beer tasters' convention—a sip here, a sip there. I'll get my crew on it right away, but it may take some time—"

"We don't have the luxury of time, Commander Scott," Kirk stonily reminded him, hazel eyes hard.

"Aye, sir, that we don't. My crew is on it." He bent over his work station, speaking urgently.

Uhura turned from her console. "Captain, Deck 6 reports life support dropping to minimal despite attempts to bring it back on-line. With your permission, I'll have the off-duty personnel transfer elsewhere." When he nodded, she swiveled her chair around again.

"Ensign Estano!" Kirk called to the man in Chekov's chair during the security chief's absence.

The young ensign sat bolt upright. "Aye, sir!"

"I want a security team of two in the shuttlebay in five minutes. They're to take a shuttlecraft across to the space station and attempt to access the station proper and locate the landing party."

"Yes, sir!" Estano's hands flew over his console, and his voice rang out. "Security guards Jaffe and Corey are ordered to the shuttlebay in five minutes, suited for a rescue operation aboard the Romulan space station." Static broke up his message. Frowning, Estano repeated it. He shot a glance at Kirk. "I *think* they heard me, sir."

"Let's hope so, Mr. Estano. It's a long walk to the shuttlebay." He rubbed his hands together. "Uhura, is it cold in here or is it just me?"

She studied some readouts on the vast panel before her. "Life support is minimally affected, Captain. Bridge temperature has dropped by several degrees."

He nodded, unease squirming through his veins. Kirk stared ahead at the viewscreen. Its image of the space station was interrupted by a flurry of static.

Frustration gnawed at him. He was doing everything he could, following up his leads, and it felt like he was doing nothing! Something was making the *Enterprise* come apart around him, stealing the power she needed in order to function, and his landing party was as good as vanished. What in hell was happening over there?

Chapter Nine

BREATHING DEEPLY through his mouth against the almost overwhelming stench in the amphitheater proved to be almost as difficult for McCoy as breathing through his nose. The stink of decomposition was a palpable thing, lying along his tongue and the back of his throat in a way that let him taste its sweet sourness.

Quelling the desire to lose the meager remains of his last meal, McCoy twisted the mediscanner on. Its self-diagnostic beep let him know it was still functioning, unlike so much else aboard the station, but who knew when it might decide to quit on him? Stepping forward, he ran the business end of it back and forth above the nearest bodies. While one part of his mind occupied itself with interpreting the sounds emitted by the mechanism, McCoy did his own scan by eye.

McCoy wasn't interested in how they had died. The scanner would tell him that and much more by the time it was done taking its readings. What he was concerned with were clues to who these people were, how they had gotten to this place, and what they had been doing here. Was this station merely an attempt on the part of the Romulans to expand their presence in the galaxy—not unlike the motive the Human race had in building its first space stations? Or had there been a more nefarious reason for its construction?

And what about the secretive Romulans themselves? Did these people laugh at the same kinds of jokes he did? Did they even laugh at all? Did they enjoy a glass of Romulan ale after a hard day's work as much as he liked to relax with a glass of Kentucky bourbon? Did they hold their friends as dear to their hearts as he did Jim, Scotty, and (God help him) Spock?

This wasn't a game the physician was playing, though it had started out that way all those long-ago years in medical school at the Academy. Back then (and, given the common thread in medical students, it probably still went on), there was a running contest of sorts among the interns and residents to see how much they could divine about a patient merely by silent observation. Their deductions would then be corroborated or refuted by the hospital's written records. McCoy had become pretty good at it, good enough that the other students in his class took to calling him Sherlock McCoy. It was fun making those educated guesses, but during the course of that fun McCoy discovered an extraordinary thing. He began using that talent to better understand his patients, to learn where they came from, where they were going, what their fears and passions were, and how those impacted on their illness or their injury.

So many physicians couldn't be bothered to take the time to really watch and know their patients, to "be where they are looking," as a Native American professor had once appropriately phrased it. In McCoy's opinion, that sort of doctor was missing out on a rare opportunity to be something more than just a dispenser of medication. It was much easier to treat someone you were familiar with, someone you knew a little something about, even if that knowledge was garnered only through intuition. Granted, there was nothing of import he could do now for these dead Romulans, but that old training perked to life under his skin. He *wanted* to know a little more about these people, to make them real in his mind even if it was only for a moment or two, to make their deaths matter—if only to him.

The doctor contemplated his cadaverous patients for a moment longer, then turned and vacated the room, closing the door securely behind him. Only then, with the comparatively fresh air of the station cleansing the fetidness from his nostrils, did he realize that the rest of the party had joined him and Hallie, probably running up when they saw her turn away, sickened. She sat cross-legged on the floor, head bent over her knees, breathing deeply. Markson and Chekov knelt on either side of her. Markson's hand was on her shoulder in support, while the security chief spoke quietly in her ear. McCoy saw her nod at something Chekov said and look up. Her eyes seemed bigger than before against the pasty whiteness of her face.

Spock was watching McCoy. "Doctor?"

He jerked his head back. "It's not a pretty sight in there, Spock, but look if you want to. It's full of dead Romulans." He waited, back turned, while Spock made an extremely brief investigation. He heard the sound of a communicator being flipped open.

"Spock to *Enterprise*. This is Mr. Spock, contacting the *Enterprise*. Come in, *Enterprise*."

McCoy didn't expect a reply but was still disappointed when none came. He would have given almost anything to hear Jim Kirk's voice right about now, even if all Jim had to tell them was that they couldn't effect a rescue right at the moment. Just knowing he was out there would be a great help.

When the Vulcan returned to his side, McCoy was looking down at the scanner in his hand. "This is damned odd . . ."

"Doctor?"

He sighed irritably and returned the instrument to the pouch at his waist. "Well, according to the scanner's readings, all those people in there died of hypothermia. But I don't see how that can be possible." He breathed heavily, and his breath smoked slightly in the cool air. "It's just not that cold in here, especially on a station carrying clothing and blankets, like we've seen." He scratched his head. "I just don't get it. I don't get it at all."

Leno spoke up. "Is it possible that life support kicked off altogether and then came back on-line later?"

"As my grandpa used to say, Ensign, anything's possible in an animated cartoon," McCoy conceded. "If I wanted to buy the premise that these people had been murdered, I could see someone taking control of life support and shutting down every area but theirs until the others were dead, then reactivating it to throw a kink in any investigation that might follow. But there are just too many loose ends for that, and I don't think that's the case. Call it a gut feeling." He glanced briefly over his shoulder and away again. "I think those people came together for warmth and it just wasn't enough to sustain them. But it should have been." He frowned, disquieted, his eyes distant. He was reminded suddenly of his remark to Jim about finding a station full of dead Romulans. "This is just too weird." Even after all his years in the medical field and the vast extent of his training, knowledge, and hands-on experience, things like this still tended to make McCoy's gut clench up like a fist. Hypothermia was a damned tragic way for someone to die.

Rubbing her arms, Ensign Hallie stood up from the floor and released a short, explosively pent breath. "At least it's not some kind of plague we could catch," she said with relief and looked around at her companions.

"Well, it wasn't hypothermia that killed that first Romulan we found," Leno replied with laconic pragmatism and jerked a thumb over her shoulder back the way they came. Hallie shot her a dirty look behind Chekov's back.

"And it wasn't plague, either," McCoy added firmly. "Unless it's a plague that can make its victims run into walls headfirst."

"Do you think there are more bodies on board?" Markson wanted to know.

The doctor shrugged. "Who knows? If there are, I don't want to find them. I've seen plenty for today."

"How long have they been dead, Doctor?" Spock asked. He stared thoughtfully at the closed doors at McCoy's back, his expression unreadable.

"The scanner estimates four to six weeks," McCoy replied tiredly. "Same as the woman down below. Due to the extent of deterioration, I'm afraid I can't do any better than that without transporting them into sickbay and performing an autopsy. Why?"

Spock nodded as though caching the information away for further pondering somewhere in that computer he called a brain. "I am merely trying to discern how long this station may have been adrift. Since the

Romulans died at least four weeks ago from the effects of hypothermia, it is safe to assume the station has been adrift that long, and possibly longer. Beginning with the four-week time frame, if we can postulate the station's current trajectory and speed as having been constant and without interference from outside source or internal tampering, we should be able to deduce from where it drifted and chart its origin on a starchart."

"If you can find a computer to access that will let you do that, *or* manage to contact the *Enterprise*. Beside, I thought we decided that this station just washed in from the Romulan Empire." The doctor folded his arms. He felt unreasonably cross with the Vulcan's calm dissertation and the entire damned situation they were in. Being irritated . . . well, it annoyed him.

"Probable, but not certain, Doctor. Current information makes that reasoning inconclusive and only one avenue of not particularly valid speculation," Spock politely pointed out. "There are others."

"I don't think I want to hear them right now," McCoy hastened to reply. He stepped away from the amphitheater turned tomb and walked back the way they had come, drawing the others after him. He had no great desire to loiter outside the place. "Frankly, Spock, at the moment I pretty well don't give a damn where this station came from. All I care about is that we're without power and cut off from the *Enterprise*." He glanced at the tall figure striding along beside him. "You said something before about finding a map of the station?"

Spock nodded. "It was not extremely detailed, but it did show the location of the station's bridge. I endeavored to memorize it before the system abruptly shut down."

"Well, in that case, we'd better not lose you, had we?"

Spock let the comment slide. "Now that I know with better assurance where we are within the station, we can more accurately direct our progress. According to the map, if we take the stairs up two more levels, we can then access a corridor that will take us to a turboshaft and, hence, to the bridge."

"Wait just one damn minute," McCoy broke in brusquely and stopped dead. Spock looked at him and blinked so patiently that the doctor was reminded of one of his uncle's Jersey cows. "Taking a turbolift might have been a fine idea before all this nonsense with the power started. If you think I'm getting into a turbolift on a station with fluctuating power that might just decide at any moment to cut out altogether, you're out of your ever-loving Vulcan mind! There's no way I'm getting turned into pâté for you or anyone else."

"Your concern is legitimate, but unfounded, Dr. McCoy." Spock placated him unemotionally. "In other circumstances, I might have suggested such a course of action. However, I would not recommend making the attempt now."

"Good to hear it," McCoy said gruffly. "So why do I feel like I'm waiting for the other shoe to drop?"

Spock continued, unconcerned by the doctor's interruption. "However, there should be maintenance access ladders along the entire turbolift system. In all probability, we can use those to access the bridge level."

McCoy grimaced. He hated heights almost as much as he hated water. "Aren't there stairs we can take?"

"According to the map, the stair system does not reach to the bridge level."

"Now, why doesn't that surprise me?" McCoy

asked wearily. He glanced at Hallie, whose color had improved. "You better learn something about landing parties right now, Ensign."

"What's that, sir?"

"*Nothing* ever goes right!" He looked over at Chekov. "It sounds like a long climb, Lieutenant. I hope your crew has thick callouses on their hands."

Chekov nodded grimly. "It comes with the territory, Dr. McCoy. It comes with the territory."

When the landing party emerged from the stairwell two levels higher than the station's shopping district, Spock paused, gestured with one graceful hand, and started down an adjacent hallway. "The turboshaft we seek should be at the next corridor junction."

The others hurried to follow him and were gratified to find that to, indeed, be the case. Unfortunately, the tall, black-hued turboshaft doors were securely barred against them, locked shut when station power dropped.

McCoy stared sourly at their latest obstacle, his eyes following the trapezoidal shape of the doors and the solid seam down the middle. This mission had ceased being enjoyable in any way a long time ago. "Well, do you have any recommendations, ladies and gentlemen? We seem to be at an impasse."

"We can try patching the generator into the wall controls for the turbolift," Chekov said, studying the fingerpad closely. "This looks like a pretty close match, and what isn't I can jerry-rig. That should produce enough power to get the doors partway open, at least, and gain us entrance to the ladder system."

"God willing and the creek don't rise," McCoy felt compelled to add. "It wouldn't work in that office down below."

"I don't believe we need the reminder, Dr. McCoy,"

Spock said. "The turboshaft system represents a more integral part of the station. In theory, it should be the main lifeline, if you will, of the station proper and may be more easily accessed, particularly given the fact that there is an appropriate conduit. In any case, we lose nothing by the attempt. Proceed, Lieutenant Chekov," Spock ordered and stepped back to give the younger man room.

"I'm surprised at you, Spock," McCoy murmured. The doctor stood with one hip sidecocked and his arms folded loosely across his chest, watching Chekov work with his typically small, precise, unwasteful movements.

"How so, Doctor?" Spock also kept his voice low so as not to distract the security chief from his task. His dark eyes kept careful watch on Chekov's progress.

McCoy fought a smile but continued to watch the Chekov, fascinated by the jerry-rig job he was performing on the turbolift conduit. "Oh, I just figured that with a Vulcan's superior strength, you'd just pry open the doors for us, like you did downstairs."

Spock's eyes never diverted from watching Chekov and his crew patch in the portable generator. Leno and Hallie held it in their arms, slung between them like a patient in a four-handed seat lift, while Chekov connected wires to appropriate circuits. "I am strong, Doctor," the first officer conceded. "However, I am not *that* strong."

McCoy cocked his head sideways and looked up. "Really? I'm disappointed."

Spock gave every impression of not wanting to continue with this conversation, suspecting a trap. The racial politeness of his Vulcan bloodline, however, would not let him rudely break it off, much as his human side probably wanted to. "And why is that, Doctor?"

McCoy shifted his weight to the opposite hip and shrugged a lean shoulder. "I just thought that once we all retired, I could get you a job as a circus strongman."

"Thank you, Dr. McCoy," Spock replied with a patience born of long association with the caustic, teasing physician. "I shall endeavor to keep that in mind once I have retired from duty to Starfleet. However, since the lifespan of a Vulcan is appreciably longer than that of a Human, I anticipate that I shall be enjoying service to Starfleet and the Federation long after you have—how do Humans phrase it?— been put out to pasture. At that time, you might want to consider a second career as a purveyor of snake oil. It would put your verbal skills to good use." With that remark, Spock stepped forward to watch more closely Chekov at work.

McCoy glared at the Vulcan's back. "Very funny," he groused. He glanced around, impatient to have them be on their way, though he wasn't looking forward to climbing up what promised to be several deck levels of the station in their bid for the bridge. Imagine sticking the command center of your station out at the end of nowhere. It was different from anything he'd encountered, but he could kind of see the Romulans' point, if they *had* done it for security reasons. It made McCoy wonder just what else they'd done aboard this station in the name of security.

Movement tickled his peripheral vision, and he turned his head sharply. Nothing was there except the long expanse of the deserted corridor, empty and dark in the wake of their passage. Funny, he could have sworn . . .

He turned back to find Markson watching him closely. An eerie knowledge seemed held at bay in the ensign's dark eyes. "Did you see something, Dr. McCoy?" he inquired softly.

McCoy shrugged and rubbed his shoulder nervously. "Just had a crick in my neck, son."

Markson nodded. "Of course." His eyes sought the corridor beyond McCoy's shoulder. The doctor turned to follow his line of vision, but of course there was nothing to be seen.

"We're ready," Chekov announced. "Here goes." He depressed a button on the turbolift fingerpad. Nothing happened, and Hallie's face fell. Chekov reached to fiddle with a dial on the front of the generator and hit the button again. The double doors silently slid apart about a foot, and the first real smile McCoy had seen in some time graced the Russian's round features.

"Well done, Lieutenant," Spock praised. He stepped closer. He and Chekov stuck their heads into the narrow opening and shone their handlamps around the shaft's dark interior.

"Looks all clear," the security chief confirmed. Precariously balanced in a way that made McCoy think of Jim's propensity for climbing mountains as a form of relaxation (his, not McCoy's), Chekov reached inside and shook the metal ladder attached to the inside wall of the shaft. "Seems secure. I don't think we'll have any problem." He straightened and turned to face them. "I'll go first. Mister Spock, you'll follow me, then Markson, Hallie, Dr. McCoy, and Leno. Ensign Leno, it's going to be up to you to disconnect the generator and bring it along."

"Right, Chief," she nodded. "No problem."

"I recommend that we strap our handlamps onto our wrists," Chekov advised, suiting action to words and watching closely while the others did the same.

"That way, we'll have both hands free to climb and we won't be shining the lights down into each other's face. Everyone ready? Let's go." He swung out into the shaft with all the grace and agility of a monkey and started up the ladder.

McCoy waited in line behind Hallie, but his eyes were on Markson standing ahead of her. What was going through his mind? It didn't take long to find out. Markson stopped at the edge of the shaft, presumably to get his bearings before swinging out into the darkness. When he didn't move after a few moments, Hallie gave him a nudge in the center of the back. "Come on, Dan. Let's move out." There was no response from the tall ensign, but McCoy saw the line of his shoulders tense.

"Dan?" Hallie reached out to touch him, and McCoy caught her arm, shaking his head sternly.

He moved around her to stand at Markson's side. "Ensign? Is everything okay?" He rested a gentle hand on the security guard's wrist and quickly counted pulse beats. The young man's heart was racing so quickly it was a wonder the doctor couldn't hear the drumming. "Dan? What's wrong, son?"

From inside the shaft came Spock's voice. "Is something the matter, Dr. McCoy?"

"We're fine, Spock. We'll be right with you. Just hang on." He winced at the inadvertent bad pun and was patently thankful when Spock didn't follow it up with some witty rejoinder.

Markson was muttering something, and McCoy had to lean close to hear him clearly. "What, Dan? What did you say?"

"The enra. It's just like the enra."

The *Enterprise* doctor was baffled by the comment. "The enra? What's the enra?" When Markson only continued to stare wide-eyed into the shaft's darkness,

McCoy shook his arm slightly. "Dan, what's the enra?"

The security guard swallowed convulsively and turned toward McCoy. In the displaced light of the handlamps, his face looked leached of blood, his eyes wide and frightened. "The enra—" He licked his lips and swallowed again. "The enra are the deep pits on Vindali 5 where the dead are buried and where their spirits rise to the surface. They're just like this, just this size, and the dead are buried in layers, and their ghosts rise up to walk—" He breathed deeply, fighting to keep himself under control. "There's this sound when the dead rise, when the ghosts come. It's like a screeching howl that announces their coming—"

"Dan." McCoy's voice was stern. Hallie and Leno were silent behind him, and he knew Chekov and Spock must be listening from within the shaft. "I don't hear anything like that, do you?" His fingers tightened on the guard's forearm. "*Do* you?"

A quick shake of the head. "No, sir."

"That's because we aren't on Vindali 5 and this *isn't* an enra. There aren't any ghosts here. There aren't any—" Well, he couldn't say there weren't any dead, that's for sure. "There aren't any ghosts here," he reiterated. He leaned closer. "Did you visit the enra as a kid, Dan? Did you see something on Vindali 5?"

Markson laughed. It was a weak and sickly sound, but it was still a laugh and it eased McCoy's concern just a trifle. "There are always things to see on Vindali 5, Dr. McCoy. Ghost walks, spirit dances, parades for the dead . . ." His eyes finally found the doctor's and settled there. A small smile touched the security guard's pale lips. "I'm okay, Dr. McCoy. Thank you."

"Are you sure?"

"Yes, sir. It was just a shock, that's all, seeing something like this after four years away . . ." He waved a hand toward the shaft. "I'm okay," he repeated.

"All right, son." McCoy patted his arm. "I'll take your word for it. You get nervous again, you just let me know."

"Yes, sir. Thank you, sir."

Chekov's voice sounded from the depths of the shaft, his tone concerned. "Is everything okay back there?"

At a final nod from Markson, McCoy called out, "We're fine, Lieutenant. We're coming along behind you right now." He gave Markson another squeeze on the arm and returned to his place in line.

Moving with infinite care and making sure to never look down, Markson disappeared into the shaft. A moment later, Hallie sprang after him like a small ape, swinging effortlessly onto the metal rungs. She smiled over her shoulder at McCoy as she ascended the ladder behind the others. "Come on, Doctor," she encouraged. "There's nothing to it."

"Easy for you to say." He stopped at the edge of the shaft and unwisely peered down. His light illuminated a good distance before being swallowed by encroaching shadows. There was nothing of note to see, no gaping mouth ready to swallow him whole, no spectral vision complete with scythe and lantern, and none of Vindali 5's walking dead. There was nothing to worry about. So why the hesitation?

"It's not a good idea to look down, Dr. McCoy." Leno's mellow voice was soft in his ear. She already had the generator secured around her strong, broad shoulders by its carry strap and was ready to follow him into the shaft as soon as she unhooked the leads.

"You're telling me." He brought his head up and trained his eyes on the ladder, promising himself not to look down again. Taking a deep breath and swallowing hard, he reached for the nearest rung, gingerly stepped out into the spotlit darkness of the shaft, and began climbing. He kept his eyes fastened on his hands, curled about the rungs before him, and only glanced up occasionally to make sure he didn't get too close to Hallie, or to reassure himself that the others were still there, their handlamps bobbing in the darkness above. Behind him, he heard the snap of disconnecting wires and Leno's easy leap to the ladder as the turboshaft doors closed behind her. Now they were locked away in the heart of the station. McCoy sternly ordered himself not to think about being buried alive.

The air in the shaft smelled stale, almost mildewy, as it had throughout the station, and was still tainted with the scent of rotting peaches, which was a whole sight better than that of rotting flesh. The odor of mildew was a familiar one to McCoy, having grown up in the more humid climes of the southeastern United States, but it was one he'd never encountered in space. The airtight environment of a space vessel usually precluded the development of mildew, and yet here was the pervasive scent of it or something very like it. He wanted to ask Spock about it, but there was no way he was going to attempt to engage the Vulcan in conversation right now and risk losing his concentration on the slender metal rungs passing beneath his hands.

Noting that his hands felt strange, McCoy paused and freed one, rubbing the chilled fingers together. The ladder felt somewhat slick, though there didn't appear to be any residue on his fingers. Carefully, he reached out and touched the cool wall. It felt the same as the ladder, as though something was there—but not there. He shook his head. *Don't lose your grip, Leonard,* he thought, and made another face.

"Problem, Dr. McCoy?" Leno's voice wafted up to him softly from below.

He wiped his hand on his pant leg. "No, I'm fine." He shivered, not completely from the cold air, and continued to climb.

They ascended in silence, the only sounds the scuff of their boots on the rungs and the sounds of their labored breathing. Their lights dipped and weaved along the shaft walls like drunken fireflies. They paused for breath periodically, and during those breaks, Chekov and Spock spoke briefly, comparing their count of levels and how many more they expected to have to climb before reaching the appropriate deck. McCoy was grateful that life support functioned, if only minimally. That meant it would never get cold enough in here to threaten their lives . . . except somehow, against all sense, those Romulans below had died from hypothermia. How was that possible when it wasn't cold enough to threaten a person's internal body temperature? His mind worried over the question like a dog with a bone.

A faint sound wafted up from below, freezing them all in mid-motion. McCoy strained to listen and thought he heard something, but couldn't be certain. "Spock?" he whispered. "Wha—" His voice died in his throat as their lights once again extinguished, dropping them into blackness. McCoy's hands clenched tighter around the ladder rung, spasming in fear and chafing painfully against the metal. Vertigo assailed him, and his senses swam in the cloying, all-encompassing blackness surrounding them. Knowledge of the drop beneath his feet made his heart thunder in his chest loud enough that he thought the others could hear. He pressed his face against the ladder and swallowed hard.

"Everyone remain still," Spock said, and McCoy was grateful for the Vulcan's calm tones. Markson made soft noises over the doctor's head, but McCoy couldn't tell if the security guard was praying or crying. His heart went out to the younger man. Markson had worked so hard to get where he was, only to be undermined by baggage from his past he probably hadn't even know he still carried.

"Are you all right, Dan?" he heard Hallie ask quietly. There was no clear response, only the muttered litany of Markson's voice. McCoy didn't like the edge on the guard's tone and wanted nothing more than to get out of the shaft and into some kind of light.

The noise from below came again. This time McCoy's ears caught it as familiar. So familiar that he really didn't want to speculate, for fear of being right.

Spock saved him from having to. "I want everyone to slide around the edge of the ladder—"

"What?" McCoy squeaked, breathless at the thought of moving with that unseen drop beneath him.

"—and squeeze into the space between the ladder and the shaft wall." Spock ignored McCoy's inadvertent interruption and spoke quickly. "Ensign Leno, you should be able to accomplish this if you let the generator hang by its strap from your arm. Can you manage the weight or would you prefer to quickly pass it up to me?"

Below McCoy, the young woman snorted in the darkness. "No offense, Mr. Spock, but you must be joking. I didn't get these biceps by knitting baby booties."

"My apologies, Ensign."

"Mr. Spock?" Given their situation, Hallie sounded extraordinarily calm. "What's happening?"

"The turbolift is coming up the shaft," he replied simply.

McCoy closed his eyes with dread and hastily swung around to the inside of the ladder. No wonder the sounds had been so familiar. "Isn't there space enough to clear us, Spock?"

"There *should* be, Doctor," came the Vulcan's voice out of the darkness overhead, "but I do not believe we are in a position to trust such speculation as certainty without light by which to see. These ladders are for use when the turbolift is inoperative. Even if there is adequate space, I do not want to risk one of us being sucked out into the shaft should the turbolift pass us at maximum acceleration."

"So who's arguing?"

McCoy felt the enormous presence of the turbolift car as it ascended the shaft. A breeze moved past his face, caressing the sweat-slickened skin and fluttering his hair. The car approached slowly, ponderously, like an elephant silently passing in the darkness and leaving you with only an impression of its size and might. He sensed distance between his narrow hiding place and its passage, and breathed deeply with relief. Even if they'd stayed on the outside of the ladder, no one would have been injured.

"If that blocks our access to the bridge—" Leno began.

"Then we shall find another way to enter, Ensign," Spock finished for her, voice firm and inarguable. Now was evidently not the time to bring up such arguments.

"Aye, sir."

From high above came the loud sound of metal against metal, and Markson let out a startled cry. Only later would McCoy speculate that the brakes, or whatever it was that held the turbolift car in place, had withdrawn or failed. (He didn't know the particulars but supposed Scotty could tell him all about it if he cared to ask . . . which he didn't.) Whatever caused the weird energy fluctuations they'd been experiencing had something to do with it, for their handlamps blazed on just as the turbolift descended, screaming with speed and out of control.

"Hang on!" Spock ordered loudly.

Eyes blinking painfully in the sudden light, McCoy had only the merest instant to realize that, for reasons known only to Markson, the young security guard had either not secreted himself safely in the tiny space behind the ladder or had emerged before an all-clear was given. Before McCoy could cry a warning, the turbolift car was upon them and past in a rush of screaming wind that plastered his clothing against his skin, sucked the breath out of his lungs . . . and sucked Markson out into the shaft behind it. The security guard fell, his screaming wail shredding their ears like claws. A few seconds later, from far below in the darkness their lights could not penetrate, came the crash of the turbolift hitting the shaft bottom, and Markson's cry was abruptly cut off.

Someone was shaking uncontrollably, and it took McCoy a moment to realize it was he. The shaft was dark again, but it was the doctor's own personal darkness. He didn't remember having closed his eyes. He wanted to say something, *anything,* but couldn't work up the saliva or the knowledge of what there was to say. He hung frenziedly on the ladder between Hallie and Leno, his mind a blank on what to do next.

From above, someone cleared their throat. "Sound off." Chekov sounded hoarse, but his voice brought a sense of reality back to the situation. "Chekov."

"Spock."

A pause. "Hallie." She sounded terrible, her throat clogged with tears.

McCoy knew how she felt. "McCoy."

"Leno. *Damn.*"

"Is everyone else all right?" the security chief asked. McCoy looked up and wondered if he was as pasty-faced as the Russian. Did his eyes look as huge as Hallie's? Even Spock appeared off-color.

They all answered in the affirmative, for they *were* all right . . . at least physically. There would be time later to assess any other damage.

"Okay." Chekov took a deep breath. "Let's keep climbing."

"But, Dan—!" Hallie protested.

McCoy reached overhead and found her ankle. She jumped at his touch and he cursed himself for not warning her. They didn't need another fall. "Hang on a second, Chekov. She's right. I need to check this out."

"Doctor, you don't really think he survived that fall?"

"People have survived worse, Lieutenant. This will only take a minute." Prying one hand off the rungs, although letting go was the last thing he wanted to do, he reached into his medipouch for his small tricorder. Holding it toward the shaft bottom, he flicked it on. His eyes hunted the readout for a few moments, then he put the mechanism away and sighed quietly. "Let's keep climbing," he said simply.

"But—" Hallie started to protest, her voice thick with emotion.

Chekov's voice cut in, strength overlying deep

feeling. "Later, Hallie. Come on people, let's go. By my count, we have only four levels to go."

It may as well have been four light-years to McCoy's way of thinking. He clutched the rung so tightly that for a moment he wasn't certain he could convince his hands to relinquish it. Only a poke from Leno in an exercise-wearied calf started him moving again, his eyes fixed on Hallie's heels as she ascended ahead of him.

The climb seemed interminable to the doctor's numbed mind. His leg muscles begged him to stop, to rest, but he followed the siren call of Hallie's boots above him until he almost stubbed his nose against her heel where she'd stopped below Spock.

"Are we there?" Leno called.

"Made it," Chekov reported. "Send up the generator."

"My pleasure, Chief," she grunted. She dipped her head, pulling the carry strap free, and hefted the piece of equipment toward McCoy. He took it grimly, the muscles of his hand and arm protesting the weight, and held it up toward Hallie. She stooped to relieve him of it with a strength belied by her tiny appearance. He flinched at the pain come to roost in her eyes. She gifted him with a small, unhappy smile and passed the generator on to Spock, and Spock handed it to Chekov.

The security chief snugged one leg around the ladder like an acrobat and maneuvered the ungainly equipment with a smooth, professional dexterity. In a moment, he'd made the connections to the inside conduit and the door slid open.

"You'll all have to climb over me," the Russian advised. "I'll try to give you as much room as possible."

"Don't worry about us," McCoy stressed. "You just

hang on." It didn't seem the right thing to say, considering, and the doctor wished he'd kept his mouth shut when silence greeted his unnecessary advice.

He followed Hallie's feet again, silently promising his aching muscles that it would soon be all over and they could rest, at least for a little while. Spock reached down a long arm to help Hallie into the room, and she helped him swing McCoy, then Leno, and, lastly, Chekov in after her.

They were in a vestibule of some sort, corridors going off in either direction, and with only one door in the opposite wall. "If the map I read was accurate," Spock said, "behind those doors is the bridge of the station."

"Hallelujah," McCoy said unenthusiastically. "Let's hope the damn generator will open this door, too."

"Here's hoping," Chekov agreed and set to work. It didn't take long. With the experience of the turboshaft behind him, the Russian made short work of the connections, and the door eased open.

The smell wasn't as bad here as it had been below, but still awful enough to goad a noise from Leno. Sighing heavily, McCoy nudged her aside and stepped forward for his first look at the space station's central hub. He came around a central console in the big room and stopped just short of stepping onto the outflung hand of one of the two dead Romulans sprawled on the deck. Suddenly, all the doctor's strength fled. He sat down fast and hard, bruising his tailbone on the cold floor, and stared straight ahead, numb to the core.

Chapter Ten

KIRK SAT IN HIS CHAIR at the conn, chin on fisted hand, staring at nothing. The pain in his side was a throbbing refrain now that the painkillers had worn off completely and the real pain of his injury had leached through to batter his senses. And now he felt cold, probably an aftereffect of his broken ribs.

Sulu had noticed and, with his captain's permission, had left the bridge momentarily to find field jackets for the entire bridge crew. It *was* cooler on the bridge than normal, but Kirk didn't like how cold he felt *inside*, where the jacket's warmth could not reach. Was it the injury? Was it worry gnawing at him? Or was it something else he hadn't yet considered?

A flash of annoyance with himself and everything around him dragged Kirk from the morass of his lethargy, and he straightened in his seat. "Uhura, has that shuttlecraft gone out yet?"

He'd never seen the communications officer look so apologetic. "Not yet, sir."

"Well, what are they waiting for? We've got a landing party stranded over there." He waved at the viewscreen. The image of the station was becoming harder and harder to see as time passed. Static had gone from snowstorm to blizzard proportions.

"They're having trouble getting the shuttlebay doors to open, Captain," Estano told him from the security station. He sounded almost embarrassed, though he didn't have anything to do with the bollixed condition of things. "Jaffe and Corey are in the shuttlecraft, ready to go. Engineering's working on it right now."

Kirk caught himself before he had a chance to say, "Well, tell them to hand crank if they have to!" He bit the words back, knowing that Commander Scott's engineering team was doing the best it could, as quickly as it could. He opted for just a nod, and turned back toward the screen. "Thank you, Ensign. Keep me apprised."

"Aye, sir."

The inactivity ate at Kirk like a tribble gorging on quadrotriticale. First and foremost, he was a man of action, a man of decisions who acted on those decisions with surety and swiftness. Yet here he sat, completely useless, while someone else planned to go and rescue his friends. The thought goaded him like a spur in the side. He was not a man who took easily to convalescence, as Bones would have been the first to tell anyone.

"Captain?" Uhura again, looking as frustrated as Kirk felt, and ever more apologetic for interrupting a thought loop that wasn't getting him anywhere, anyway.

Don't snap at your crew, Jim. They're the best you've got, the best in the world. Don't take it out on them, even if you do *want to slap yourself silly.* "Yes, Uhura?"

"More reports coming in from all over the ship, sir."

Control the sigh. Don't let them see it's getting to you . . . "Read it slowly, Commander."

Malfunctions of all sorts continued unabated. Doors either behaved like the jaws of a trap, sometimes seriously injuring crew, or didn't open at all, leaving stranded personnel little option but to use emergency hatches, if they were available, or try to call for assistance that would be a long time coming because work crews from engineering were dealing with problems elsewhere (including the shuttlebay doors). Currently, several of the crew were stranded in their rooms, the botanical garden, and a number of lavatories. And still it went on.

Food dispensers had made a gluey morass of several areas. One moment the computer could be used, and the next there was nothing but dead silence in response to repeated inquiries. The list was as long as Kirk's arm and as diverse as a mongrel's genealogy, and continued growing by the moment. The only plus side to the entire situation was that there were no severely ill patients in sickbay and no dangerous individuals being held in the brig. Considering it now, though, Kirk would have been happier tackling a wild-eyed murderer armed to the teeth and running rampant through the *Enterprise* than dealing with the starship's traitorous systems. Scott could check and recheck all he wanted to, but Kirk was convinced the problem lay outside the ship, and he was willing to bet he knew exactly *where.*

Kirk waved Uhura to silence partway through the list. "That's enough, Commander. Continue sending out a distress signal beacon. Attempt to contact Starfleet Command, and keep trying to reach the landing party. And find out what the hell's going on with that shuttlecraft!"

"Aye, sir!" Swathed in the deep red of her field jacket, the commander turned back to her board.

"Captain!" Estano called from his place at the security station. "Shuttlebay doors have been successfully opened. Shuttlecraft *Valgard* is under way."

Kirk's fist clenched in a gesture of victory. *Finally!* "Patch me through to the shuttlecraft, Uhura."

"I'll try, sir."

He watched her, waiting for her nod. "This is Captain Kirk to the *Valgard.*"

Static greeted his sending, overlaying some type of conversation he couldn't quite make out. "Uhura—"

"Working on it, sir. Try again."

Kirk repeated his hail. This time the contact was clearer, the response understandable, though still scratchy. *"Valgard* here, Captain. This is Jaffe. Corey and I are under way."

"Well done. How are systems?"

Her voice crackled, overlayed with static. "A little jumpy, sir, but nothing we can't handle. It should be fairly routine to gain access to the space station."

Jaffe's optimism almost scared Kirk. It was just the sort of good feeling Fate routinely liked to chew and swallow whole. "Carry on and good luck. Try to keep us posted of your progress."

"We will, sir. *Valgard* out."

Kirk watched the viewscreen closely, waiting for the shuttle to come into view. What he did not expect was Uhura's excited exclamation. "Captain! I have Mr. Spock!"

Adrenaline rammed through Kirk and left his nerve

endings tingling. "Put him through!" He heard the scratchy channel open. "Spock!"

Vicious static snarled any response, if there was one, and then Uhura said, "Go ahead!"

"Spock!" Kirk called again. "Can you read me?"

". . . interference . . . unable . . . read you . . . one moment . . ." Suddenly the signal came in a bit stronger. It was nothing approaching clear, but Kirk could at least make out the words. "Captain, this is Spock."

Kirk smiled. "It's good to hear your voice, Mr. Spock. Is everyone all right?"

"Ensign Markson has died in an accident. Other than that, we are fine. Dr. McCoy and the others are currently exploring our present level."

Sorrow touched Kirk's heart. He hadn't known the security guard at all, though he knew Markson had been a new crewman aboard the *Enterprise.* Knowing him or not, Kirk felt despair at the loss of one of his men. "What happened to Markson?"

"He fell in a turboshaft. However, the details are not pertinent to our situation at this time, Captain. Since we cannot, with any assurance, determine how long our contact may last, we need to exchange important information while we have an open channel."

"Correct as always, Spock. Report."

"Captain . . ." Static flared, and Kirk feared they'd lost their tenuous, all-too-brief contact. Then the signal cleared, and he could once again hear Spock's voice. "We have made no headway in discovering why the station is here; however, we have discovered a score or more of dead Romulans on one of the lower levels. Dr. McCoy's findings indicate they died of hypothermia."

"Hypothermia?" Kirk felt a chill that had nothing to do with his injury. "Are you in danger?"

"Undetermined, Captain. We should not be, as the ambient temperature is not low enough for hypothermia to be a risk."

"Then how—"

"Unknown at this time," Spock cut in. "We have reached the station bridge, and I have managed to successfully tie in the generator to access the communications and computer system, hence my ability to contact you. I do not know how long this will last, but in the time allowed I will attempt to gain as much information as I can through the computer system as to why this station is here and why it lost power—"

Kirk spoke over his first officer. "Speaking of power, the *Enterprise* is suffering a power drain of some kind, Spock. It's affecting first one part of the ship, then another. Systems are redlined all over the ship. We can't trust the transporter enough to beam you back at this time."

"Fascinating." Kirk could practically see his first officer's eyebrow go up. "Captain, we are also currently experiencing some of the same difficulties, though on a much smaller scale. The drain is unusual in that even our handheld weapons and lights are affected."

"Then it's *not* just the *Enterprise!*" Relief that his suspicions had borne fruit flooded through Kirk in a wave, and he flashed a look at Scott, who grinned in return. They weren't out of the fire, but it did both men good to know that the problem didn't lie somewhere in the ship.

"Affirmative. I have every reason to believe that the space station is con . . ."

Static interfered, and Kirk's heart raced. "Uhura, get him back!"

"I'm trying, sir!"

Spock's voice came back on line. ". . . unable to hold channel much longer. I will endeavor to learn more on my hypothesis before exploring engineering. I . . ."

"Spock! We're sending a shuttlecraft to the station to access one of the airlocks and get you out."

"Inadvisable at this time, Captain. Power is too . . ." The line cut into howling static so loud Uhura had to turn down her speakers.

"Dammit!" Kirk pounded the arm of his chair and instantly regretted it when pain shot up his side and down his arm, freezing his breath in his lungs as though he'd just tried to inhale an iceberg. He squeezed his eyes shut tightly, forcing back the blackness, and all hell broke loose.

"Captain!" Sulu called from helm. *"Valgard* has cleared the ship, but she's skewed, sir! She's going off course!"

Kirk pried open his eyes and stared at the screen, trying to see through the interference. The shuttlecraft's forward momentum was a memory. The small vessel was cocked at an angle, her running lights already dimmed. Evidently, whatever was causing their problems was sucking the shuttlecraft dry of power as well. What had Spock been trying to tell him? The space station is con . . . Con what? Contributing, maybe? That made sense if Spock was planning to check out Engineering. . . . And what hypothesis was he planning on checking out? *Damn,* but he wanted to talk to his first officer!

"Captain!" Scott called urgently. Kirk only barely refrained from yelling back at him. God, but his side *hurt!* "I had diagnostic sensors trained toward the station when Mr. Spock's communication cut off. I don't know how far I can trust their readouts, sir, pertaining to levels and such, but there's definitely a drain, and it's coming from that ugly piece of garbage out there."

Though it wasn't an official description, Kirk found it oddly appropriate. He glared at the station. So, he'd been right. Spock's cryptic words confirmed it, and Scott's reading nailed the lid on the coffin. If that was the source of the drain, then *that* was the enemy. *That* was what he had to defeat to get his crew and his ship back in his hands.

Only how?

Chapter Eleven

McCoy PAUSED in the doorway before leaving the station bridge and looked back at Spock. The Vulcan was seated at one of the consoles with the generator at his elbow, preparing to tie the separate power unit into the station's computer and attempt to contact the *Enterprise*. "You going to be all right on your own?"

The first officer didn't even look up, eyes intent on his work. "I fail to see how I could be other than 'all right,' Doctor. There is little ill that could happen to me while trying to access the computer banks."

If you can. McCoy thought to himself, suddenly uncomfortable with his natural role as general curmudgeon. He grunted. "Can't prove it to me by this place," he said aloud. He didn't doubt the Vulcan's prowess with computers and their ilk, though he'd rather have dropped into the sea without a life preserver than admit that in anyone's hearing, least of all Spock's. Just as he didn't want to admit to himself how worried he was that none of them would ever reach the *Enterprise* again.

Had the others made the same deductions as he? They couldn't raise the *Enterprise* on their communicators. It was safe to assume, knowing Jim Kirk as well as he did, that Uhura must have tried to reach them when they didn't check in after a reasonable length of time. With no response forthcoming from the landing party, why hadn't Jim ordered Scotty to just beam them all back immediately, as was the usual procedure? The answer to that, of course, was that even with Scotty at the controls, they either couldn't locate the landing party or didn't have the power for a return beaming. Which, in turn, meant they were having the same troubles as the space station. Either thought was enough to scare the hell out of McCoy.

He glanced over his shoulder at the wide windows circling the station bridge. Each was shielded by a heavy panel, giving the room the appearance of an enormous metal shipping crate. McCoy wished the baffles were down, even if it was only a crack. He wanted to see out, to see the *Enterprise,* even if she was far away and unreachable. He wanted confirmation that she and Kirk were still out there, that hope was still out there.

He suddenly realized with a start that Spock was staring at him, hands folded in his lap. How long had McCoy been standing here, lost in thought?

"Is there something else, Dr. McCoy?" the Vulcan inquired solicitously.

"No!" the doctor snapped, embarrassed at having been caught with his guard down. He started out the door, then paused. "Ah . . . good luck, Spock."

The first officer regarded the doctor through eyes that McCoy could read quite well at the moment.

"And to you." The Vulcan's head bent back to his work, and McCoy left the room and joined the others in the hallway.

Chekov looked all business, almost stern and a little withdrawn into himself. Leno was harder to read, being that McCoy didn't know her very well. She seemed okay. He didn't know Hallie very well, either, but she wore her heart on her sleeve. The skin around her eyes was tight and shadowed with pain, but she was doing her best to keep it all together until the mission was over. She was going to be a professional if it was the last thing she did, and McCoy felt a rush of pride in the young officer.

"How can he stay in there?" Leno asked, jerking her head toward the door. "Mr. Spock, I mean. How can he just sit in there with those two dead Romulans?"

"They can't hurt him, Ensign," Chekov replied, probably more brusquely than he'd intended. "And Mr. Spock's enough of an officer to do what needs to be done, whether the circumstances are pleasurable or not."

McCoy rubbed his chilled hands together and shivered. "Okay, Lieutenant Chekov, you're the chief. What's our plan of action?"

Chekov's dark eyes regarded them all coolly, one after the other. "Ensign Hallie and Dr. McCoy, you'll take the right-hand corridor. Leno and I will explore to the left. Keep in mind that equipment is acting oddly, so don't rely on it. You'll be better off relying on your own skills and the skills of your partner. If you lose lighting, remain calm. Don't move unless you know precisely where you are in relation to the things around you." If anything, his expression grew more stern. "We don't want any more accidents." His eyes flicked toward Hallie and away. "We can't be certain the communicators will be useable, so don't get out of voice range of your partner. Under no circumstances is anyone to enter a turboshaft. Any questions?"

That was one concern Chekov didn't need to worry about, so far as McCoy was concerned. There was no way this side of anywhere that the doctor was going to let Hallie climb into a turboshaft without him, and he wasn't about to go with her. In fact, he had every intention of not getting within ten feet of a turboshaft if he saw it before it saw him.

"All right, then," Chekov concluded when he saw that no one had any questions. "We'll rendezvous back here in no more than one hour. That should give Mr. Spock plenty of time to do what he needs to if he can, and it's more than enough time for us to do a cursory check of this floor. Let's go." With a curt nod, he turned away and started down the left-hand corridor with Leno coursing at his heels like an eager hound on a freshly scented trail.

"I wish I could be like that," Hallie said quietly, watching them disappear around the corner.

McCoy followed her gaze. "How do you mean?"

"They're both so cool, so calm about everything. Looking at them, you'd never know that Dan . . ." She sighed, and her mouth tightened bitterly.

"Let me tell you something, Ensign." McCoy started down the right-hand hallway, drawing her after him with his voice. "I can't speak for Ensign Leno, but I've known Lieutenant Chekov a long time. Don't be fooled by his outward demeanor. He feels things just as sharply as you do. But he's learned through the experience of years, as you will, that grief has its time and place, and the center of a mission isn't it." He smiled gently. "Trust me. They're hurting inside, too, probably Chekov most of all. He takes it very personally when he loses a team member. Now, come on. Let's get moving." He lengthened his stride and wasn't really surprised when Hallie sped her pace until she preceded him by a few cautionary steps. Despite her grief, this was one young woman who took her security post very seriously. She wouldn't hear any complaints out of McCoy in that regard. He was grateful for her presence. Left to his own devices, he wasn't certain he would ever have left the dubious security of the station bridge, Spock's orders notwithstanding.

The corridor they traversed was as murkily lit as the rest of the station had been, and empty. The first door they encountered stood open, admitting them into a small lounge, or some type of briefing room. McCoy barely took note of the furnishings as his eyes lit upon the two tall, narrow windows directly across from the doorway, their view not obscured by baffling as were the wide windows of the bridge. He hurried across the room and stared out at the heart-catching sight of the *Enterprise,* stark white and shining like Arthur's Grail against the backdrop of stars.

"She's pretty on the inside and I'm proud to be part of her like I've never been proud of anything else in my life." Hallie spoke quietly from behind him, where she stood on tiptoe to see over his shoulder. Her voice was hushed and reverent. "But she's one *gorgeous* lady from the outside."

"That she is, Ensign. She's the proudest ship in the fleet." McCoy's chest felt tight with longing to be aboard her once again.

Hallie's small, strong hand rested on his shoulder and squeezed briefly. "We're going to get back to her, sir. All of us." Utter faith colored her tone. "You can be sure of that."

The doctor was warmed by her conviction. "I *am* sure of that, Ensign," McCoy replied stoutly, sure of no such thing. It was an amazing and endearing aspect of Humanity that, no matter what the odds, you could rest assured that they would make the best effort to bolster one another's failing confidence, whether or not there was any fact upon which to base that bolstering.

Hallie's hand dropped. "We'd better get going, Dr. McCoy, if we're going to cover our end of things before our time is up. Besides, we don't want the chief to come along and catch us sightseeing."

The remark reminded McCoy poignantly of Kirk, standing cocksure and proud in the transporter room, confident in his abilities and those of his crew. Jim wouldn't have let any of this get him down, at least not for very long. He'd keep busy, keep his brain churning over the problem at hand until he found a solution, or so exhausted the problem with his attempts that it rolled over, belly-up and all four legs in the air, and surrendered. McCoy could do no less than follow his captain's excellent example.

"Right you are, Ensign Hallie. Let's finish in here and move on." He turned away from the window after a final, brief look at home, and did not dare look back for fear of never being able to tear his eyes away again.

Austere and elegant black furniture with upholstery the color of dried blood stood gathered together in various conversation nooks around the room's perimeter. There were no trappings to indicate recent occupation of the room by the station's inhabitants. Rather, the contrary was true. The room had the air of never having been used at all. The walls were devoid of decoration and, when McCoy reached out a tentative hand and ran his fingers along a panel, were cold and faintly moist to the touch, like the walls of the turboshaft. He smelled his fingertips but detected no aroma. His skin felt vaguely slick when he rubbed his fingers together, another sensation reminiscent of the turboshaft climb. With a grimace, he wiped his hand against his trouser leg.

"Something the matter, Dr. McCoy?" Hallie paused in the doorway, ready to leave, and glanced back at him. When he shook his head, hurrying to join her and resume their exploration of the corridor, she nodded. "It's creepy, isn't it? Kind of like being in one of those haunted houses people used to put up during Halloween."

McCoy chuckled. "Now that you mention it, it *is* sort of reminiscent of that. A big, old, empty place with echoing corridors." *And dead bodies.* Better not to think about that. "The only difference between a haunted house and this station is that the station doesn't have any haunts wandering down the halls toward you with their head under their arm."

"But that sort of makes it worse, don't you think?" she asked. The ruddy illumination on her face from the emergency lights cast strange shadows against the delicate structure of flesh over finely sculpted bone. She looked about seven years old and more vulnerable than she actually was. "We don't even know what it is we're up against. When you can see something, it's easier to evaluate it and determine how to deal with it."

"Sort of like what shaman have said about knowing the true name of something." When Hallie blinked confusedly at him, McCoy explained. "Some cultures believe that everything in the world has two names, the name you know it by—like you knowing me as Dr. Leonard McCoy—and its real name. The everyday name is nothing, it's powerless. But the *real* name—" He paused ponderously, waggling a finger in the air, and she smiled. "That's something else again. When you know a person's or thing's real name, you have power over it. You can control it." He shrugged. "At least that's what they say."

"I think I understand what you mean." Hallie's nod was a sharp, birdlike gesture. Her eyes never rested on any one thing but moved continuously, alert for danger. "When you don't have the assurance of knowing something's real name—or knowing for certain if something's really there, waiting in the dark—you have no power over it or your situation. Your imagination can take over and sometimes make things worse than they really are."

"You can pretty much *guarantee* it'll make things worse than they really are," McCoy amended. "It's the nature of the human beast. If a person isn't careful, their imagination can really run away with them. It's an interesting trait. A lot of different species have it, even some of the so-called 'lower' species. It's not really a sense, in the strict definition of the term, but it can affect all your senses and make you experience any number of things. All that seems to matter is whether or not you believe, and how strongly you hold that belief."

Hallie stopped abruptly and turned toward him, her expression serious. "Do you think that's what happened to Dan? Did his imagination get too big for him, become too real? Is that why he died?"

He thought this might be where this whole conversation had been heading. No amount of medical or psychological training really prepared a person to try and answer these kinds of questions, and Leonard McCoy had both in spades. Unfortunately, he still hadn't satisfied his own mind as to how much of Markson's death was pure accident and how much was a result of his fear. But Hallie wanted some kind of answer, and it had to be an honest one. She'd know in a moment if he wasn't being up front with her.

He kept walking, his eyes tracking sideways where she strode along beside him. Her expression was grave, her dark eyes unwaveringly on McCoy's features. "I don't know anything for certain, Suzanna. I know that's not much of an answer, and I apologize for that, but only Dan knew what was going on in his head. Only he knew the depth of his feelings, be they fear or something else. I think your guess is as intelligent a deduction as any, particularly since you knew Dan as a person, as a friend. I wish I could say I had, but I just can't know every single person who ships aboard the *Enterprise*. I didn't know Dan Markson except as a name tag on a medical record." The admission made McCoy sorry, even as he understood the futility of that sorrow. "For all I know, maybe he thought the sounds coming out of the shaft when the turbolift engaged were the sounds of the dead in the enra, and his childhood fears just took over. I think the situation and his past came together in just the wrong way for him, Suzanna, and he suffered a horrible, tragic accident." McCoy knew Hallie would eventually make up her own mind about Markson's death. All McCoy could do was offer suggestions.

Hallie scratched her chin, quietly pondering his words. "Then you don't believe in ghosts?"

"I don't believe in Commander Scott's ship-burning, blood-covered haunts, no."

"That doesn't precisely answer my question, Dr. McCoy," she said archly.

He grinned. "No, Ensign, I don't suppose it does." He paused to peek inside an open doorway. Another small office. Nothing remarkable. "I've watched a lot of people die, Hallie, some of them very close to me."

His eyes grew momentarily distant, thinking about his father. "Some died tragically, some fearfully, some with the greatest dignity you can imagine."

"But have you ever *seen* a ghost?" She seemed to want real assurances in this regard. What did she think, that Daniel Markson was going to reappear protoplasmically?

"You want my *personal* opinion on the matter of ghosts?"

"Please." She nodded eagerly.

"Okay," McCoy said seriously. "Despite Commander Scott's seemingly bottomless wealth of stories about phantoms of all shapes, sizes, and dispositions, I swear to you by my oath as a doctor of medicine that in all my years as a practicing physician, I have never seen anything to make me even remotely believe in ghosts, goblins, spooks, gremlins, or haunts that didn't have a rational explanation. I work very closely with the ephemeral, Ensign. I've brought babies into the world and ushered out friends and strangers alike, and I've certainly been in a position to have had a visitation if one was forthcoming. Hell!" he expounded. "It's practically due me!"

"Belief is the weirdest thing," she said with exasperation. "It's so hard to understand how two groups of people can believe in such radically different concepts."

"That's what makes us who we are, Ensign. Talk to Mr. Spock about the IDIC sometime, if you really want to give your brain a workout," McCoy chuckled. "Belief *is* a weird thing, yes. It's also a very cultural, very personal thing. Just like the imagination. Which brings us full circle."

Hallie smiled. "I guess so. Thanks, Dr. McCoy."

"For whatever little I've done, you're welcome."

A few yards on, the corridor split into a T. McCoy

stopped and looked in either direction. "What do you say, Ensign?"

She followed his lead, staring first one way, and then the other. "Well, going to the left probably leads back toward Leno and the chief." She flashed her handlamp in that direction to get a clearer view, but there was nothing noteworthy to see. She trained the light in the other direction. "We've still got time on the clock, Dr. McCoy. Might as well make the most of it, don't you think?"

McCoy wasn't certain he should tell her what he really thought. "I would get saddled with the one who wants to see everything in the universe," he groused good-naturedly.

"You don't want the chief and Ensign Leno to grab all the glory, do you, Dr. McCoy? Think of what we might find."

"I *am* thinking about it, Ensign." He sighed and straightened his shoulders. "Why do I think I'm going to be sorry I didn't tell you ghosts are real?"

Her light laughter drew him down the hallway after her, their footfalls sounding a twinned cadence on the metal decking. There were more doors along this section of hallway, but most were securely locked or jammed. The ones that stood open seemed to be sparse living quarters. Beyond those they found a small botanical garden full of withered and dead plants and, still farther on, a mess hall.

"At least we'll know where to get food if we want it," McCoy commented from the doorway. Several foodpacks lay strewn across the floor as though dropped in someone's hurry. It was kind of sad, really. Had those poor souls in the amphitheater tried to stay alive no matter what, hoping rescue would come, only to succumb to something they could not avoid? McCoy shook his head. "I never thought I'd see the day when I'd be trying to jimmy a Romulan cafeteria, but weirder things have happened to me since I joined Starfleet. Let's go."

They turned away and continued down the corridor, unsuccessfully trying doors as they progressed its length. McCoy glanced over at Hallie and caught her shivering. "Are you all right?"

She nodded and chafed her hands together. "Just a little cold, I guess. Doesn't it feel colder in here to you?" She flipped up the collar of her field jacket, framing her face in white.

He thought about it. No, it didn't feel any colder. But *he* felt colder, deep down inside, like he used to feel as a kid when he was coming down with the flu. It was a cold that, unchecked, could go all the way to the marrow.

Something very much like a fist grabbed McCoy's guts and knotted them with a quick twist. Knowing it was useless, knowing it was stupid and having to do it anyway just to make certain, he pulled out his mediscanner. "Hold still."

"Why? What's the mat—?"

"Just hold still!" he ordered, voice gruffer than he'd intended. He ran the scanner the length of Hallie's slender frame, then turned it on himself. The results made him very grim.

Hallie saw it immediately. "What's the matter, Dr. McCoy?"

He shook his head in perplexity. "Our internal body temperatures have dropped."

"What's causing it?" She wrapped her arms around herself.

"I don't know. It shouldn't be happening at all. It's not cold enough in here to warrant it." He ran the scanners over both of them again, to reaffirm his findings. They were the same. Both he and Hallie were down by about four degrees. He could only assume the same was true for Chekov and Leno. And probably Spock. "Look, let's finish up here and get back to the bridge. I need to check on the others and—"

The sudden force of Hallie's arm across his chest slammed him up against the wall hard enough to make McCoy cry out in surprise. He stared at her. "Do you have a personal vendetta against me, Ensign, or—"

"Shush!" Her head was turned away from him, her eyes on the corridor.

"What is it?" McCoy whispered.

She shook her head in a sharp, angry gesture to quell anything else he might feel compelled to say. Her eyes searched the corridor ahead where it turned a corner. "I don't know." Her voice was so faint, McCoy read her lips more than heard the actual words. "I saw something. I *know* I saw something move, and this time it wasn't our lights along the bulkhead, because our lights aren't on. I'm going to take a closer look. Stay here."

"But—" Her fierce grip tightened and cut him off.

"Security's orders, Doctor, for your own safety. Stay here and wait for me. I'll be back before you know it." Before he could even attempt to voice an argument, she slid away from him as smoothly and silently as oil on water. Phaser ready in one hand, she held her handlamp against her chest with the other, readying it to flash into the intruder's eyes and give her the advantage of the opponent's momentary blindness. Hugging the wall like a shadow thrown by lamplight, she catfooted along the corridor toward her objective.

At the corner, she glanced back for a moment. "Be careful," McCoy whispered unnecessarily. She couldn't have heard, but she gave him a brief nod nonetheless before turning away. The rise of her narrow shoulders gave clue to the deep breath she inhaled before rounding the juncture and entering the other corridor, disappearing from McCoy's view.

A scream to rend vocal cords and leave them bloody echoed through the corridor and drove a spike of fear into the doctor's heart. He jumped to his feet and started forward. *"HALLIE!"* At that instant, the emergency lights died without a cluing flicker, dropping the doctor into a darkness more absolute than the bottom of a mine shaft and freezing him where he stood.

Chapter Twelve

CHEKOV MOVED ALONG the corridor as smoothly and silently as if he glided on ice. Leno followed two paces behind him, a watchful attendant, and he felt extremely secure with her presence at his back. Though a little slower in hand-to-hand combat than he would have liked, the ensign made up for it by being a crack shot with a phaser. If someone (or something?) came at them from behind, she would drop them in their tracks, Chekov had no doubt of that.

He was coming to hate this mission, and was more unhappy than he could presently let on by the recent turn of events. No commander enjoyed losing any of the men or women serving under them and Chekov, like Kirk, was particularly prone to the feelings of helplessness rage and frustration that the death of one of his crew invariably produced. While Chekov was confident that every member of his security staff knew the dangers inherent in the job when they chose to sign on as security guards, that didn't make their loss any easier to bear. Notifying families of the death of a loved one was one of the worst aspects of his job.

And, dammit, he had *liked* Dan Markson! True, the kid was pretty green around the edges, but he was a new graduate, after all. Markson, and Hallie too, had come aboard the *Enterprise* only a short time earlier, bright and shiny from their Starfleet Academy graduation ceremony and eager to do their best, proud to have been assigned to the foremost ship in the Federation fleet. Gregarious Suzanna had settled in a little more readily than Dan, making friends right away and carving out a niche for herself in the squadron of security guards. Dan had been more reticent but just as eager to please. In him, Chekov had seen something reminiscent of himself back in those long-ago but clearly remembered days when he first stepped aboard the *Enterprise* as an impassioned new crew member, ready to conquer the universe singlehandedly.

He remembered how excited and enthusiastic he'd been . . . and how scared. Nervous and overly zealous to make a good impression, particularly with Captain Kirk, he'd done a better job of annoying people and making a nuisance of himself. Then one day during his off time, while he sat in the botanical gardens brooding and miserable and questioning everything he had ever thought he knew as the truth, Captain Kirk had just "happened" to stroll by and ask him along on a walk.

Chekov had long since forgotten how many repetitive circuits of the gardens they made that day, but he'd never forgotten a word of what Kirk had told him. The captain made the effort to take the time to encourage the young ensign to talk about himself, his home, his aspirations and dreams . . . and, finally, his fears. James Kirk had imparted to Chekov a vastly important kernel of wisdom: No one is completely unafraid. No one is untouched by personal fears. And that means none of us is truly alone. Rather than drive us apart from one another, that knowledge should only serve to bring us closer in our understanding, and in our common bond of Humanity.

Dammit! He had wanted the chance to tell that to Markson, to pass along the favor and the knowledge, as Kirk himself had. But now it was too late. The only thing left to do was to gather up Markson's body at the end of this damned mission and ship it home with a sincere and polite note of condolence.

Sometimes Chekov hated his job.

The room coming up on his left was open, the door gaping like a toothless mouth onto the dark corridor. He held his phaser hand in the air as a signal to Leno. Her footfalls stopped immediately, and she slid in quietly behind him, weapon at the ready. Chekov's eyes flicked briefly sideways, caught her ready nod, and returned one of his own. Drawing a deep, silent breath, he paused for an instant, then swung around the doorjamb in a smooth movement, phaser aimed before him. Leno followed in a well-orchestrated motion, staying close to the floor and sliding in under his arm. Between the two of them, they had every inch of the room covered.

Not that there was much to cover themselves against. The room was completely vacant of life, or former life, for that matter. Just to make certain, Chekov hand-signaled to his partner and she obediently went in one direction while he went in the other. They met on the far side of the room, having thoroughly circumnavigated it.

"Anything?" Chekov whispered.

"Not a thing, Chief." Handlamp strapped securely to her wrist, Leno flashed it around the room again. " 'Not a creature was stirring,' as the legends say." She shook her head in amazement. "Boy, would you look at this place! Guess besides not trusting any other race in the galaxy, the Romulans don't much trust each other either."

Chekov didn't know if that observation was true or not, and didn't much care. The room *was* quite a sight to behold, though.

Easily as big as the station bridge, he could only assume it might be the central office for whatever sort of security force the station might have been designed to require. A large desk console occupied the central portion of the room. It was bare but for two computer screens and an immense keyboard imbedded flush with the desk surface. The wall facing the desk was made up of twelve-inch viewscreens, many of them shattered, ostensibly used for observation of the station's various areas and their inhabitants.

Chekov walked over and gingerly ran a hand along the edge of one screen, then bent over the desk to consider several keys before tapping out a sequence. As expected, nothing happened. "This would be really convenient right now, if only it worked. We could check out the entire station *and* find out if anyone else is on board, all at the same time."

"Yeah, and if wishes were horses, as my mother used to say," Leno responded from behind his back. When she spoke again, her voice was muffled. "Chief, come take a look at this."

Chekov turned, curious at her change in tone. The wall directly behind the desk was made up of narrow doors, which Leno had discovered were lockers. She had one open and was shoulder-deep inside it, rummaging like a terrier. She emerged as he approached, her expression gleeful. "Wait'll you see it! This stuff is great! I could have a field day in here!"

Chekov peered in over her shoulder, then reached

past her to push things aside and see for himself. The locker was full of equipment, everything from what looked like a sleek environmental suit to various pieces of body armor, several kinds of weaponry, and who knew what-all else. Curiosity dug at the lieutenant, and he answered the ensign's wide, anticipatory grin with a smile of his own. "Couldn't we both, Leno. Unfortunately . . ."

He closed the door on her petulant, "Aw, but Chief!" and shrugged apologetically. "We don't have the time right now, Leno. Maybe the Captain will let us dig around in here later, if Starfleet decides to let us really take this baby apart. How's that sound?"

"It sounds great, providing it actually happens. I wonder how much convincing Starfleet and Captain Kirk will take?"

The Russian laughed lightly and gestured for her to follow him. "Ensign, there's something I came to understand about Captain Kirk a very long time ago, and you'll eventually realize it for yourself if you're fortunate enough to really get to know him. His curiosity is immense and it includes *everything*. We'll probably have to beat him aside to get to it first."

Eyes wide, she took a step backward and feigned horror. *"You* beat him aside, Chief. *I'm* hoping for a long and distinguished career in Starfleet Security."

Leno stopped so abruptly in the corridor that Chekov ran into her broad back with a grunt. She was rigid and as unmoving as stone, one arm half-raised in caution for silence. The security chief's eyes searched the corridor, but he spied nothing of concern. "What?" he whispered.

She shook her head. Chekov was standing so close that stray wisps of her hair tickled his nose. "I don't know, Chief," she whispered. "For a second I thought I saw something. It was just at the edge of my vision . . ." She shook her head again, hard. It was a snapping, angry motion. "My nerves must be getting to me," she said with disgust. "I thought I was cooler than this."

"I've worked with you for years, and you're always cooler than ice, Leno," he assured her. "We've had a tough day. No one could go through it without getting spooked."

She looked over her shoulder. "Even you, sir?"

For just an instant, she was a new recruit again, needing his assurance. He nodded. "Even me, Ensign. The eeriness of this place aside, and I don't like it when my men die."

Her eyes flicked forward again. "Yeah." Her voice was hard, containing her emotions. "It stinks."

Chekov made a mental note. Once back aboard the *Enterprise,* he would have to work Markson's death out of her, probably by taking her on in the gymnasium. He wondered idly if they would both end up visiting Dr. McCoy afterward, as they had the last time they paired for sparring. Not that it made any difference. He didn't want any of his team carrying around that kind of emotional baggage. It could tie you in knots if push came to shove.

He nudged her. "Let's move out."

"Aye, sir."

They continued down the corridor. Locked doors they passed after one inspection. If any stood open, they paused to flash their lights around the interior and moved on. There was little of interest and nothing that they thought important to bring to the notice of Mister Spock or Doctor McCoy. Certainly there was nothing to lend further clues to why this station was here or why it was under minimum power. Let Starfleet Command be concerned with vacant living quarters and half-finished drinks on tabletops.

The hallway ended in a T. The right-hand arm led back toward Dr. McCoy and Ensign Hallie. The left arm dead-ended, beyond several closed doors, at the gaping maw of a second turboshaft. Chekov nodded with satisfaction and tried to ignore the pit. "That's it, then. Let's head back and see how Mr. Spock's doing. Maybe we can help him while we wait for the others."

"Maybe they've already beaten us back, if they found as little of interest as we have," Leno observed.

Chekov suppressed a smile. "Hungry for some action, Ensign?"

She shrugged. "Not that I want anything bad to happen, Chief, but a little activity sure would beat this aimless walking around."

The security chief held up a finger. "Be careful what you ask for, Ensign Leno. You may . . ." His voice trailed off, and he stared beyond her shoulder at the open turboshaft. "Oh, my God . . ."

"Chief?" She frowned at his reaction and slowly turned around to follow his gaze.

Something was coming up toward them out of the shaft's lower darkness, but it wasn't using the ladder to make its ascent. Pale and diaphanous, almost transparent in places, it glided in midair, emerging several feet off the floor from between the open doors and rising rapidly without the support of legs or arms . . . or anything else, for that matter.

Leno pressed back, stepping away from its advance, but Chekov was immoveable behind her, his eyes trained on the vision. Pale and stroked with faint colors like the inside of a seashell, it glided a long length into the corridor and stopped to seemingly regard them from nothing that looked like eyes. It started forward again, moving in a wavelike motion, and a long, gossamer wisp disengaged from the main body and reached toward them.

Leno raised her phaser and sighted down it. "Keep back!" she warned.

Whatever this was facing them took no heed of her, if it even understood what she said. As it continued to undulate toward them, Leno squeezed the trigger. The phaser wheezed and spat a weak stream of energy, hitting the thing head-on.

It reared back sharply, an amazing array of colors pulsating under the skin. Abruptly, it was gone, trailing rapidly down the turboshaft like water draining out of a sink. With a sharp cry, Leno bounded after it.

"Christina! Wait!" Chekov started after her, and the lights died. "It's too early to start shooting." He stopped short, and his heart rammed into his throat as he heard her stumble, crying out as she fell . . . and catch herself, swearing profusely. She appended the profanity with a completely uncontrite, "Sorry, Chief."

Somewhere behind them, a scream ripped free, killing Chekov's reply in his throat.

Eyes wide with fright, McCoy stared into the un-yielding darkness. "Hallie!" he called again, not caring if there was something else out there to hear him. His thumb frenetically clicked the button of his flash again and again, with no success. It was dead, just like everything else. Just like Hallie?

Hands outstretched before him, McCoy disobeyed Chekov's strict orders and slowly shuffled blindly down the corridor, the fingers of one hand trailing along the wall for guidance. Adrenaline surged the blood through his veins, and his pulse pounded so loudly in his ears he wasn't certain he'd hear anything until it came up and tapped him on the shoulder, and he was utterly confident that if anything touched him in the darkness, he would explode into a billion pieces, like shards of glass or a nova, and probably take whatever it was with him.

He paused uncertainly as the emergency lights overhead came back on. A faint, hardly perceptible light of a different quality illuminated the corridor's turn, sketching a charcoal line against the red-hued darkness. It came closer, brightening as it advanced. "Hallie?" McCoy whispered hoarsely, knowing full well that this approaching illumination was not the brilliance of the returning security guard's handlamp.

Beyond the turn came a whimper of reply. No words, just sound, but it was enough to get McCoy moving forward again. Despite what he might be moving toward, Hallie was there, and she needed him.

Something incomprehensible drifted around the corner and killed in his throat any other words McCoy might have had. He felt as though someone had pushed the 'stasis' button in his brain. Mental function ceased as his mind came up empty-handed of a name to call this thing, and he froze in fascinated shock.

Whatever this was glowed with a pale bluish-white phosphorescence touched with swirls of pale pink, green, and lavender. There was a slight, definite shape to the thing, but certainly nothing McCoy could readily identify. A central core roughly seven inches in width appeared horizontally around the turn in the corridor, drifting about five feet off the floor. It undulated slightly, as though the station corridor were filled with deep ocean swells and not stale, unmoving air. Cilialike filaments of varying lengths sprouted from the mass at irregular intervals, and they twined and danced with a life seemingly separate from the central trunk. As it drew closer, McCoy could almost see through it. Colors danced under the "skin," though whether these passages were comparable to his own blood vessels was impossible to say. It drew ever nearer to the motionless physician, and the tip of one tendril rose back on itself like a creature testing the wind for scent or a cobra pulled back to strike. It crested and slithered toward McCoy, dancing in the air a scant few inches in front of his insignia pin. McCoy's breath came in rapid, shallow gasps, the race of blood echoing in his eustachian tubes, as it reached out and stroked his cheek.

The searing cold from the creature's touch was like a blow across the face. McCoy gasped with pain, slapping a hand to his cheek, and broke and ran.

He shot away, not back the way he had come, but forward, toward Hallie. Behind and beside him, the thing reared back, then retreated before him, slithering away out of sight like a snake down a hole.

McCoy slammed around the corner and stopped short, almost tripping from his own momentum. Hallie lay on her side, back against the corridor wall, knees pulled up against her chest. Her eyes were closed, and she looked very pale, even under the ruddy cast of the overhead lights.

The doctor fell to his knees at her side, experienced hands reaching to touch her. "Ensign Hallie? Suzanna?"

Her thin lips parted, though her eyes didn't open. "Cold . . ." she whispered. "So cold . . ."

She *was* cold. He cupped her face in his hands, gauging temperature even as his fingertips counted the thread of a pulse in her neck. McCoy dug the mediscanner out of his pouch and ran it over her. No injuries, but her internal temperature had dropped several more degrees. As an afterthought, he turned the scanner on himself. His temperature was down, too, though not as severely. For now, he would forgo an injection. He didn't have much stimulant and he had a feeling they were going to need all he had before this was over.

McCoy tabbed open the front of his field jacket. Unmindful of his roughness, he hauled Hallie up by the shoulders and pulled her within the warm circle of his arms, tucking the loose sides of his jacket around her. He held her there with one arm while, with his free hand, he inserted into the hypospray something to bring her temperature back up, at least for a while.

He pressed the spray home through the sleeve of her jacket and waited. After a few tense moments, her eyes opened and she looked up at him. Her lips weren't quite so blue now. "Dr. McCoy?"

"Alive and in person," he said gently. When she tried to disengage herself, he caught her arms and held her. "You just stay right where you are, Ensign, and get warm. Are you all right?"

Her nod was rigid, mocking normal human movement like a marionette parodying its Human counterpart. She blinked at the question as though trying to focus her thoughts. "Fine, I think," she finally replied. "I was so disoriented . . ." She drew in a sudden breath that clattered between her teeth, and grabbed his arms in hands that were strong and punishing when she shook him. "Did you see it?! Did you see that thing?!"

He nodded, letting her pull away and sit up on her own. "I saw it."

Breath gusted out in an explosive sigh that shook her entire willow-thin frame. "Thank God! At least it wasn't my imagination." Her eyes searched his face. "Though I don't know which is worse, having it be my imagination or having it be real. What *was* that thing, Dr. McCoy?"

He shook his head. "I don't know, Hallie. I thought

I'd seen or read about nearly every strange thing in the galaxy, and I can't even make an educated guess."

"But it *was* real? You weren't just saying that to make me feel better?"

He managed to find a chuckle somewhere deep inside and draw it to the surface. "I almost wish I were, Ensign, but no. It was real."

Her eyes challenged him. "You said there were no ghosts, Dr. McCoy, but I think you're wrong. I think we both just saw our first. And I think it was Dan Markson."

That bizarre thought caught the doctor completely off guard. "That's a little bit far-reaching, don't you think, Ensign?"

"Is it?" she challenged, her tone hard. "You said yourself that you've never seen anything else like it, so what else could it have been?" she demanded, then appended, "sir."

"Just because I don't know what it was doesn't automatically make it a ghost, Ensign. It could have been a lot of things, and I'm sure there's a better explanation than to call it Markson's ghost or a Romulan ghost or any other kind of ghost. Ghosts *do not* exist, Ensign Hallie." Irritation built, burning away the remnants of his fear. "I can't prove that to you, but I accept it as an empirical fact. If my word isn't good enough for you, you're welcome to take this up with your commanding officer when we're back aboard the *Enterprise.*" Not only was she welcome to, McCoy would insist that Chekov order her to if this attitude persisted. Just such a compulsion may have contributed to the death of one crewman. They didn't need another believing in things that go bump in the night. "We don't have time for it right now."

Her eyes dropped their challenge. "Yes, sir," she said quietly. "I apologize if I was rude, sir."

"Apology accepted. Now, let's—"

"Dr. McCoy! Ensign Hallie!" Chekov's voice and the sound of running feet reached them from beyond the corridor's turn.

McCoy climbed to his feet, pulling Hallie up with him. "Chekov! We're here!" He started forward to meet them.

The security chief and his companion raced toward them from the far end of the corridor. McCoy nearly laughed aloud. He recognized those pale expressions. Evidently someone else had had a visitation, too.

Chekov skidded to a stop. "Are you both all right? We heard someone scream . . ."

Hallie hung her head. "That was me, Chief. I'm sorry."

"She had every reason to scream," McCoy defended the crewman. "I nearly screamed, too."

"You saw it, didn't you?" Leno broke in. "I thought just the chief and I were going nuts! I hit it with a phaser shot but it got away."

"Did you injure it?" McCoy asked.

"I don't know." Leno said. "What was it, Dr. McCoy?"

"Well, it *wasn't* a ghost," McCoy stressed before anyone else voiced the dreaded G word. "Beyond that, I can't even begin to guess. It wasn't like anything I've ever seen before. How are you two feeling? Any problems with the cold?"

They stared curiously at him. Chekov shrugged. "It's cold in here, but I—" He stopped, startled, when McCoy ran the mediscanner over him, then turned it toward Leno. "What's the matter, Doctor?"

McCoy pressed his lips into a thin line of annoyance as he read the results. "We've got trouble." He glanced up and down the corridor just to make certain the thing wasn't lurking nearby. "We need to get back to

Spock right now," he urged without telling them anything more, and started down the corridor back the way they'd come. Worry chewed at him.

"But, Dr. McCoy—"

"Maybe Mr. Spock will have some good news for us," Hallie expressed hopefully, falling into step beside him.

McCoy smiled at her but didn't reply. *Maybe*, he thought to himself. *But considering everything that's happened so far, I wouldn't bet on it.*

Chapter Thirteen

"SULU!" Kirk cried frenziedly. His ears sought the sound of Spock's voice, knowing it was gone, while his eyes tracked the *Valgard*'s cockeyed progress. The shuttlecraft was not altogether adrift. Someone, either Jaffe or Corey, was periodically hitting weak thrusters in an attempt to keep the craft level and on something close to its original course. "Get a tractor beam on that shuttle!"

"Aye, Captain! I'll try!"

"Don't try, Mister Sulu, just do it!" Kirk ordered. "Get them back in here before their systems fail completely and they're adrift, too."

The helmsman immediately turned away to work frantically at his console.

Kirk sat rigidly at the conn, staring at the static-filled viewscreen, his mind awhirl. He'd had a bad feeling about this station from the moment they had gotten their first glimpse of it. The only occasions in his life when he'd ever really gotten into trouble was when he didn't pay attention to his intuition. Why hadn't he listened to his instincts and gotten the *Enterprise* the hell away from here, let somebody else investigate things for a change?

He knew the answer to that as surely as he knew anything, and it only made him feel worse. It was one thing to endanger himself and his crew, and quite something else to consign another ship to its fate.

He was abruptly reminded of his remark back in the rec room all those thousands of years ago when Scotty was telling a harmless ghost story. Kirk's words came back to haunt him now . . . . "Whatever their goal, they evidently thought it worth the risk . . . it's the same risk you make in taking an active part in life . . . or becoming a Starfleet officer." Each one of the men and women serving aboard the *Enterprise* had known what they were getting into when they signed on, had known the risks. Each of them had known they might not come back.

But he didn't want it to be because of *him!*

Some of his inner turmoil and doubt had to do with his injury. The pain didn't help his mood. Loss of his landing party had raised his hackles till he was like a wolf on the defense. Add to that the power failures and a shuttlecraft gone adrift, and it was a wonder he wasn't chewing off his own leg to get out of the trap.

The only good news since the arrival of the space station had been Spock's call, letting him know the landing party was, for the most part, still well (except for Markson, of course . . .), and Scotty's discovery that the ship's problems were being caused by, as the chief engineer so succinctly put it, "that ugly piece of garbage." At least Kirk wasn't cold at the moment. Frustration pulsed his blood so hard through his veins, he wondered if he'd ever feel cold again.

He caught himself finger-drumming a rapid, monotonous tattoo on the arm of his chair and quelled it, curling his fingers tightly against the palm and clenching them into a white-knuckled fist. Starship captains weren't supposed to have nervous tics. And even if it happened that they developed one, that sort of thing wasn't supposed to be aired where the rest of the crew could see it.

But it sure beat losing it altogether.

"Mr. Sulu?"

The helmsman didn't turn, so intent was he on his controls. "I'm able to get partial power to the tractor beam, Captain, but not enough to pull the shuttle in. I can maintain their distance from the ship for an indefinite period with a pulse beat on the tractor beam." He glanced over his shoulder. "That should save us some power, rather than initiating a steady pull, and it will keep them close by."

Kirk nodded. "Very good, Mr. Sulu. Do so. Uhura, try to get a message through to Corey and Jaffe and let them know what we're doing. I don't want them to think we're going to just leave them out there."

"Aye, sir." She sounded exhausted from relaying the uncountable inquiries, status reports, and all the other messages flooding her board, but bent to the task immediately, her mellow voice not even giving hint of all that went on as it reached across the distance to the shuttlecraft and the security personnel within.

"Captain?"

Kirk turned to Scotty, who now stood beside the conn. "Yes, Mr. Scott. What is it?"

The chief engineer looked troubled, as well he might. He didn't even glance down at the status board in his hand, just held it out to Kirk. "Update on current conditions, sir. I'm afraid it doesn't look very good." He was the most apologetic Kirk had ever seen him, as though this entire thing were his fault.

Would that it were, but Kirk knew exactly at whose feet the blame must be laid. He glanced at the board. Life support was failing on several decks, despite efforts to bring it back on line. On other decks, systems continued to flip on and off like the lights on an old-fashioned Christmas tree. Both cases had prompted the evacuation of personnel to the large areas of the officers' and crew lounges, rec room, mess, and gymnasium. Systems shipwide were steadily and resolutely failing with no way to boost or preserve them. It was only a matter of time before the *Enterprise* was as dead in the water as the Romulan space station.

The long list made Kirk feel as though someone had punched him under the heart. "I've blown it, haven't I, Scotty?" he asked quietly.

"I beg your pardon, sir?"

"Me," Kirk explained. "I missed our chance to escape from—" He waved a hand toward the screen. "Whatever that is over there. My first priority is not to endanger this ship or her crew, but I've done it in spades. The minute I knew there was something wrong, I should have had the ship withdraw—"

"And leave behind the landing party?" Scott was aghast.

"It's not my first choice, Mr. Scott, no. But I have to consider the welfare of the rest of the crew, balancing the lives of six against those of four hundred and ninety-four." Kirk felt like such a traitor saying it, but it was the truth. Spock, Bones, and the others knew the risk when they signed onto a Federation starship. There was never any guarantee you'd be coming home from any particular mission, and none of those aboard the station would want him risking the lives of the rest of the crew just for them. "Maybe we could have beamed the team back aboard from a greater distance, instead of sitting here letting our energy reserves get sucked away. Or we could have sent for help from Starfleet Command. If we'd had another ship here . . ."

"That other ship would be as disabled as the *Enterprise* is right now," Scott predicted sternly. "Captain—" He stepped closer, lowering his voice to give them the semblance of privacy on the crowded bridge. "Captain, we lost contact with the landing party first. There was no indication of any other trouble at that time that would have warranted withdrawal of the ship."

"But—"

Scott spoke over his captain's protest, something he had almost never done in all his years serving under James Kirk. "The minor aberrations that were initially reported were so small as to fall under the category of any of the minor routine fluctuations and malfunctions we get aboard the ship from time to time. There was no way to tell it would lead to the *Enterprise's* losing power. Captain—" The chief engineer laid a gentle hand on Kirk's arm. "Don't blame yourself. There's no way you could have known."

"But, I *should* have known, Scotty!" Kirk maintained strongly. "The *Enterprise* is my ship, and I—"

The crackling sound of Christine Chapel's voice came over the intercom. "Sickbay to Captain Kirk."

Kirk's eyes closed almost by themselves. He hurt so badly. Worse, his ship was hurt, was dying around him, inch by inch. If this was one more crisis . . . "Go ahead, Doctor."

"Captain, I've just taken temperature readings on several crewmen reporting a sensation of cold. In every case, internal temperature has dropped by several degrees."

"Cause?"

"Unknown, Captain."

A chill worse than he'd felt to date, a chill that had nothing to do with the minimalization of life-support systems, coalesced around Kirk's heart like a sheen of ice. In his brief contact with Spock, the Vulcan had said something about Romulans dying of hypothermia in conditions where it couldn't possibly exist, and now the same thing was happening to the crew of the *Enterprise*.

His sixth sense shrieked, clawing its way up the inside of his skull with taloned feet. This time he would pay attention to it. "Dr. Chapel, I don't have details so you're going to have to trust me on this, but I have every reason to believe that the crew is going to suffer hypothermia."

"Hypothermia? But, Captain, the ship's ambient temperature is—"

Kirk cut her off. "I know all about the ambient temperature, Doctor. Just trust me. There is a very real danger of hypothermia. According to Mr. Spock, several Romulans aboard the space station suffered the same fate despite station temperatures that would indicate otherwise. Take what precautions you can to ensure the safety of the crew."

"Yes, Captain," her crisp tones replied. "Chapel out." She might not completely understand what he was getting at or why, but she'd follow his orders to the letter, of that Kirk was certain. But her efforts would do little good if they couldn't get out of here soon.

"Scotty." Kirk tugged the chief engineer's sleeve. "We need a plan and we need a plan *now,* otherwise the landing party and everyone on this ship is going to die. Is there any way at all to gain enough power to distance the ship from that damned station?"

Scott shook his head. "Captain, I've tried everything I can think of and I'm clean out of miracles. Besides, sir, if we left the landing party—". Kirk's eyes meeting his cut the chief engineer off in mid-sentence. The captain had already made it quite clear what he was prepared to do, if need be, to ensure the safety of the greater portion of his crew.

Kirk's mind raced. There had to be something they could do. He had never believed in the no-win scenario, and he wasn't about to start now.

A reverse tractor beam, to push the ship farther away from the station, was out of the question. They were having a hard enough time keeping Corey and Jaffe within reach with just small pulse bursts.

Kirk leaned forward. "Scotty, could we do a fast evacuation of the air in the shuttlebay to propel us away from the station?"

Scott nodded. "In theory, Captain, though I don't think there'd be enough air in it to move us far enough away to make it worth the effort."

"We have to try *something,* Mr. Scott."

"We can't do it, Captain." Sulu turned and looked back at them sadly. "The shuttlebay doors never reengaged when *Valgard* took off."

Dammit. Kirk closed his eyes briefly. "What if we divert all remaining power to our shields? Can we raise them strongly enough to protect systems and get them back on-line at least long enough to get us away from here?"

"I'll let you know in a minute, sir." Scott stepped over to his console.

The captain knew he wouldn't like the answer before Scott opened his mouth. The chief engineer's face said it all. "At present capabilities, Captain, our shields would only raise forty-eight percent, if that. That's enough to give us power to coast out of here only if we have a big hill to give us help."

Kirk's eyes sought each face on the bridge. "Does anyone have any suggestions?" They were all silent, staring at him, waiting for him to make the inevitable decision, which he didn't want to make . . .

. . . but which he would, as captain. "Scotty—" His voice caught and he cleared his throat. "Do we have enough power to initiate self-destruct?"

The silence on the bridge was deafening. Scott nodded, expression stoic. "Aye, sir, but not for long—less than a half hour."

"Understood, Mr. Scott. Sulu, leave off the pulse bursts to *Valgard*. On my order, you're to use the same to draw us closer to the space station. We want to make certain we take it with us when we go."

"Aye, aye, sir," the helmsman said numbly.

"Uhura, if you can, let Jaffe and Corey know what's coming. And see if you can raise the landing party one more time. They should know about this as well, so they can . . . prepare themselves."

Kirk sat straighter in his chair, not wanting to think about what he was about to do, and unable to think of anything else. He touched a button on the chair arm. "Captain's log, supplemental. There seem to be no further alternatives open to us. The Romulan space station continues to leach our energy, putting the entire ship's crew, as well as the landing party, at the mercy of slow death by hypothermia. Every attempt to reverse this process has resulted in failure, or inability to even make the attempt due to power loss. It is only a matter of time before my ship is as dead and adrift as the Romulan station. Once Starfleet is aware that we have lost contact, they will send Federation ships to seek an explanation. We are unable to send a subspace message warning Federation and other ships away from this sector, and both the *Kongo* and the *Lexington* will be here shortly. I cannot allow another vessel to suffer the same fate as the *Enterprise;* therefore, there is only one recourse open to me." He glanced briefly at Scotty, Sulu, and Uhura, and was profoundly touched when each of them nodded accord with his words. Kirk took a deep breath. "We will use our remaining power to get as close to the station as we can in order to destroy it when the ship . . . explodes." The word tore out of him, leaving him feeling raw and wounded. "Upon my order, Chief Engineer Montgomery Scott will jerry-rig every photon torpedo aboard the *Enterprise* to ensure their detonation at the time of self-destruct as an aid in destroying the space station. Commendations are in order for the ship's entire complement of crew. Full responsibility for these actions is mine. Kirk out." His finger jabbed the button hard and he stared stonily at the viewscreen.

Maybe he would have to start believing in the no-win scenario after all. Then again, maybe not.

Kirk glanced around the bridge at the solemn faces of his crew. "Ladies and gentlemen, we have twenty minutes before we will be close enough to the station to institute the self-destruct. That gives us twenty minutes to come up with another solution." His fingers curled into a fist and he pounded gently on the arm of his chair. "And I intend to do it."

Chapter Fourteen

THE FIRST THING McCoy noticed as they neared the station bridge was the smell of cleaner air. The stench of the Romulans' decomposing corpses was alleviated, and the scent of rotting peaches had all but vanished. He took a deep breath and for the first time in his life was pleased by the sterile smell of recycled air aboard a space craft.

The second thing he noticed was Spock.

"Spock! Have we got something to tell—!" As he and the others came onto the station bridge, McCoy's excited greeting died on his lips. The Vulcan looked awful.

Spock was exactly where they had left him, seated at a computer console with the generator at his side. Anyone other than McCoy would probably have noticed nothing other than the Vulcan's peculiar stillness, and might have put it down to the singular concentration that often characterized Spock. But McCoy was nothing if not utterly himself, and what he saw sent him rushing across the room before the others could even register that something was wrong. The Vulcan's color was off. Spock's skin had developed a waxy sheen, like a corpse filled with embalming fluid.

"Spock!" McCoy gripped the first officer's shoulders firmly and swung him around, then scrabbled the fingers of one hand into his medipouch at his side. A quick scan showed him that Spock's internal body temperature had dropped drastically from its standard 91 degrees to 85 degrees. It might not seem like much to the layman, but McCoy knew that unconsciousness would set in for the Vulcan at 79 degrees, and those six tiny units could slip by awfully fast if you weren't careful. After that . . . Hell, if Spock were Human, he would have been unconscious already, slipping his way toward coma and death.

It wasn't as though the doctor hadn't anticipated this event, and McCoy reached for the hypospray he'd administered to Hallie. Changing the dosage slightly to account for the Vulcan's different metabolism, McCoy pressed it home through the material of Spock's field jacket and waited.

Funny, how a minuscule amount of time can seem inordinately long when you're worried half to death. Beneath McCoy's fingers, Spock was frighteningly still, though occasionally his body shook with tremors that let the doctor know he was still alive.

Finally, the Vulcan blinked sleepily, licked his thin lips, which were practically devoid of color, and slowly raised his head. "Dr. McCoy—" His voice was raspy and hoarse, a broken parody of his normal tones. "I have been . . ." He sighed heavily, tiredly.

"Take it easy, Spock," McCoy urged. "It'll keep for a few minutes. Let the medicine take effect first." He looked over his shoulder at the others crowding in behind him. "It's the hypothermia, though I can't understand why Spock's being affected so radically before the rest of us. He tolerated the cold temperatures of Sarpeidon's ice age better than I did, and that was one hell of a cold place. This just doesn't make any sense." His mouth twisted wryly. "But, why should it? Nothing else has. How are the rest of you doing?" Before any of them could reply, he ran the mediscanner in a long sweeping gesture across the three of them.

"How *are* we, Doctor?" Chekov asked, and McCoy was reminded that he hadn't answered the lieutenant's question earlier. The doctor was fairly certain the security chief could read his expression quite adequately.

"We all have lowered internal temperatures. They're not as radical as Spock's, mind you, but they're still something to be concerned about, particularly if we can't find a way to bring them back up and maintain them there. I can't figure it out. It's chilly in here, sure, but more like a brisk autumn day. It's definitely not cold enough in here to induce hypothermia."

"Ensign, that's what it is, though it shouldn't be a problem at all. We need to get warm, and soon."

Spock's fingers curled loosely around McCoy's wrist and squeezed to get the doctor's attention. "What is it, Spock?"

"Doctor—" Already the Vulcan's voice sounded better. His eyes were open now, the vision clearer and brighter. The sight did a world of good for McCoy's spirits. "I have much to report. I have been successful in tying in the generator to some of the station systems, though, naturally, it does not produce enough energy to power up everything."

"Naturally. I noticed the air smelled a whole sight better." McCoy took a deep breath through his nose. "That peach smell is all but gone."

Spock nodded. "Air is being recycled at slightly better than minimal. In addition, heat production has been brought up marginally as well."

"Well, that's good news, but it doesn't do much for us when we don't know what's causing our temperatures to drop. We need to find a way to maintain our body heat at safe levels without letting it drop so far we succumb to unconsciousness."

"I'm on it, Dr. McCoy," Leno announced suddenly and vanished out of the room at a run.

The doctor stared after her. "Where's she going?"

"I don't know . . ." Chekov snapped his fingers. "Yes, I do! And she'll probably need help. I'll be right back." He took off after his crewman.

McCoy blinked at Hallie. "Do you know what that's all about?"

She shrugged. "Beats me. How are you feeling, Mr. Spock?"

"Much better, Ensign, thank you for asking." The Vulcan sat straighter and took a deep breath.

McCoy noted with completely detached, utterly professional, joyous enthusiasm that Spock's color was much better than before. He made another pass with the scanner. "Well, your internal temperature is back up to safety levels, but I don't have any guarantees on how to keep it there, since I don't know why it's dropping in the first place. This is damned peculiar." He slapped the scanner against his palm in irritation, as though maybe it was acting up and hitting it could make it work correctly again. He knew that wasn't the case, but the physical gesture did wonders for his outlook.

"I have spoken with the captain." Spock made the announcement with all the aplomb of a remark about the current weather conditions.

It made McCoy want to hit him but, being a physician, he didn't like to manhandle his patients, even when they deserved it. "You talked to Jim?! Is everything all right?"

"Evidently, Doctor, everything is far from 'all right.'" Spock sat back in his chair, looking better by the moment. "We were only able to speak briefly due to the energy fluctuations we are currently experiencing."

"Why doesn't that surprise me?"

"But our conversation was long enough for me to learn that the *Enterprise* is also suffering from power drainage, which is why they could not beam us back when we lost contact with the ship. Evidently, they are attempting to send out a shuttlecraft to enact a rescue, but I do not put much faith in the attempt, given the current parameters of our situation."

But Kirk was trying. That was all that mattered. Leonard McCoy had known Jim Kirk long enough to know that the starship captain would try every trick in the book to get them back. And, when those were exhausted, he'd try a few more. And if those didn't work . . .

. . . McCoy didn't want to think about that.

"I lost contact with the ship shortly thereafter," Spock continued. "And so I turned my attention to—" He blinked over McCoy's shoulder. "What do you have there, Lieutenant?"

McCoy turned. Chekov and Leno were back, their arms filled with yards of shiny black material. Leno grinned, unable to contain herself. "Romulan environmental suits, Mr. Spock, from the security office, or whatever it is back there!" She indicated the direction with a jerk of her head.

"Chances are, Ensign, that if the Romulans did not endeavor to use these suits to save at least part of their number, they will be no good to us."

"Oh, put a sock in it, Spock!" McCoy growled. He stood and took a suit from Leno's outstretched arms, smiling reassuringly at her suddenly wobbly expression. "Give the woman a little credit for trying, will you? Maybe these won't help in the long run, but if they aid in any sort of heat retention, even for a little while, it helps our position until we figure out a way to stop the drop in our temperatures or come up with a way to get back home. Hell, they're better than what we have now. Don't mind him, Ensign," he added for Leno's benefit. "He's always difficult to deal with."

He shook out the e-suit and held it up against him. "Well, I can't say it'll be a perfect fit, but I'm not about to quibble." He took another and tossed it at the Vulcan. "Here you go, Spock. Climb in. Doctor's orders. And everyone make sure you pull up the cowls. Heat loss is greatest through the top of your head. The longer you keep that covered and insulated, the better your chances of retaining heat for a longer time."

The next few moments were spent in getting out of their bulkier clothing and into the sleek lines of the environmental suits. The soft, smooth material clung to their bodies like a second skin or a thin, insulating barrier of fat. Alpine skiers and deep sea divers in the twentieth century had first discovered the practical use of such a suit, and mankind had wisely taken it with them into space.

McCoy snugged the open-faced cowl up over his head and immediately began to feel warmer than he had in the bulky field jacket. "How's everyone doing?"

Their replies in the affirmative made him feel better than he had in hours. Even Spock looked pleasantly surprised by the difference he felt once inside the environmental suit. Hallie's suit sagged here and there, as it was made for a much taller person, and McCoy took note of that fact. The suit's poor fit would probably make her more susceptible to further heat loss than the rest of them, if it happened that these suits did not do their job and halt the loss of body heat.

He didn't for a minute think it would go any other way. If so, the Romulans would have used these suits to try and save themselves, as Spock had said. For now, it was a help, and it was at least an attempt on their parts to stay alive just that much longer, but he would have given almost anything to know why the Vulcan was so much more affected than the others.

While they dressed, Spock told Chekov and Leno what he had told the others about his short conversation with Kirk, then resumed his recitation. "I turned my attention to accessing the computer banks and learning what I could about this station. It appears that much of the records have been wiped, probably out of fear they would fall into the wrong hands."

"I'll bet the computer didn't tell you anything about what we saw in the corridor," Leno said darkly. Her face flushed when Spock looked her way, one eyebrow cocked in silent encouragement for her to continue. He listened attentively to all of their descriptions, his head cocked curiously to one side.

"You only *saw* it," Hallie said almost accusingly after Leno and Chekov had finished their part of the story. She still looked shaken by her experience.

"Whatever it was, it *touched* me." She shivered and hunched her shoulders.

"And me," McCoy added, resting a comforting hand on her shoulder where she sat beside him on one of the consoles, her feet dangling several inches off the floor.

"And me," McCoy added, resting a comforting hand on her shoulder where she sat beside him on one of the consoles, her feet dangling several inches off the floor.

"Did it seem intelligent?"

"I didn't give it time to show me its diplomas, if that's what you mean," McCoy stressed, wide-eyed. "It didn't act like it was trying to say howdy, but how would I know anyway?"

Spock was annoyed. He didn't show it, but McCoy could tell. "What sensations did you experience at its touch?" the Vulcan pressed.

McCoy paused, thinking about it, remembering the feel of that tentacle along his face. He'd immediately wanted to say revulsion, but that hadn't been part of it at all. There had been nothing to be repulsed by, no sliminess or slickness or anything of that nature. In fact, the touch had been surprisingly dry and smooth, almost like the touch of a snake. He told Spock as much. "And cold. It was really cold." The doctor rubbed his cheek where the thing had briefly caressed him.

Hallie nodded vigorously. *"Very* cold. It kind of leaned up against me, and it felt like all the heat in my body had . . ." She trailed off, turning wide eyes up to McCoy's face.

He shook his head wonderingly. "Spock, could there be a . . . a *creature* . . . who leaches out body heat as a form of energy consumption and induces . . ." He shook his head again. It all seemed so far-fetched, but so had Vulcans before humans met them. "Am I just grasping at straws?"

"On the contrary, Doctor. Given my other findings, that is a most interesting theory."

"Well?" McCoy asked, when further explanation wasn't immediately forthcoming.

Spock paused, deep in thought. "After losing contact with the *Enterprise,* I attempted to access the ship's log or other records in order to find out the reason behind the station's existence or some information pertinent to energy loss or equipment malfunctions. There was singularly little to go on. I did discover that this station was intended to be the first of many such outposts in Romulan-held territory—"

"Terrific," McCoy muttered.

"—and that there were hopes it would manifest itself into a gathering spot of some kind."

"Sounds pretty nefarious to me," Leno observed.

Chekov, seated beside her, nodded grimly. "When were the Romulans ever up to something that wasn't?"

"What about station power, Mr. Spock?" Hallie encouraged him to continue.

"I could not access the command log, Ensign. Either it is under some type of strict locking code, or no longer exists at all. I had hoped to find records or reports on the malfunctioning of their central power source but, as I stated earlier, there is nothing of the kind. Be that as it may, the situation exists."

"So?" McCoy prompted. Where was Spock going with all this?

Spock held up one fist, uncurling one finger for each point raised. "First, we have a space station that has suffered energy loss. If our present experience holds true, that loss presented itself in a series of fluctuations before power dropped to minimal standards." His middle digit joined the index finger. "Second, since speaking with Captain Kirk, I have discovered that the *Enterprise* has suffered much the same sort of affliction and can only deduce that, given enough time, her systems will also drop to minimal and she will begin to drift, as did the station." Spock ignored the looks that the remark raised on the faces of his companions. "Since the *Enterprise* did not suffer a power loss until coming in contact with the space station, I think it safe to speculate that the power drain is caused by the station itself, either something aboard the station or in the vicinity."

Another finger came up. "Third, your reports of this entity you encountered in the corridors pose some interesting theories about loss of energy and how Romulans could die of hypothermia when the temperature makes it unlikely if not impossible. I don't think I need to remind you that body heat is a form of energy, just as are electrical impulses or the power that drives a starship." His look held them. His little finger joined the rest. "Fourth and last, when I lost contact with the *Enterprise,* I took a tricorder reading. If the reading can be trusted as even marginally accurate, and I believe it can be, there were indications of a power drain emanating from directly aboard this vessel."

"Excuse me, Mr. Spock," Chekov interrupted. "You tried using the tricorder earlier, when we first came aboard the station, and it didn't register any power drain. Why now?"

"I suspect, Lieutenant, that is because the creature is growing stronger as it draws more energy from the *Enterprise,* if it is, indeed, the creature that I am reading on the tricorder. If I interpret my reading correctly, and the creature is doing what I am suggesting, then it is logical to assume that the center of our problem lies in engineering."

"And no Scotty within reach," McCoy lamented.

Spock's head dipped in a brief nod. "I agree that it would facilitate matters if Mr. Scott were here, should the station's power source indeed prove to be the problem; however, I suspect that is not the case."

"Why do I think I hate the sound of that?" McCoy watched while Spock stood and reached to disengage the generator from its conduit. "What are you doing that for?"

"We may need it in engineering," Spock answered simply.

"Oh." McCoy swung his foot and shared a look with the others. "What about that"—his head jerked toward the open doors—"whatever it was, that *thing,* out there?"

Spock quickly coiled wires and slid the generator back into its sling. "When we find engineering, Doctor, I believe we will find your 'thing,' as well."

"Great." McCoy levered himself off the counter and picked up his equipment from atop his discarded field jacket. "Just great."

Chapter Fifteen

THE SIX MEMBERS of the landing party paused in the vestibule outside the station bridge and glanced up either leg of the corridor. Most of them studiously ignored the half-open doors of the turbolift directly in front of them, but McCoy caught Hallie studying the doors and the wide emptiness of the dark shaft with an expression of deep sorrow in her eyes. It was hard to lose a friend, and harder still to lose them under tragic circumstances. It probably didn't help matters that she just couldn't understand where Markson's fears had come from.

"Ensign Leno," Spock said, interrupting McCoy's quiet observation of Hallie. "You said that there is another turboshaft farther along this corridor?" His hand gestured to the left. McCoy appreciated his friend's tact. Spock knew that none of them, especially Hallie, wanted to climb down the shaft they'd come up. They would prefer the risk of meeting the creature, or whatever it was, head-on rather than be faced with Dan Markson's remains lying at the bottom of the shaft.

Leno nodded. "That's correct, Mr. Spock. That's how that thing came at the chief and me, like a snake up a sewer pipe." She gestured. "This main branch of the corridor ends in a T. One leg circles back to the right to connect with the right-hand branch. The turboshaft is at the end of the other leg, at a dead end."

McCoy didn't particularly like that specific turn of phrase. "I suppose we have to climb a turboshaft again?" he asked unhappily, already knowing the answer.

Spock shifted the weight of the generator's carrying strap on his shoulder. Sheathed in the sleek dark suit, all he needed to complete the picture was a face mask and a pair of goggles, and he would have looked like a salamander. "Unfortunately, Dr. McCoy, if we wish to reach the lower levels and descend to engineering, that is precisely what we will have to do." His eyes flicked over them all. "However, we will not have to go down the turboshaft all the way to the bottom. Given that we dare not trust the mechanics of this station any further than we must, I propose for us to go down to the first level, which houses a stairway system. At that point, we will switch over and make the rest of our descent much more quickly and, I assume, safely."

"Well, I don't think any of us are outrageously keen on getting into a turboshaft again, Spock," McCoy said for the benefit of the others. "But I don't see as we have much choice." He nodded. "Sure, it sounds like a good idea." The others nodded their agreement of the plan as well, though Hallie had to be reminded to do it by a jab in the ribs from Leno.

"Then let us proceed." Spock led them down the hallway toward their objective. Almost by routine, they fell into their usual order, with Chekov pacing forward to precede Spock, and Leno bringing up the rear. Markson's absence was a notable vacancy at the Vulcan's side.

Walking in the e-suit felt markedly different than in the clothing McCoy was used to. The material flowed with the motion of his frame, never binding, never restricting. Unencumbered by his usual boots, his feet glided almost soundlessly over the decking, the slightly waffled sole of the suit foot feeling pleasantly pebbly against the bottom of his foot.

"Are you okay, Ensign?" McCoy asked Hallie quietly as they walked.

She jerked slightly, as though startled by the question or goaded out of some inner reverie. Her head bobbed once in an abrupt nod. "I'm fine, sir."

She didn't look fine to McCoy. Her face seemed even paler against the dark circle of the close-fitting cowl, and her wide eyes were cold. "Are you sure, Hallie?"

"Yes," she said absently. Then she shook off whatever she was thinking and turned to the doctor. "I'm fine, sir," she repeated neutrally. "Thank you for asking."

"You're welcome," he replied, stunned by her chill response. The rest of the short walk was made in silence.

The doors to the other turboshaft were still open, leading into darkness. Leno took it upon herself to hang on the open doorway and brazenly stare the length of the shaft. "Nothing down there I can see," she reported, straightening. She patted the edge of the door frame, her eyes pensive. "I almost took a header down this shaft in the dark," she mused. "That critter owes me one."

"Two," Chekov said. When she looked at him curiously, he added, "For almost stopping your chief's heart in the process."

"Three," Hallie appended stonily, and nobody had to ask her what she meant.

McCoy stood back from the open doorway, not eager to get any closer to it than he had to until it was time to make the descent. The thought of going down there for the express purpose of encountering whatever it was they had previously confronted made nervous sweat break out on his palms and the small of his back. They had all been lucky last time. What if their luck didn't hold out this time around and the creature turned out to be more malevolent than it had first appeared?

"We'll descend as we ascended," Chekov said, drawing McCoy's attention away from the worthless introspection. "I'll go first, with Mr. Spock behind me. Next will come Ensign Hallie, then Dr. McCoy, then Ensign Leno. Keep your handlamps attached to your wrists, but pointed *down*. That way, you won't blind the person coming down behind you, but you'll light the way for yourself and the rest. Mr. Spock, how many levels do you anticipate we'll have to go before we reach a stairwell access?"

"Assuming this turboshaft is twin to the one we originally climbed, Lieutenant, we have twelve levels to descend before reaching a point where we may switch over to the stairway system."

"Okay," Chekov said to the group. "It was a long climb up, and it's going to feel just as long going down. If you get tired, speak up, and we'll take a breather. I don't want anyone getting fatigued. We don't want any more accidents. Any questions?" He nodded when there were none. "Let's go."

Swinging into the shaft this time was probably one of the hardest things Leonard McCoy had ever had to do in his entire life. What if that creature was waiting for them, waiting to suck away every ounce of warmth their bodies held, as he suspected it could? What if the turboshaft came by again and pulled them all to a quick death? What if—

Stop it, Leonard! he sternly ordered himself. *You're doing just what Dan Markson did.* And look where that got him.

In retrospect, moving up the ladder had been comparatively easy. Oh, his legs and arms had gotten tired, but at least he'd been able to look *up* and try to forget the vast drop below him. Now it was there, stretching beyond the bodies of his companions as far as the eye couldn't see, which made the whole thing just that much worse. Light pooled across the dark expanse of Hallie's suited head and shoulders from McCoy's handlamp, ran together with her own, and spilled downward over Spock to light Chekov. The Russian's light cleft the darkness only so far before being swallowed. McCoy centered his concentration on Hallie's slim, black-sheathed hands on the rung beneath his feet, and he tried not to step on her in his haste to finish this stint on the ladder and get back on solid ground.

They descended as they had climbed, in silence, the quiet broken only by their breathing. This time, McCoy couldn't hear their feet on the rungs, even taking into account the fact that his hearing was just slightly impaired by the thin material over his ears. He lost track of time with nothing to reference but the top of Hallie's head and the feel of Leno descending after him, so he was a little startled when Chekov called an unexpected halt shortly after they had taken a break.

"What's the matter?" he asked no one in particular.

Chekov swore softly in Russian before replying. "Our way is blocked."

"By?" Did he really want to know?

"A turbolift car."

Terrific. "What are we going to have to do, climb back up and cross over to the other turboshaft?"

"We could . . ." McCoy didn't like the sound in the Russian security chief's voice. It meant he was thinking.

"What is your recommendation, Lieutenant?" Spock asked, his spotlit head bent in Chekov's direction.

Chekov looked up and squinted in the bleaching glare of the Vulcan's handlamp. "Well, Mr. Spock, we could do as Dr. McCoy suggested, but that would cost time that we may not be able to afford if we want to avoid freezing to death."

If? McCoy wondered.

The trail of light from Chekov's handlamp flashed in a circle below them. Straining to one side, McCoy saw the top of the turbolift below them. The Russian's light was trained on one particular section. Suddenly the doctor knew what Chekov was going to suggest, and knew just as certainly that he was going to hate it.

"There's an access hatch in the top of the car, Mr. Spock. I've been keeping track of our levels of descent and the reference marks on the inside of the shaft, probably put there for the maintenance crews. According to your count, we're coming up on the first level where we can access the stairs, and I'm fairly certain we're coming up on a deck access, as well. If this car is even slightly in line with the door, and the door is open, we should be able to crawl through the car and access the corridor."

Crawl was an appropriate word, because that was exactly what McCoy's skin was doing under the fine sheath of e-suit material. "You're not serious!"

"It would behoove us to try the Lieutenant's idea, Doctor," Spock said, looking up and squinting in the light from the lamps above him. "Otherwise, we *will* lose time that could be put to a better use. I cannot speak for the rest of you, but I am beginning to again feel the cold and fatigue associated with the onset of hypothermia."

"Are you all right, Spock?" McCoy asked worriedly. "Any dizziness? Do you want another shot?"

"I am experiencing no dizziness at this time, Doctor, and making the effort at this point to crawl over Ensign Hallie to give me another dosage would further waste what time we have. I recommend we attempt what Lieutenant Chekov has suggested."

"I'm all for it." Leno's voice reached them from above. "I'd like a break from this ladder. My hands are getting stiff."

Loss of manual dexterity . . . and even within the small protection of the e-suit. In his mind's eye, McCoy could see the medical reference manual and the page on hypothermia. He shook his head, torn. To go up and around the "safe" way (as much as anything was safe aboard this tin can), or cut corners and go down through a car that might suddenly decide to move and make lovely designs with their bodies on the ceiling of the shaft. What a choice.

"Let's do *something.*" Hallie's voice goaded them.

"But what if the car starts to move?" McCoy felt he had to say it, had to put his fears into words.

Lit by his light, Hallie's shoulders moved in a smooth shrug. "You can't live forever, Dr. McCoy," she replied flatly.

"No? Watch me." He sighed and nodded. "Okay, Chekov. Let's give it a try."

"Right. Keep your lights trained on the car top. Don't any of you come down until I give the all-clear." His fierce gaze stabbed at them from below, squinting against the glare from their lights. "That's an order, even to the senior officers." He went down several rungs until he was just above the top of the car. Hanging on with one hand, Chekov stretched across the intervening space and put his foot on the turbolift, slowly easing his full weight onto it.

McCoy swallowed hard, suddenly realizing he'd forgotten to breathe. His eyes worriedly followed the security chief's careful, precise movements.

Chekov paused. There was no telling what went through his mind in the few seconds before he let go of the ladder altogether and stood alone on top of the turbolift. He waited a moment, arms out. When the car didn't move, he swiftly knelt, pried up the hatch in the roof, and bent to flash his handlamp around the interior of the car. The look he shot up at them was expectant. "Something is going our way, finally! The car stopped halfway through the level, but the corridor door *is* open. If we climb into the car, we can squeeze through the opening on the other side. Don't anyone come until I call the all-clear, then come only one at a time when you hear your name called. Move quickly. Don't hesitate. I'll be waiting for you on the other side."

Without waiting for any reply from the others, Chekov disappeared into the dark opening. McCoy half expected the car to pick that moment to plummet toward the shaft bottom, but it didn't. He heard movement inside, like a mouse trapped in a can, and the Russian swore virulently once or twice. Then they heard his voice. "I'm through! Mr. Spock, you're next."

The Vulcan moved without hesitation, following Chekov's lead into the turbolift car, lowering the generator and following after it. A few moments later, he spoke. "Ensign Hallie."

She moved with single-minded determination, and McCoy wondered again just what was going through the young security guard's mind. She disappeared into the opening with the ease of a newt sliding under a log. "Dr. McCoy, it's your turn."

Dammit. He didn't want to get in there, didn't want to trust his safety to the vagaries of a space station with a mind of its own. But he also didn't have any choice, if they hoped to reach engineering and find an answer to all their questions. Swallowing fear with a taste like bile, he climbed down the last few rungs and, praying fervently to anything who might be listening, stepped onto the top of the turbolift.

It didn't so much as quiver under his feet. He released the rungs with hands that shook and stood there a moment, feeling weak in the knees.

"Dr. McCoy? Are you coming?"

Spock's voice. "I'm on my way," the doctor assured them. "Don't rush me." He lowered himself into the car, hung by his fingers for a second or two, and let go. His feet struck the floor, and *that* was when he expected all hell to break loose. But it didn't. Three handlamps lit the interior, and he held up a hand to shield his eyes.

Chekov, Spock, and Hallie were on their knees, peering in at him from the top half of the open shaft doors. The men each reached an arm toward him. "Come on, Dr. McCoy," Chekov encouraged. "Grab on and we'll lift you free."

They didn't have to tell him twice. McCoy's hands grasped theirs readily and he half-walked up the inside wall, bending to slide the rest of the way on his stomach. He paused on the lip, half-in and half-out of the turbolift, like a fish beached on a sandbar, and a horrible thought abruptly badgered its way into his brain. What if this damned thing started moving *right now?*

His hands tightened around theirs even more strongly, and his feet scrabbled uselessly for purchase. "Get me out of here!" In two seconds, he was in the corridor and getting to his feet.

Nothing had ever felt so good as the solidity of the corridor floor beneath his hands and knees. At least that wasn't in any danger of going anywhere. "Come on, Leno!" the doctor called, listening to the pound of his heart against his ribs, and ignoring the slickness of his skin inside the e-suit. "Last one in is a rotten egg."

"It's about time." They heard the skitter of her feet along the steel rungs, the thump as she landed on the roof and slid through the hole. Their lamps lit her way as she quickly took in the situation and held up her hands. "Here I—"

The car moved suddenly, dropping. Leno cried out and the others snatched their hands back to safety. The turbolift didn't drop far, only several inches— McCoy breathed a sigh of release—but it effectively cut off Leno's escape route. There was no way she was going to squeeze through that tiny opening now.

She swore with the facility of a longshoreman, and Chekov didn't call her on it. Doubtless, he felt like doing a little swearing himself. McCoy certainly did.

This was too damned close to what he'd imagined. "Now what are we going to do?" Hallie asked.

"You're going to go on without me," Leno practically spat, surprising them all with her vehemence. "You're going to have to get to engineering and check out Mr. Spock's theories, if we hope to have even a chance of survival. You don't have the time to fool around here trying to get me out. Mr. Spock, was the chief right? Can you reach the stairs from this level?"

"I believe so, Ensign."

"Then go and do it."

"Spock—"

"Ensign Leno is absolutely correct, Doctor." Spock's eyes were trained on what little they could see of Leno through the small opening. "If the creature is, indeed, drawing off our body heat and affecting the power supply of this station and the *Enterprise* as I have surmised, we only have a limited amount of time left to us in which to take some kind of action, if we can. Ensign—"

"Save it for later, Mr. Spock," Leno said brusquely. "I'm not sunk yet. What level is engineering on? I'll meet you there."

The woman's bravery warmed McCoy to the bone. Even Spock looked impressed. "Engineering is located on the lowest level of the space station." He nodded gravely. "I look forward to seeing you there, Ensign."

"You're on. Now the rest of you get out of here and let me get to work."

They spared one last look at her defiant eyes, then moved off down the corridor with Spock in the lead.

"How is she going to get out of there, Chief?" Hallie asked, trotting along at McCoy's heels.

Chekov shook his head. "I don't think she is,

Hallie." He murmured something in Russian, his voice awe-filled. "We'll come back for her when this is all over."

They raced along at Spock's heels, arms pumping in rhythm. The Vulcan held the generator against his chest so it wouldn't bounce against him and led the way toward the stairs.

Though McCoy had amazing faith in the Vulcan (not that he ever would have told him that), he was still surprised when Spock halted beside a door and opened it to reveal the stairway system stretching away below them. "Spock—" He panted, chest heaving. "You remembered this was here from the map you saw below?"

"Yes, Doctor."

McCoy shook his head, utterly amazed at the capacity of the Vulcan's memory. "When you die, I want *that*"—he pointed at Spock's head—"in a jar on my desk. I've never seen anything like it!" He panted and blinked up at the strange look the first officer was giving him. "It's a compliment, Spock!"

"I shall endeavor to remember that, Doctor." He stepped onto the landing.

McCoy swallowed hard as he followed the others into the stairwell and let the door close behind them. They shone their lights around the dark shaft, but there was nothing to be seen. If that thing had been there, waiting for them, McCoy wasn't certain what he would do, but he suspected it involved lots of yelling.

Spock glanced their way and started down the winding course of stairs. "Come along. I recommend we stay close together."

"You'll get no argument from me," McCoy vowed.

Spock did not pause. Their feet whispered against

the metal risers as they rapidly descended toward their goal. "That will be a pleasant change."

"Was that a Vulcan joke?" McCoy called, not expecting a response, and his expectations were not disappointed. He hurried along in the Vulcan's wake, the beam of his handlamp trained on the small of Spock's back.

They moved downward level by level, around and around, until McCoy lost all notion of where they might be in the vast station. Had he been alone, he would have been turned around on himself and irretrievably lost. "Spock," he finally asked when they passed yet another landing and its welcoming door. "Are you *sure* you really know where we're going?"

"It is not much farther," the Vulcan assured him without even a backward glance.

"That *doesn't* answer my question."

Several additional flights later, Chekov pulled up short, and a mild oath escaped his lips. "Is it my imagination, or is it getting warmer in here?"

Spock stopped on the stairs and turned around. "Your imagination is not playing tricks on you, Lieutenant. It is, indeed, markedly warmer here than on the previous levels."

"But, why? I didn't think there was enough power on this station to generate this much warmth."

"And if it's so warm in here," Hallie added, "why don't I *feel* any warmer?" She rubbed her arms briskly and hugged herself within the loose confines of the e-suit. In the light of her handlamp, her lips looked blue. McCoy's heart turned over in his chest.

Spock did not reply. He continued down the few remaining stairs to the next level and opened the door.

A blast of moist air assailed them, rushing into the stairway in a wave of warmth that McCoy felt against his face but which did not seem to reach through the e-suit. They hurried to follow Spock, catching the door before it could close on the Vulcan's retreating back.

It smells like a greenhouse in here, was McCoy's first thought.

They had come out onto a lattice-work of catwalks, suspended high over the station's central energy core. The walls trickled with moisture, tracking runnels down the smooth surface and dripping to puddles on the distant floor. The smell McCoy associated with rotten peaches was heavy in the air. There were other underlying odors, but nothing McCoy could put a name to.

Spock stood at the very edge of the catwalk, staring down into the room below. "I believe you will all want to see this." He motioned them forward to join him, already turning aside to take a long stairway to the floor of the room.

McCoy started after him and stopped dead in his tracks. Beside him, Chekov released a low sound. Hallie, wherever she was behind him, was silent. He stared over the slender banister at the room beyond. Eyes huge, brain daring itself to believe what he was seeing, he tried to take it in all at once and felt his mind begin to overload. Piece by piece, he sorted out images and scents, trying to build himself a cohesive, understandable explanation when the words really weren't available with which to do it.

Scents sorted themselves out first. Still the not-really peaches, plus something briny, salt-tinged, and sealike. Mustiness . . . wood . . . leaf mold . . . a smoky scent of undefinable odors McCoy couldn't even attempt to put a name to. There were others, but by then his eyes were full of all there was to see.

The round chamber below them was huge and

vault-ceilinged, several times the size of the *Enterprise*'s copious engine room. The floor was a confusing jumble of work stations, computer banks, conduits, and more things than McCoy, with his layman's knowledge, could put a name to. In the center of the room rose a towering vastness, stretching from floor to ceiling, which McCoy assumed was the central core for all the station's power. Only it wasn't just the central core anymore.

Surrounding the core from floor level to about halfway up, and spreading partway into the room, was a creature the likes of which McCoy had never seen, nor even contemplated. Its vast bulk filled half the central chamber but without a sense of immense weight. It was diaphanous, shimmering with colors and hues like the inside of an abalone shell caught by the sun and yet not anything like that at all. Tiny lights played along the gently expanding and contracting surface (or within the surface, it was hard to say). Ropes of color that might have been veins and arteries plied the body like colorful streamers around a maypole, shimmering as they twisted, giving off sparks of light. A faint sound filled the air, but when McCoy tried to listen more closely, it seemed to evaporate from his hearing.

It was, unequivocally, the most beautiful thing McCoy had ever seen in his life, and he was suddenly overwhelmed with emotion.

"Evidently," Spock observed dispassionately, "power loss was not caused by a malfunction."

"I—" Chekov was at a loss for words. "What *is* it, Mr. Spock?"

"I do not know, Lieutenant. I shall, however, endeavor to find out."

McCoy caught at the first officer's arm as he turned away. "It's *huge,* Spock. How did it get in here?"

"I would speculate that the creature was not this large when it arrived and took up residence within the space station, perhaps entering through an exhaust duct. I believe it safe to conjecture that it was much smaller and grew as it ingested the energy output from the station."

"Kind of like a hermit crab taking on a new shell," McCoy said quietly.

"Much like that, Doctor, yes," Spock agreed.

"Except hermit crabs take on vacated shells," Chekov pointed out. "They don't go in and kill the current resident."

"Perhaps the creature did not see the Romulans as residents, Lieutenant," Spock pointed out. "Perhaps it did not see them as living entities at all, but merely as an energy resource."

"Then that *is* what killed them?" McCoy asked, waving a hand toward the gently billowing bulk of the creature. "They died of hypothermia in the warm confines of the station because that thing sucked them dry?"

"That is a not quite accurate description, Doctor, but it will suffice for now." The first officer turned and started down the stairs.

"Just where do you think you're going?" McCoy demanded, starting after him.

"Down to the main level, Doctor," Spock said without looking back. "Ensign Leno reported that, even with a weak charge, when she shot her phaser at the creature, it recoiled from her and Lieutenant Chekov. I would like to test a hypothesis."

"Which is?" McCoy heard the others descending behind him.

"That the combined efforts of our phasers might actually stun the creature into unconsciousness, breaking its drain on this station and the *Enterprise* long enough for us to effect a rescue and escape. At the very least, our phasers should suffice to upset or disturb the creature."

"If all we do is upset it, let's just hope it's not heavily into revenge," McCoy added darkly.

Chapter Sixteen

THE FOUR REMAINING MEMBERS of the landing party descended the stairway from the catwalk as rapidly as they could, their eyes almost constantly on the creature as they moved.

If McCoy thought it was impressive from above, it was more so from beside. He wanted to call it a jellyfish or a krill, but those words just didn't encompass all this creature seemed to be. It bugged him that, with all his education, he couldn't come up with one or two correct adjectives to describe this damned thing.

They gathered in a line several yards back from the shimmering bulk. "Energy level readings," Spock said, loosening his phaser into his hand.

Chekov glanced at his own, then looked to either side to double-check McCoy's and Hallie's. "Well, there's power, Mr. Spock, but I don't make any promises."

"I don't recall asking for any, Lieutenant," the Vulcan replied calmly. "As it is to be expected that our beams will be weak, we may need to step closer to effect any response from the creature. Please wait to follow my lead." He brought up the weapon and sighted down it. "Begin."

McCoy absurdly felt like something out of *Shootout at the OK Corral* as their phasers all came up in identical smooth motions and their fingers depressed the triggers. A weak stream of energy, curdled as old milk, slipped forth and splashed against the creature like a wayward seaside wave. Colors spread along its side, and it seemed to flinch in response.

"Closer," Spock ordered, and they stepped several feet nearer. Their second volley sent up another spray of color along the creature's side, but it did not attempt to retaliate or repulse the attack.

McCoy glanced sideways at all the machinery. "Are we having any effect? Is its hold weakening?"

"I do not yet know, Doctor," Spock replied. "I recommend we get somewhat closer."

"Just how close are you expecting to take us, Spock? I don't exactly want to become bosom buddies with this thing."

"This will suffice," the Vulcan said, taking his place only several feet from the creature's pulsating form.

"It's probably just trying to decide if our phasers taste good," McCoy grumped to Chekov.

"A weak beam just doesn't seem to be having any effect," Hallie said. "Can't we up the power, sir?"

"I would prefer not injuring this creature, if possible," Spock informed her. McCoy could tell from her look that she wouldn't have had any problem at all with injuring it, or even killing it for that matter. "Let us try one more time."

Chekov glanced down at his phaser. "That's about all we have left, Mr. Spock. After that, we'll be without weapons."

"Understood, Lieutenant. Is everyone ready? Then, fire."

An indescribable rainbow of color rippled over the creature's surface, and it suddenly reached toward them. No . . . not toward *them* but toward Hallie. It writhed up the energy beam from her phaser, sliding over the weapon and her hand like it was made of jelly, and drew her inside itself before any of the men could move. Her body twitched hard within the color-shot mass, and she struggled to turn around, staring at the men with eyes that were huge, panic-stricken, and pleading, the white showing all around the dark iris. Her hands reached toward them beseechingly, begging for help. Her slim form shuddered, then snapped violently backward, her back bent like a strung bow. One hand dug at her chest while the other reached toward them, fingers crabbed into the palm.

"NO!" Not thinking about what he was doing, not daring to think about it because he wouldn't do it if he did, McCoy started in after her. Behind him, Spock roared his name in a voice that must have hearkened back to the Vulcan's more violent roots, and someone's hands grabbed the doctor's arm. McCoy struggled against the tight grip, winning forward by inches, and thrust his other arm up to the shoulder inside the creature.

He had left his arm in snow, in someone's freezer, beneath the iceberged waters of the planet Nordstral. The cold was pain, sharp and bright, the e-suit all but useless, but when Hallie's limp fingers brushed McCoy's, he lurched for them, caught them in his own, and leaned back, letting the force of whoever had him drag them both to safety.

McCoy sagged to his knees, and Hallie slid out at his feet like a baby fresh from the womb. Her face was as blue as death. Her lips, the edges of her nose, and the corners of her closed eyes were violet. She lay unmoving, unbreathing.

The doctor lunged over her and tore at the front of her e-suit, rending it open to expose the pale flesh beneath. His right arm and hand were cold and unresponsive from their journey inside the creature. He had to reach across with his left hand into the medipouch at his side, finger-picking unerringly through the equipment, finding what he needed by touch, and sliding the vial into the hypospray in a smooth motion. He pumped the medication into the center of her chest, tossed that vial aside, and rammed home another.

"What is it?" Chekov asked, breathing heavily behind him, and for the first time McCoy knew who it was who had dragged them both to safety.

"Cardiac arrest!" he snapped. Laying the cold flesh of his right hand against her body and cupping his left over it in the age-old gesture for cardiopulmonary resuscitation, he pumped Hallie's chest rapidly several times, then tilted her head back, pinched her nose, and breathed into her mouth. He listened for a moment, then repeated the routine. And again. And again. And again.

"Come on, Hallie," McCoy grated from between clenched teeth. "You've come this far. Don't let me down now." Why the hell hadn't the medication done anything to restart her heart? His mind rifled through what else he had in the pouch that might be effective, and came up empty-handed. If he had her in sickbay, then he could do something. Then he could perform a miracle worthy of Montgomery Scott. But here . . .

He stopped pumping an instant before Spock's hand touched him. McCoy threw off the touch with a rough jerk of his shoulder and sat back on his heels, his hands curled and useless between his knees, his head bowed in defeat.

A wordless noise of regret escaped Chekov. He knelt beside the doctor to gently close up the front of Hallie's e-suit and fold her hands together over her stomach. He sighed. "The suits may afford us some protection, but evidently it's not enough," he said quietly.

McCoy stirred, drawn away from memories, and rubbed his right arm. He was beginning to get some feeling back into the useless appendage. Sparks of sensation tingled along his skin, and he flexed his fingers slowly. *Loss of manual dexterity* . . . "But why did it go after her?"

Chekov shrugged, his eyes on his team member's silent form. He frowned suddenly and touched her hand, where her fingers still curled around the butt of her weapon. "Maybe this had something to do with it." He turned the phaser so the others could see. Hallie had set it nearly on full. "I guess she didn't agree with you, after all, Mr. Spock. So much for whether or not it's into revenge."

"Either that, or it went after the strongest beam, the one that posed the greatest danger, or possibly the strongest source of food," Spock postulated.

"What difference does it make?!" McCoy snapped. "Hallie's dead either way!" He shook his head helplessly. "We have to get out of here."

"Where do you suggest we go, Doctor?"

McCoy's head snapped around, and he glared up at

the Vulcan. "Anywhere on this station that's the farthest point from that thing! You saw what it did to Hallie! It leached away every ounce of energy and warmth she had in her entire body. You think it won't do the same to us, even if we don't touch it? The farther away we are, maybe the longer we'll have."

"Distance did not save the Romulans on the bridge," Spock pointed out.

"But maybe it bought them time!" McCoy spat. "We have to try something!"

"Leaving engineering will not aid our attempts, Dr. McCoy. We have discovered the cause of the energy drain affecting the station and the *Enterprise*. Only through observation of the creature can we hope to learn how to counteract—"

"And just how long do you think we'll be able to observe this thing before we drift into unconsciousness and coma?" McCoy wrenched free the mediscanner and turned it on Spock. It warbled apologetically but produced no readings. *"Dammit!"* McCoy stopped short of flinging it across the room and jammed the piece of equipment back into his pouch.

"Mr. Spock's right, Doctor," Chekov said quietly. "We have to try. Running to the other side of the station won't do anyone any good. Even if we don't survive, maybe if we stay we can help someone who comes later."

"Yeah, yeah, right. Okay, we'll stay." McCoy didn't feel like arguing, but his blue eyes challenged the Russian. "I'm not happy about it," he felt obligated to add. "We'll stay, but let's find someplace away from that . . . *thing.*"

"For the moment, I concur," Spock agreed. He assisted McCoy to his feet with a hand under the doctor's elbow. All three men glanced briefly at Hallie's body, but there was really no point in moving it.

They turned away, and McCoy stopped dead. "I really don't need any more of this," he said to no one in particular.

A body was propped up against the front of one of the consoles. None of them had noticed it before. The desiccated Romulan sat with his legs stretched out straight before him, his hands in his lap. One death-stiffened hand clutched a writing stylus. Beneath the other rested an open book.

"What do you suppose he was doing down here all by himself?" Chekov asked, kneeling to get a closer look. Unlike the other bodies they'd discovered, the smell wasn't so bad down here. Maybe the overwhelming odor of peaches the creature put out had something to do with it. "Why didn't he gather together with the others?"

"His rank insignia identifies him as a physician," Spock supplied, his dark eyes studying the peaceful corpse.

McCoy looked at it in a different light, then, for this man had been a kindred spirit, for all that their races warred against one another. Would he have liked the Romulan? Could they have carried on a sociable conversation, sharing information and learning medical techniques? He liked to think so. But what had this man been up to, down here alone while his fellow crewmen slowly froze in comradely death, his fingers growing numb and hard to maneuver before unconsciousness claimed him and death carried him away?

Spock tugged free the book from beneath the corpse's hand and began to flip through it. "This is most curious. It appears to be a diary of some kind."

Chekov stood and peered around the first officer's

arm, shaking his head at the spidery Romulan script. "It's not often you see anyone keep written records anymore."

"Too true, Lieutenant," McCoy agreed. He was as dependent as the next person on the computer for his record-keeping, but sometimes he lamented the loss of the truly *written* word and thought that humanity was a trifle less for its absence from their lives. "So, does it say anything interesting, Spock?"

The Vulcan did not answer at first, so intent was he on skimming pages. Then his eyebrows rose high on his forehead in the largest expression of surprise McCoy had ever seen on that saturnine face.

"Well . . ." the doctor prompted.

Spock turned to look at his companions. "There is much here of interest, Doctor, particularly to the captain. We must endeavor to contact the *Enterprise.*"

"I'm all for that, Spock, but don't you think that is going to be difficult? I was under the impression you had a hard enough time doing it up on the bridge. Now you want to try it down here with this thing sucking away at—"

"On the contrary, Doctor. In light of the information in this journal, I realize that my successful attempt at contacting the *Enterprise* was extraordinarily easy."

McCoy cocked an eyebrow, for the moment not caring if he looked like Spock. "Come again?"

"According to this diary, and as we have observed in our own experience, this creature feeds sporadically."

"In fits and starts, you mean."

"Precisely. Part of that may have to do with metabolism. This Romulan physician also theorized that the creature must recalibrate its internal system every time it comes upon a new energy source."

Chekov snorted. "Between us and the *Enterprise,* this thing must think it is having a banquet."

"In a manner of speaking, Lieutenant, except that it must find some of the banquet unpalatable, at least initially, hence its proclivity to 'taste' each source in order to understand it and best define how to consume it in the most expedient manner."

"Which is why you got through to the ship?"

Spock nodded. "I believe so, Doctor. The generator has a unique fusion pulse system, and it was never tied into the system long enough for the creature to get a good 'taste,' if you will. When I used it on the bridge, there was some interference, but I believe the problem lay with the *Enterprise,* not with the transmission."

"The creature must have been drawing energy from the ship at that time," Chekov said, eyes wide.

"Possibly so. Owing to its unfamiliarity with the generator, I was able to reach the ship. This entity is leaching energy from a variety of sources, all new to it, which must require some effort. That, coupled with the fact that the generator is something of an unknown quantity, should allow us enough power to contact the ship."

"Providing their systems aren't so depleted that they can't hear us." McCoy almost wanted to slap himself for saying it.

"We must take that risk," Spock said calmly, and continued. "The creature has evidently not become proficient in draining Human beings—"

"How can you say that?" Chekov demanded, waving an arm toward Hallie's silent body. "It took everything out of Hallie in only moments!"

"Because she merged with the creature, Lieutenant. I suspect that the creature drew the heat because of its own low body temperature, causing it to draw the heat from Ensign Hallie's body according to the laws of basic thermodynamics. In addition, if the creature had previously experienced humans, you would all have been feeling the results of its leaching much sooner and with much more severity than you have."

"Which explains why you felt so bad on the bridge," McCoy supplied. "Vulcans and Romulans have the same physiology."

"Exactly, Doctor. We can use its inexperience with the energy produced by Earth Humans to our advantage. If the creature finds new, unaccostumed energy sources disturbing or disorienting, you and Lieutenant Chekov can act as additional buffers around the generator."

McCoy shrugged. "I don't have any problem with that, Spock, except for this—it drained Hallie dry, throwing her into cardiac arrest. That may have been all it needed to learn everything about us. Despite the best intentions, we may do you no good."

"There are no guarantees, Dr. McCoy. It is merely the only option we have open to us. The creature must digest what it has learned in order to accomplish a realignment of its systems."

"Let's just hope it's a slow eater," McCoy observed.

It took longer than Kirk had anticipated for Scotty to manually jerry-rig all the photon torpedoes aboard the *Enterprise,* but the Scotsman wasn't about to leave it to just anyone to do. As chief engineer, it was his job, his prerogative.

Kirk had followed him with his mind's eye, watching him take the long walk from the bridge back down to Deck 7 and Engineering, where he picked up the necessary tools. Then it took a little longer for him to get from there to the foundation levels of the connecting dorsal at Decks 12 and 13, where the photon-torpedo launch system was contained. Kirk envied him the opportunity for one last stroll around the vast ship. Why shouldn't he take his time? It wasn't as though hurrying to get there was going to radically change anything. They were all in danger. They were all going to die. A few more minutes either way wouldn't make that much of a difference to anyone.

Scott had his orders, and Kirk knew that he would follow them to the letter, even if regret tore at his heart. It was Scott who'd stayed with the *Enterprise* throughout the years, nursing her through the troubled times when Kirk left her to pursue the Admiralty he thought he wanted. Scott had eased her through a rigorous refitting and all the troubles that entailed. Even when the others went off on shore leave, more than likely he was to be found sitting with the engines, reading quietly, just he and his girl.

They had both done right by her all these years, and together they would do right by her now. If she had to go out, then Kirk knew that Scott would arrange that she go out in a blaze of glory, by God.

So, if Scott had taken the time and care, going from torpedo to torpedo, checking their charges, priming them, and connecting them via their magnetic loading plates until the torpedo bay looked like it was strewn with streamers for a New Years Eve party, who could blame him? Then he had made the long, slow climb back to the bridge . . . saying goodbye to this grand lady every step of the way.

Kirk glanced up when Scott climbed out of the floor, and read the reality of the chief engineer's emotions on his craggy face. Chances were, he didn't look much better. He felt more haggard and careworn than he ever had in his life. It was a certainty that these events were going down his throat no easier than they were Scott's. They both loved the *Enterprise,* for vastly different reasons, but love her they did.

"All set, Mr. Scott?" Kirk's voice was subdued and taut with emotion.

"Aye, Captain." The chief engineer nodded. "She's all set. When she goes, she'll make a fireball that they'll see all the way to Antares."

Pain sliced Kirk's heart. "Thank you, Scotty. I'm sure she appreciates it. Uhura, were you able to get through to *Valgard* and tell Corey and Jaffe what's going to happen?"

She shook her dark head. "Not that I can tell, sir, but I sent the message."

"Very well." It wasn't the sort of surprise he'd wish on anyone, but he didn't suppose the two security guards would have time to ponder it any longer than would anyone else. "Any luck raising the landing party?"

"None yet, sir. I'm still trying."

That rankled him more than anything. He at least wanted to hear Spock's and Bones's voices one more time, to tell them good-bye, to tell them . . .

They already know it, Jim. Well, he supposed that was true, but he still would have liked to deliver the message in person. Kirk cleared his throat. "Uhura, can I get shipwide communication?"

"You can try, sir. I don't know whether or not all sections will read you."

It was worth a try. Kirk hit the button on his chair. "This is Captain Kirk. I am about to initiate the self-destruct sequence. I deeply regret that it has come to this. I—" Emotion clogged his throat, and he swallowed hard. "It has been an honor and a privilege to work with each and every one of you. Kirk out." He sat back in his chair, feeling that it wasn't enough and knowing it was all he had. His eyes strayed briefly around the bridge. Everyone was watching him—Uhura, Sulu, Scotty, Estano, and all the others. Watching him. Trusting him.

He cleared his throat. "Commander Scott, if you please. Lieutenant Commander Sulu, you'll fulfill Mr. Spock's role as acting science officer."

"Aye, sir." The helmsman rose to come and stand with his captain and the chief engineer around a free computer screen.

Kirk then took a single deep breath and kept his voice even. "Computer, this is Captain James T. Kirk. Request security access." The screen flared to black. A beep sounded, and the words SECURITY ACCESS—IDENTITY ACKNOWLEDGED appeared. Kirk licked his lips, not daring to look at the two officers with him, not daring to look at the bridge crew, not daring to think of Spock and McCoy. "Computer, destruct sequence one, code one-one-A." The computer fed it back to him, words as everlasting as an epitaph. DESTRUCT SEQUENCE ONE. CODE: IIA.

Scott leaned forward, heartbreak and resolution kindred spirits in his eyes. His voice never wavered as he gave the command. "Computer, this is Commander Montgomery Scott, chief engineering officer. Destruct sequence two, code one-A-two-B." Again, the words were repeated on the screen.

Sulu drew a steadying breath. "Computer, this is Lieutenant Commander Hikaru Sulu, acting science officer. Destruct sequence three, code one-B-two-B—"

"Captain!" Uhura's voice was incredulous, her face as bright as a child's on Christmas morning. "I have Mr. Spock!"

"Computer, hold self-destruct!" Kirk snapped, and

felt the trickle of ice water throughout his body. "Spock?"

The connection was terrible, but it was Spock, no doubt about it. "Yes, Captain. I'm here with Dr. McCoy and Lieutenant Chekov."

Oh, no . . . "What's happened to Hallie and Leno?"

"Ensign Leno has become trapped in a turbolift, Hallie is dead."

Damn, damn, damn . . . No time for this now. Not much time for anything much longer. "Spock, we've been trying to reach you. We have very little power left and no way to rescue the landing party or save our ship. Several crew have fallen unconscious due to lowered internal temperatures. We are in the process of initiating a self-destruct sequence—"

"Jim! No!"

"Bones, I—"

"Captain." Spock's calm tones overrode them both. "We have discovered the cause behind the energy loss and ship malfunctions."

Relief made Kirk's knees feel rubbery, and he sat down hard at the conn, hardly noticing when the pain flared in his side. "Does it have something to do with the station's power source?"

"In a manner of speaking. There is a creature living aboard this vessel—"

"Did I hear you right, Spock? A creature? What kind of creature?"

"A creature that ingests energy, Captain." As quickly as possible, Spock told Kirk the little they had observed about the creature, including Hallie's death and the discovery of the diary.

"Then, that settles it," Kirk said finally, a real sense of purpose making him feel better than he had in some time. "In order to save the ship and rescue you,

215

we need to discover a way to kill the creature, and do it before we lose all ability to function."

"I would advise against trying to destroy the creature, Captain."

Kirk frowned. "But why, Spock? It's endangering not only your lives but the lives of every person aboard this ship. If we don't destroy it, we're condemning five hundred people to their deaths."

"Doctor Rinagh kept quite good records, Captain. He reports the initial malfunctions aboard the station, the discovery of the creature, and their inability to either kill it or induce it to leave the station. By that time, of course, it had realigned its internal systems to their energy output and was rapidly draining the station to minimal power."

"Why only minimal power, Spock? Why not drain it altogether?"

"I have only conjecture in that regard, but I postulate that the creature needs a certain reservoir of energy in order to survive. When power reaches limits too low to consume, it maintains the status quo by going into some form of hibernation."

"I see. Go on."

"When it became obvious that they were doomed, Doctor Rinagh chose to leave his companions and come to Engineering in an effort to learn more about this creature before his death, to warn others who might come this way. He felt that the creature was intelligent and possessing, perhaps, rudimentary sentience."

Kirk's heart fell. He didn't want to hear this. He wanted to hear that the creature that threatened his crew was a dumb brute beast.

Spock was continuing to speak. "He reports that it reacted to emotion in waves of color, which I also noticed when Ensign Hallie died."

"Did that thing murder Hallie?" Kirk asked.

"Killed," McCoy stressed. "Not murdered. It . . . *drained* her of body heat, inducing hypothermia, cardiac arrest, and death."

"Then it *did* kill her."

"You could just as easily say it was self-defense on the part of the creature. We were attempting to stun it, but Hallie had her phaser set on kill."

"Have you seen any indications of hostility?"

"None, Captain," Spock said. "We have been almost within reach of the creature, and it seems to barely take note of our existence. As for Ensign Hallie, I don't believe it did harm to her with a sense of purpose."

"Captain." Chekov this time, his voice sounding strained. "Hallie was part of my team, but I must concur with Mr. Spock and Dr. McCoy. We need to discover for certain whether or not this creature is truly sentient. We cannot destroy it. We need to learn more about it."

But it's endangering my crew. "Can we do something to drive it out of the station?"

"Uncertain, Captain. I postulate that this creature operates on somewhat the same level as an Earth hermit crab. Given that, I cannot imagine it leaving the space station when its current size is considered."

That got Kirk's attention even more fully. "Just how big is this thing?"

"Jim, you've got to see it to believe it," came McCoy's laconic reply.

"I'd give anything to do that, Bones." And it was true. Much as he was worried about his crew, much as he was uncertain of how to proceed, Jim Kirk was, first and foremost, an explorer. And he desperately wanted to get a look at this thing for himself. "So it won't leave?"

"Ostensibly, it would probably leave were its home destroyed. Other than that, I imagine it would not leave until it outgrows its present home, which does not seem likely in the near future, or another energy source comes along."

"Like the *Enterprise*. So why didn't it come aboard?"

"Like I said, Jim," McCoy broke in, "there's no room for it. And why should it move when it can just take what it needs from right where it is?"

"Good point, Bones." Kirk plucked at his bottom lip, deep in thought. "Is there any way we can cut off its ability to feed?"

The silence on the other end of the connection went on for so long that Kirk thought they'd lost the away team again. Then Spock came on, his tone thoughtful. "The creature evidently needs time to recalibrate itself to each new, previously untried food source. Captain, how much power does the *Enterprise* currently have available?"

It was Scotty who answered. "We're not down to minimum yet, lad, but it's a close call. We have enough power to use the tractor beam on short bursts to bring us into the station. We'd planned on initiating self-destruct and boosting it with every photon torpedo we have."

"Might I recommend an alternative, Mr. Scott?"

Scotty exchanged looks with Kirk. "Please do, please do."

"I suggest you reroute all remaining power to the ship's engines. It has been our experience that the creature has not yet completely recalibrated itself to the configurations of Human physiological energy output. That is essentially why we are able to contact you now. In theory, you can use the ship's company as a Human barrier to buffer the engines and allow power to build. If you can use that power to manufacture a frequency matching that which is put out by Humans, and continue to change it slightly every few minutes—"

"Then the creature won't be able to feed, and the power drain will stop!" Scott finished, amazed. "Captain, I might then be able to get the engines up to impulse, and that would be enough to let us retreat out of the creature's range."

"Correct, Mr. Scott," Spock continued. "Once the ship is out of danger, you could attempt a long-distance transport of the landing party. In the event that is an impossibility, Captain, I urge you to leave us behind and notify Starfleet. They could recommend how best to proceed in that eventuality. However, I strongly suggest not destroying the creature unless it must absolutely be done. We have never met anything like this, Captain. For all we know, it may be the last of its kind. To lose this opportunity would be a great tragedy and a greater loss."

As would your places in my life, Kirk thought, but didn't say it aloud. Spock was right. When they joined Starfleet, they put their lives on the line for a greater cause. Knowledge was their siren song, no matter what the cost.

"All right, Mr. Spock. We'll try it your way. But if it doesn't work and we're left adrift, I'm not consigning my entire crew to freezing to death."

"Understood, Captain. And thank you."

"You're welcome." Kirk turned sideways. "Mr. Scott? It's time for you to make a trip to the engine room."

Chapter Seventeen

KIRK SAT AT THE CONN, legs crossed, arms folded tightly across his chest. He knew he looked a lot calmer than he felt.

Scott had been down in Engineering for several hours, putting Spock's plan into effect and pulling in crew from all over the ship to cram into the warp engine room, the horizontal intermix chamber, and, with appropriate suiting, the dilithium reactor room. Anyone who could be freed from duty was ordered to report to Scott. Packed in as they were, they were all going to be very good friends by the time this was over.

Without a doubt, Kirk was willing to bet that most of the crew thought this was nuts. He could hardly blame them for the sentiment, but all the same, he suppressed a smile at the thought. Any of them who had shipped with him more than a few months had probably seen him do something stranger than this at least once. The first rule of thumb when you were a starship captain was to learn to fly by the seat of your pants. He liked to think he'd become pretty good at it over the years.

And there was always the self-destruct, if they needed it. He just prayed that Spock was right and they wouldn't. So far, things were progressing much as Spock had said they would. Power was still very low, but they seemed to be gaining some ground, enough that they now had almost continual contact with the landing party. That was a benefit that Kirk wouldn't willingly give up.

"Captain?" The cautious tone of Sulu's quiet voice immediately pulled Kirk out of the respite of his momentary reverie. "I think we might have a problem, sir."

"What is it, Mr. Sulu?"

"I'm not certain, Captain." The helmsman frowned. "Systems are so erratic that it's difficult to be completely certain, but I think there's an unidentified ship approaching."

Kirk perked up immediately. "One of Starfleet's?"

"Inconclusive, sir."

"On-screen." For all the good it did. Kirk leaned forward, trying to peer through the rain of static. There *was* a ship out there, but damned if he could tell whose it was.

They didn't need to give the creature another Federation ship to munch on, not while they were getting the *Enterprise* back on-line. "Uhura, warn them off if you can. Tell them we have a priority-one situation here."

"Aye, sir."

Sulu suddenly called out. "Captain, I still can't discern the make, but she's approaching rapidly, and I think her shields are up."

"Yellow alert!" Kirk snapped. His heart sank when

no familiar klaxon answered his command. He glared away Sulu's apologetic look and stabbed the communications button. "Scotty! I need shields!"

Never in Kirk's memory had Montgomery Scott sounded so put out. "I'm sorry, Captain, but there's just no way I can do that. I've barely begun implementing Mr. Spock's idea. We've got improved communication capabilities, but that's it. If you want power to shields and weaponry I can maybe get some of it for you in a wee bit, but that means we're dead in the water so far as going anywhere."

"Mr. Scott, that's not good enough."

"Yes sir," Scott replied. "Begging the captain's pardon, I wish it were different. I wish there was something I could do, but my bag of tricks is empty. The crew and I are working as hard as we can, but the lass just doesn't yet have it in her to give."

Kirk suppressed the storm of emotions roaring through him. "Scotty, we have an unidentified vessel approaching with shields raised. If we don't get some protection, it may not matter much longer." He cut the connection before the chief engineer could respond. Uhura, open all hailing frequencies to the approaching vessel."

"I'll try, sir," she said dubiously. "Communications are better, but nowhere near what I'd like." Her clear voice filled the room as her hands played across her console. "This is the Federation starship *Enterprise* to unidentified vessel. We have a priority-one situation at present. For the good of your ship and crew, keep your distance. Please identify yourself."

Static crackled across the viewscreen, turning it into a raging blizzard. Somewhere in that mock storm, the wind abated for an instant, clearing the screen and letting them all see what bore down upon them.

"Captain!" Sulu's strident voice identified it for them all, not that Kirk thought there was any question. "Romulan bird of prey off the starboard bow!"

Oh, hell. "Red alert! Scotty, there's a bird of prey out there! I need everything you can give me!" *How are we going to get out of this one?*

"Captain!" Uhura called sharply. "The Romulan captain is hailing us!"

Kirk's mind tumbled. Now what? He had no choice. "Put him on screen, Commander."

"I'll try, sir," Uhura responded.

She did a good job, considering the dicey reception. Kirk decided it was just as well. With the lurid scar across his cheek and a nose that looked as if it had been broken half a dozen times, the Romulan commander was certainly no beauty.

He sat in his seat, straight and regal, with his dark robes around him, rank insignia gleaming shiny gold against the blackness of his sleeves. He looked like a Humanoid shark. "I am Telris of the Romulan Empire and captain of the bird of prey *Elizsen.*"

Kirk's mind jumped. What to do? On the one hand, he had to consider the safety of his ship and crew. Could he ask the Romulans for assistance? Did he dare show weakness to this enemy of the Federation? Negotiations were no closer to a permanent treaty with the warlike race than they were with the Klingons. It was Kirk's personal bet that they never would be, but that didn't mean he wanted to aggravate the situation, either. How far could he trust them, if at all?

Kirk cut in before Telris drew another breath. "Greetings, Captain Telris. I'm Captain James T. Kirk, of the Federation starship *Enterprise.* I—"

"We know who you are, Kirk," the Romulan commander growled, his tone ugly. "Your reputation precedes you."

All thoughts of establishing trust went right out the window. Kirk wasn't certain just how, exactly, he was supposed to take that remark but felt safe in guessing he should feel insulted. Well, he would . . . later. When he had time. "You are now in direct violation of Federation treaty. If you return to Romulan-held space immediately, no formal charges will be filed." *How's that for bravado?* Kirk asked himself.

Disconcertingly, Telris laughed, a long and hearty bellow of sound, echoed by his men in the background. When he stopped, his expression was less than humorous. "Your sarcasm amuses me, Kirk. Thank you. It has been a long time since I had such a good laugh." His thick fingers caressed the arms of his chair. "I find it highly unlikely that you will press charges of any kind or take any action against me or the Romulan Empire."

"Oh, really?" Kirk said calmly. "And what makes you so certain?" His eyes strayed to Sulu's broad, round features in supplication, and the helmsman shook his head very slightly and very slowly. *Come on, Scotty,* Kirk silently prayed. *Where are those shields?*

Telris leaned forward, and his face filled the screen like something out of a bad movie. "Because our sensors indicate your ship has not yet raised her shields. I find it highly unlikely that you trust me so fully, Kirk, which means your *Enterprise"*—he said the name with a decidedly oily slur—"is without power to raise those shields . . . or to do much of anything else, either, if our sensor readings be true." He sat back in his chair, the picture of satisfaction. "As for the rest, a thief and saboteur should not consider himself in a position to point the finger of accusation."

Kirk blinked with surprise. "I beg your pardon?"

"You're very good at playing the idiot, Kirk," Telris praised. "But this time it will not save your life or the lives of your crew. Your 'priority-one situation'"—his voice was laced with heavy sarcasm—"is a *Romulan* space station, which I have tracked and now find within Federation boundaries and chaperoned by not only a Federation starship but the jewel of Starfleet's puny armada." He vehemently thrust his forefinger at Kirk. "James Kirk, I charge you with trespassing into Romulan space, theft and sabotage of a Romulan space station—"

Kirk barked laughter he didn't feel. "Theft?! How do you propose this station got here? That we *towed* it? The *Enterprise* does not have that kind of power and you know it. This station was found derelict and adrift within our borders."

"A likely story from the murderer of a station's crew!"

"Murderer?!" Kirk was so flummoxed by this latest charge that he momentarily ignored the others.

"Our sensors indicate life signs aboard the space station from only four individuals. *Four,* Kirk, when there was a crew of over one hundred. Your men, I presume."

"That proves nothing!" Kirk broke in angrily, rising to his feet on a wave of pain and stepping toward the screen, his hands balled into fists at his sides. "I deny your allegations! We found this station adrift and unmanned within Federation borders! I readily admit that some of my crew are aboard! They were sent to investigate how a Romulan space station came to be where it does not belong." The jibe didn't seem to bother Telris in the least. "They reported to me that the station crew was dead a long time before their

225

arrival. They died of hypothermia caused by the presence of a creature aboard the station—"

"A creature, indeed!" Telris laughed sardonically. "Save me your pretty speeches, Kirk, and do not attempt to place your own blame upon a fabrication. Your glib words may work among your Federation sheep, but they do not work with me! The charges stand, and you will pay the highest penalty!"

Kirk wanted to hit something. That was the problem with Romulans . . . you were damned no matter what you did. "It's the truth! My people have seen it. At least one of my crew has been killed by it. I can't help it if you don't have the sense to believe me. Go ahead and make your claims, Telris. Make all the charges you want against me with the Federation. They'll go along nicely with my countercharges of infiltration beyond treaty borders and espionage. It's taken as common knowledge that the Romulan Empire resorts to *attempting* to plant spies within the Federation, but I never thought you'd have the unmitigated gall to try and set up an outpost within our very borders!"

Telris applauded slowly and contemptuously. "Bravo, Captain Kirk. A sterling final performance. You misunderstood me in one small detail, however."

Kirk's eyes narrowed. He felt the bridge crew behind him, taut and breathless. "Oh?"

The Romulan captain nodded. "Yes. I have no intention of bringing charges against you with the Federation." His eyes widened mockingly. "Does that surprise you? I see that it does." He slowly stood. Under different circumstances, Kirk might have been awed by the sheer presence of the man. "I prefer to take care of things by myself as they arise. I see no reason to bother higher authorities with the details of your eradication." He smiled as the wolf might have smiled just before it ate Little Red Riding Hood's grandmother. "I consider myself particularly fortunate to have found the *Enterprise* without power. True, it takes away the thrill of the hunt," he acknowledged with mock sadness. "But it makes the ending most expeditious." He chuckled. "First, though, I'll take care of your boarding party." He gestured over his shoulder to someone out of sight. "Beam aboard with your men, Sacul."

"No!" Kirk cried. "My crew is innocent!"

"Nothing innocent ever thrived within the confines of the Federation, Kirk!" Telris snapped. But a moment later, someone yelled off-screen, and the Romulan commander whirled in. "What?!" His voice rose to a furious howl. "Then get them back here!"

Kirk had a sudden sneaking suspicion, and his hopes rose on a cresting wave. Spock had said that the creature needed time to recalibrate itself to *new,* previously untried food sources. It stood to reason that it would eagerly go after something it could consume without recalibration. And *Elizsen* and *Reltah* were both *Romulan*-built . . .

"Something the matter, Captain Telris?" he inquired lightly, resisting the urge to cross his fingers behind his back in a hopeful wish.

Telris rounded on him. His face was a mottled whorl of fury. "What have you done, Kirk? I'll kill you for this!" His fingers clenched as though he could feel the soft flesh of Kirk's throat under the curved nails. "How did you do it?! You have no power! How did you interrupt our transporter beam?! You've left my men smoking hunks of meat, Kirk!" He shrieked, his voice rising to a ringing cry. "I'll kill you for this! *FIRE!*"

"Scotty!" Even if the chief engineer had contrived to suddenly give them full power, there was no way shields could have been raised in time. "Hang on!" Kirk cried, bracing himself for the blast that would scatter the *Enterprise* and her crew across the universe. It never came.

On the screen, Telris shook in a towering rage, his face suffused with blood. He spun about, muscular arm swinging, and slammed a crewman out of his chair and onto the floor. "Not the space station, you vermined idiot! The *Enterprise!"*

Blood ran from the cowering Romulan's lacerated lip. "My lord!" he cried beseechingly, holding his hands up to protect his face. "I aimed for the ship, my lord! I swear it! The shot went wild!"

"So, weaponry aims itself now, does it?!" Telris kicked him savagely in the side, then hauled him up by one arm and flung him back into his chair. "It's your life, fool! Fire on the *Enterprise! Now!"*

The crewman's shaking hands sought his controls. Even with bad reception, Kirk saw every ounce of color fade out of the Romulan's face. "Captain Telris, we have a power drain! Weapons systems are failing!"

Relief washed through Kirk in a head-rushing wave. "Welcome to the family, Telris. You're going to keep losing power until you're down to minimals, just like the station did." Just like the *Enterprise,* too, but he wasn't about to say it. After all, they had Mr. Scott and a crew of over four hundred eager volunteers busy at work in the ship's belly. Who knew what might come of that? Something better.

Telris spun about and glared at the screen. "If that is the case, then we shall use what energy we have left to rid the universe of you!" He turned and slapped the helmsman soundly across the back of the head. Blood spewed from the crewman's nose. "Ram the *Enterprise!*"

To Kirk's horror, trajectory changed slightly, and the bird of prey turned toward them and began to accelerate.

Chapter Eighteen

PERCHED WITH THE OTHERS atop the lattice-work cat-walk in the space station's engineering section, Pavel Chekov listened with McCoy and Spock to the sounds of the *Enterprise* putting the Vulcan's theory to the test. It would take time to assemble all the crew personnel and get them where they needed to be, and probably longer still for the buffer action of their bodies to work any change on the ship's engines, but if there was a way to make it work, Mr. Scott would find it. Chekov had a fleeting thought that they were going to be cutting this one awfully close.

They had climbed back up here to put some small distance between themselves and the creature but still retain the ability to use that backwash of energy Mr. Spock had been so certain of. He'd been right, of course, which hadn't particularly surprised the Russian. In all his years aboard the *Enterprise,* he'd kind of gotten used to the Vulcan being correct in most of his assumptions.

It had done them all a world of good to hear Captain Kirk's voice again. Chekov and McCoy had stood close together, protecting the generator as best they could with the barrier of their bodies while Spock filled the captain in on what had occurred and how best to proceed. Now it was only a matter of time.

So they waited.

Standing with his arms cocked atop the railing, one boot toe sticking between two of the spires supporting the banister, Chekov stared across the vastness of the big room without really seeing it. The static of the open channel they maintained to the *Enterprise* crackled in the background. Every now and then, he thought he recognized a voice—Kirk giving a command, Uhura or Sulu responding. Once he even thought he recognized Estano's voice, and he wondered how the ensign was holding up in his role as security chief for a day.

His foot jiggled with excess energy. He wanted to pace and burn off some of his frustration, but Mr. Spock had stressed that they needed to stay near the generator and strive to maintain the open channel as long as possible, or until the *Enterprise* could take over with a stronger, clearer signal. As Chekov understood it, if they could be successful in blocking the creature's ability to feed off the ship, it would look elsewhere. Unable to find anything in the vicinity (or so they hoped), it would go into stasis, adding to the ease of their escape.

His gaze drifted downward to settle on Hallie's silent, inert body beside the slightly pulsating form of the creature. Sorrow tugged at Chekov's heart.

The young Russian had gained a wealth of knowledge in the years since he had first come aboard the *Enterprise*. Time and missions clocked drove home a plethora of lessons during his climb to the coveted position of security chief. When he began, he thought it would be best if he didn't form lasting attachments to these men and women who had pledged to give up their lives in the defense of ship and crew. It would make losing them that much easier to bear, when the inevitable end came. (The old adage was only too true—there were old security guards and bold security guards, but no old, bold security guards.)

He learned in a fairly short length of time that it was impossible to put that theory into practice. His people were more dear to him because of the role they filled aboard the ship. More than anyone else, they were in danger every day of losing their lives in service to Starfleet and its ideals. One did them a great disservice in not becoming close, in not squeezing every last ounce out of the friendships coined like precious currency.

He turned his eyes toward Spock. Protected in the e-suit as he was, the Vulcan was still feeling the depredations of the creature's feeding. More like a Romulan than a Human, Spock's physiology was more familiar to the creature, hence it could drain energy from him far easier than it could from Chekov or McCoy. Spock was beginning to look awful, his skin pallid, his movements lethargic. If things didn't turn around for them in the next couple of hours, it would all be moot as far as the Vulcan was concerned.

"What the hell?"

McCoy's exclamation brought Chekov out of his reverie and he realized he hadn't been listening for some time. He blinked and turned all the way around. The doctor and Spock were staring at the console. "Did he say something about a *Romulan* ship?"

Chekov stepped closer. "What was that, Doctor? What did you say?"

"It appears the *Enterprise* has an unwelcome visitor," Spock supplied.

"Yeah," McCoy growled. "Seems like the Romulans have shown up looking for their garbage."

They listened closely, catching through the interference of the channel enough snatches of Kirk's end of the conversation to know that they were all in big trouble.

Kirk's voice rose, strident, demanding, and incredulous—"Murderer?!"—and they shared a silent look of concern. What did that mean? Had Kirk been accused of murder, or was he doing the accusing? Had another of their company been killed?

It was agony, not being able to hear clearly the other end of the conversation from the unseen Romulan. What was he saying? More importantly, what was he going to do? It never occurred to Chekov that the Romulans wouldn't do *anything*.

Chekov clenched his teeth and swore the most vile Russian oath he could conjure, damning the channel for not being clearer, damning the creature, damning the whole situation. He looked at the others. They were no happier than he. Spock leaned forward, listening intently, perhaps divining more from the conversation because of his superlative hearing. McCoy stood, tense and strained, hovering between the generator and Spock, and looking as though he wished he could squeeze himself through the connection and end up on the *Enterprise*. Chekov could sympathize with that desire only too well.

Kirk's voice came through at them again, growing louder on a rising tide of anger, then subsiding as he listened to whatever it was the Romulans said. "Oh?" he inquired softly, and it was quiet again. They tensely waited for more.

When it came, it sent the three of them rocking to their feet. Kirk's voice yelled, "No!", followed immediately by the annoying, rising, insectlike whine of a transporter in use.

"Someone's coming aboard!" Spock warned.

"Is it Scotty?" McCoy asked, turning as the air above the catwalk began to shimmer. It moved like heat off Death Valley's famous salt flats. Granules of light and color careened within four confined spaces. There was an instant in which to recognize the stonelike, serious faces of the Romulan warriors before the transporter beam flared in a blindingly brilliant flash of light. Chekov threw a hand up to shield his eyes, then blinked beyond his upraised arm, nose wrinkling at the stench. A single young Romulan crewman, looking very alone and extremely startled, stood near them on the catwalk. He stared around him in momentary confusion, then looked down at the marbled lump of steaming flesh near his feet. Revulsion rippled his features, and he stepped aside quickly, then turned and saw the *Enterprise* crew for the first time. For an instant, they stared at one another, the tableau frozen in time. Then, with an oath and the smooth movement of a man well trained to arms, the Romulan raised something in their direction.

"DOWN!" someone roared. Later, Chekov couldn't be certain if it was he, Spock, McCoy, or all three of them together. They each scrambled for what meager cover was available, just as an explosion rocked the station, throwing them all off-balance. The Romulan rocked like a ship on unsteady seas and stumbled a few steps sideways.

Behind Chekov, McCoy cried out, his voice a sharp wail of terror. The security chief spun in the doctor's direction, and a blast from the Romulan's weapon nearly lifted the Russian off his feet, spinning him back around the way he'd come. Pain bloomed and rushed pell-mell for his brain. He clutched the wound, and sagged to his knees on the floor.

Legs wide and braced, the Romulan lifted his weapon again and aimed it not at Chekov but beyond him. "Let him go, Vulcan," he hissed.

Chekov blinked hard against the pain and turned, and his sweat turned icy cold.

When the unexpected explosion shook the station, McCoy was hurled off-balance. He grabbed at the catwalk's narrow banister, trying to catch himself, but his hand slid along the surface made slick by the creature's residue. Unable to gain a solid hold, he hit the banister hard and flipped over the side.

To McCoy, it seemed like slow motion. Black-clad fingers grasped like claws, clutching for a hold and sliding along the damp metal uprights. As he fell free, twisting, a hand shot out from between the uprights and snatched him by one wrist. The doctor came up short, gasping, pain tearing through his shoulder as it wrenched backward by the pull of his full weight.

It was Spock. The Vulcan's fingers dug tightly, painfully, into McCoy's wrist, and hauled back. The doctor twisted in the first officer's grasp, his own fingers clawing for purchase on Spock's wrist and lower arm, securing a frenzied hold around the narrow limb with both hands. McCoy looked up, eyes swimming with tears of pain and fear. Far above the tiny life-saving thread of their joined hands, Spock's face was contorted with effort, his pallid cheek pressed tightly against the railings.

"Let him go, Vulcan."

Spock turned toward the voice, strain etched deeply into the ascetic lines of his face. "I cannot do that," he answered simply, as though it were the most logical thing in the world to say. His fingers tightened around McCoy's wrist in silent reassurance. If he had anything to say about it, Spock would not let the doctor fall, but he was weakened by the creature's draw on his energy reserves. How long could he hope to hold on?

"I said, let him go," the Romulan repeated. "Or this one dies."

"Spock . . ." McCoy grunted. And then all hell broke loose.

From above McCoy's head came the sound of battle, as two bodies collided and fell, hitting the floor hard enough to make both combatants grunt with pain. Voices yelled, but he couldn't make out the words through the red haze of pain in his arm. Something skittered across the floor, and flesh struck flesh with so solid a crack that it made the doctor's wince in sympathy.

Then, suddenly, Leno's face was beside Spock's, cheek against metal as she sprawled on the floor beside the Vulcan, thrust her right arm between the railings, and stretched downward. "Give me your other hand!" she demanded.

Pain raged in McCoy's shoulder, a living thing with tearing teeth. Biting his lip against the agony, he gingerly released his hold on Spock's forearm and clutched at the rescue promised by Leno's outstretched hand. Flailing fingers brushed with an agonizing sweetness. Leno drove herself hard against the railing, and her thick, strong fingers closed around McCoy's wrist in a tight grip.

"Now!" Spock grunted and McCoy felt a lurch as they hauled back on his screaming arms. Using their free arms for leverage, and then their feet as they swung around on their rumps, they pulled McCoy in like a prize catfish out of the Mississippi.

It seemed to take forever until McCoy felt the stability of metal under his hands. He grasped for it feverishly, sweaty face against his arms, willing his fingers to close tightly over the slick uprights.

"Hang on!" Leno encouraged. "We've almost got you!"

McCoy didn't know if he could, didn't know how he did, but he managed long enough for them to reach over the banister together and gain new purchase. The doctor clutched them in a death grip and, inch by weary inch, the Vulcan and the security guard brought him back from the brink.

McCoy toppled over the railing, landing hard and bruisingly. He didn't care that it hurt, didn't care that his arms were numb while his shoulders bleated pain like a terrified sheep. It was wonderful to feel the pain and to know he was *alive!*

Gasping, he raised his head and focused on the others through a fall of sweat-soaked hair. Spock was ashen against the black cowl of his e-suit, his chest heaving for breath.

"I may have arms like a neanderthal from now on," McCoy panted. He reached for Spock's hand, unable to tell whether or not he squeezed it as hard as he hoped. "Spock . . ." He swallowed hard, working up saliva. "If I ever again say anything nasty about you . . ." He licked his lips. ". . . and I probably *will* . . . I don't mean it."

Spock's breathing was a rough rasp. "I shall endeavor to remember that," he replied quietly, and his other hand rested briefly on the doctor's shoulder.

"And *you!*" McCoy focused on Leno. He had never in his entire life seen anyone so dirty. Her cowl was pushed back, her hair free and wildly tangled. The right sleeve of her e-suit was torn almost free of the shoulder. Head to toe, she was smeared with grime. "I never thought . . . !" He shook his head. "Come here." Leaning forward, he surprised her by hugging her fiercely. "What are you doing here?"

"I told you I'd meet you here," she reminded him, her voice quiet in his ear. Her hands pushed gently at his arms. "Careful, Dr. McCoy. I'm pretty dirty."

"Pretty dirty!" He sat back and looked at her. "You look and smell like you crawled through a sewer to get here!"

Her small smile was cockeyed and not quite happy. "That might have been one of the places."

Only then did he notice the dried blood under her fingernails and the blotches of it on the knees of her e-suit. "Leno!"

Her hands caught him, keeping him away. "I'm all right, Dr. McCoy," she assured him. "It's not mine." Her eyes became hooded, distant. "When I got out of the turbolift car, I had to come around to the first shaft we climbed and go down the rest of the way from there. I, uh . . . I had to move Markson's body in order to get past the wreck of the turbolift car."

Ohmigod . . . McCoy sat back on his heels, shaken. "Well, what *happened?*" He looked up, focusing on the room beyond for the first time, and saw Chekov holding a weapon on the unconscious Romulan, who lay sprawled at the security chief's feet.

Chekov gestured with the plasma gun. *"He* happened. But not for long, thanks to Leno."

She shrugged. "I showed up at the right time, that's all. But I can't take all the credit. We make a good team, Chief."

"Yes, we do," Chekov responded and winced.

"You're hurt!" McCoy struggled to his feet and, making a wide circuit around the snoozing Romulan, hurried over to inspect the Russian's arm.

"It's not bad, Doctor," Chekov said stoutly. "It was meant to debilitate, not to kill."

"I don't care what it was meant to do!" McCoy took a few moments to tend the wound. "What was that explosion?" he demanded.

"And where's Hallie?" Leno asked, looking around. Their expressions told her all she needed to know, and she shut her eyes with a world-weary sigh.

"I believe the station was fired upon," Spock answered the doctor.

"Jim wouldn't do that," McCoy argued. "Not with all of us still aboard."

"The captain may not have had any choice in the matter, if the *Enterprise*'s weapons systems are malfunctioning as is the rest of the ship," Spock reminded them.

McCoy curled his lip. "How convenient. We can be blown up by our own ship. We're damned lucky it wasn't a photon torpedo."

"Very lucky, Doctor. Given the unanticipated appearance of our visitor, we must consider the possibility that the Romulan ship may have opened fire on the station."

"With one of their own men aboard?" Leno demanded. "That's sick!"

"Not if they would rather lose the station than see it fall into Federation hands," Chekov reminded her. "We came pretty close to our own version of that." He quickly filled her in on how close the *Enterprise* had been to self-destruct. The news made her fall silent, her expression troubled.

McCoy grunted. "Well, why did that Romulan weapon work when ours have been drained?"

"I surmise that the immediacy of the situation worked in the Romulan's favor," Spock replied. "He had just beamed aboard. The creature would need at least a few moments to recognize the food source, even were it already familiar. As he fired his weapon so soon after his arrival—"

"Time was on his side," Leno finished. She eyed the weapon in Chekov's hand. "Do you suppose it still works?"

"Unknown, Ensign."

Her expression was grim. "Can we try it out on him and see for ourselves?"

"I think it would be more to our advantage to wake our friend and see what he has to tell us," Chekov suggested. He nudged the prone body with his toe and raised his eyes toward McCoy. "Doctor?"

"I think that's a splendid idea, Lieutenant."

Spock shifted. "While you do that, I shall endeavor to contact the *Enterprise* and learn what has transpired. I am concerned that if the Romulans fired on the station, they may likewise have fired on the ship. And she is without shields."

"But if your idea is working, Spock, and they're able to raise power—"

"I doubt very much if the ship has had time to raise adequate power to shield against a direct attack, Doctor."

"Wait a minute," Leno interrupted. "The ship has power now? When did that happen?"

"It's a long story, Ensign," Chekov replied.

Spock tiredly got to his feet, and McCoy rose with him. "Spock, we have to get you out of here soon," the doctor said quietly. "Your reserves are being depleted by the creature." He didn't need to use his mediscanner to see how badly the Vulcan was doing.

"We cannot leave the generator so long as it offers us a tenuous contact to the *Enterprise,* Doctor," Spock said quietly. "And moving me will gain us little. If we are not rescued or effect an escape on our own, it will not matter shortly."

McCoy wanted to swear, wanted to argue with the Vulcan's logic but, as usual, there was no point to it. Spock was right. "I don't have any of the stimulant left, Spock," he apologized. "I pumped it into Hallie when I tried to resuscitate her."

"As you should have. No regrets, Doctor."

McCoy met the Vulcan's eyes in a look of deep understanding. "No regrets, Spock." He cleared his throat. "Now, go see if you can get in touch with Jim and let him know we're all right. We'll take care of this guy."

"Thank you, Doctor." Spock turned away and settled again before the generator, his hands on the console controls.

McCoy turned back toward the others. "Leno, if you'd be so kind as to assist me?"

"Gladly, Dr. McCoy." She lifted the Romulan by his armpits and knelt behind him, securing her arm firmly under his chin in a headlock. When she was settled and sure of her hold, she nodded.

McCoy shook the Romulan, who stirred groggily and opened his eyes. When he saw the two Federation officers staring down at him, and his own weapon pointed at his chest, he tried to lunge to his feet, but Leno held him firmly against her, her upraised knee against his spine. "Give me an excuse," she murmured quietly in his ear. "Please." She pulled him back toward her, letting him feel the pressure of her knee against his backbone and the surety of her hold. "You know I can do it, and you know that I *will* if you give me just cause."

"That's enough, Ensign," Chekov said lightly. He

kept the weapon pointing at the Romulan's stomach in the silent threat of a gut shot. "You don't need to harass the prisoner just yet."

"Prisoner?!" The Romulan spat like an angry feline and struggled against Leno's grip. "You have no right to—"

"We have every right!" Chekov snapped, and Leno tightened her hold. "You beamed aboard this station armed—"

"To protect what is ours! To put an end to your depredations aboard a Romulan station! *Reltah* is not your property! What have you done with her crew?"

The doctor leaned forward. "Seems to me, son, that we're the ones in the position to ask questions. Suppose you tell us what a Romulan space station is doing in Federation territory?"

"The Federation is peopled by thieves and liars! You stole this vessel from the Romulan Neutral Zone and murdered its crew to gain our secrets! You will not succeed in your bid for dominion over us!"

Chekov leaned over and pressed the business end of the weapon he held up against the Romulan's chest. "Shut up," he said tiredly, and didn't look at all surprised when the alien closed his mouth with a nearly audible snap. The Russian looked up at the others. "Do we have any way of tying him up?"

"Well . . ."

"This e-suit material is pretty strong. We can use what's left of my sleeve to tie his hands and ankles together."

"That sounds fine, Ensign," Chekov said. "Remind me to give you a commendation when we get back aboard the ship."

"You're on, Chief." She freed the binders from the Romulan's waist and handed them to the security chief, who quickly fit them around the alien's wrists.

242

"Must stink, being confined by your own gear," she purred in his ear and grinned. She held out her arm for McCoy to tear away the rest of her sleeve. Only when the Romulan was adequately bound did she release her hold on his neck and scoot back. She massaged her arm and surveyed their handiwork with pride, then looked up. "So, did you ever find any sign of that creature we saw?"

Chekov and McCoy exchanged looks, and the security chief reached out a hand to pull Leno to her feet. "You might say that, Ensign." He drew her toward the edge of the catwalk and the view of Engineering.

McCoy watched the strong play of emotion that washed over the ensign's face when she got her first real look at the creature. She tried several times to say something but fell silent before each attempt bore fruit. Finally, she turned and cocked her head at the watchful Romulan. "Has he seen this thing yet?"

"In all the hubbub of his arrival, I don't think he noticed," McCoy replied.

"Oh, this I gotta see!" Leno walked over and snagged the Romulan's arm. He bucked under her touch, but she held on and dragged him toward the edge. "I'm not going to throw you over," she assured him, though McCoy thought the idea might appeal to her. "I just want to prove to you that the Federation isn't at fault here." She hefted him up and turned his face outward. "What do you think of that?"

The Romulan's reaction was every bit as good as Leno's had been. His eyes widened, and he stared as though unable to comprehend the sheer size of the creature. "What is this thing?" he murmured finally.

"We're not certain," McCoy supplied. "All we know is that it drained this station of its power."

The Romulan turned hollow eyes toward the ship's doctor. "Is the station crew dead?"

McCoy paused, weighing the factors in imparting this piece of information, and decided it didn't much matter. "Yes."

"Killed by that creature." It wasn't really a question.

"It drained them of energy," McCoy said. "Just as it's draining Spock. Just as it will drain all of us."

"There must be a way to destroy it!"

"We don't want to destroy it, and if we did, I'm not sure we could," the doctor snapped.

The Romulan had the temerity to laugh. "Leave it to Starfleet to protect its murderers!"

"Hey!" Leno admonished, yanking the binders and bruising his wrists. "Are you serious, McCoy? Is there a chance we'll still get out of this?"

"If all goes as Mr. Spock plans," he assured her. "Scotty's working on changing the energy patterns on the ship's engines often enough that the creature can't realign to them so readily and feed. If that works, we'll get out of here." He patted her shoulder. "Don't worry."

Famous last words, Leonard. Famous last words.

Chapter Nineteen

"Scotty!" Kirk's voice caroled out, watching in horror as the big bird of prey started toward them.

"Power coming on-line," came the commander's cheerful reply from down in Engineering. "If you can give me just a few more minutes, sir, we should be able to—"

"We don't have a few minutes!" Kirk barked. "Sulu, evasive action! Zee minus ten thousand meters! Now!"

"Aye, sir!" the helmsman cried.

Oh, but it was slow! It was agony for Kirk, with his memory recalling a glorious vessel who jumped to fill his every command, not this sluggish ship who could barely get out of her own way. The Romulan vessel continued to bear down upon them, and Kirk thanked God and the creature that the *Elizsen's* weapons systems had gone awry and prayed that they would continue to do so. If the *Enterprise* made it at all and cleared *Elizsen's* attack, it would be by only inches.

"Sulu! We need shields!"

"Unavailable, Captain, if we want to continue our trajectory!"

And that was their very best choice in a bag full of rotten ones. Shields would be minimal and never stand the brunt of *Elizsen's* attack. At least with a small bit of maneuverability, maybe they had a chance. "Brace yourselves!" Kirk ordered.

The necessary few inches were not granted. *Enterprise* dropped under the bowline of the Romulan vessel, but one of the bird of prey's wings dragged across one edge of the saucer section in a glancing blow.

The sound reverberating through the hull set Kirk's teeth on edge, even as the warning klaxon began to scream. "Uhura! Damage reports! Scotty, I need power!"

Scott's voice from engineering overrode whatever it was Uhura called from her post. "I'm giving you all I can right now, Captain! I no sooner get a buildup than it gets expended—"

"I don't have much choice in the matter, Mr. Scott! Get more crew in there or change the frequencies more often if you have to, but get me power! Let me know as soon as we have impulse capabilities!"

Scott's sigh was a rattle in his chest. "Aye, sir!" The line went dead.

"Sulu, where's that ship?"

The helmsman worked feverishly over controls only barely functioning. "Coming around slowly above us, Captain. She may drop to our level."

"Can you scan her for damage?"

"Not at this time, sir."

"Put her on-screen." The topside cameras came into play, their reception only slightly better than it had been before. *Elizsen* was coming about.

Kirk rubbed his hands furiously over his face and scrubbed through his hair. What now? What move would the Romulans choose next, and what could he hope to do to counteract it in a ship with little power? Kirk stared at the Romulan vessel with narrowed eyes, almost insane with the stress of anticipation. What was happening over there? What was Telris waiting for?

He was somewhat surprised that the Romulan captain hadn't called for their surrender, for all the good it would do him. Kirk had as much intention of giving the *Enterprise* over to Telris as Telris had of turning his ship or the station over to the Federation.

Elizsen sat above them, like a hawk hovering over a chicken, but made no move. Had something overloaded and taken out Telris and his crew? It was a horrible thought but one Kirk willingly courted nevertheless.

Come on, he thought, sending the call across the intervening space to the creature inside the station. *Dinner's out here. Aren't you hungry? It's Romulan. You've had that before.*

"Uhura." Kirk's quiet voice was tinged with urgency. "Try to contact the landing party." What had happened aboard that cursed space station? Had anyone been hurt in the blast?

Uhura's fingers fairly danced over her console, striving to find power enough out of depleted stores to reach across to the stranded crew. Kirk didn't expect much, so he was very surprised when her face lit up. "I have Mr. Spock, sir! *He* contacted us!"

Relief flooded through the captain in a heady rush of emotion. He clutched the chair arms so hard his knuckles went white from the pressure. "Put him through, Uhura. Boost it as much as you can."

"Yes, sir. Go ahead."

"Spock!"

"Here, Captain." Oh, those calm, logical tones! There was much that Kirk wanted to know, wanted to ask, but the Vulcan cut him off, dispensing necessary information with the care of a Federation pharmacist.

They were well. The creature was there, seemingly unaffected by the attack on the station though it had begun making a humming noise for no apparent reason. Leno had rejoined them and with the addition of her to their ranks, they were able to shield the generator just that much better, hence their ability to call the ship, though there was no guarantee on how long their luck would last.

Kirk was startled when McCoy broke into the connection. "Jim, what's happening with that Romulan vessel?"

"How do you know about that?"

"Let's just say they sent us a little gift in the package of a Romulan warrior. An intact one, I mean. You wouldn't want to see the others. Or smell them. And don't you ever again tell me the transporter isn't something to be worry about."

"I wouldn't think of it. Is he all right?"

"He's in one piece, if that's what you mean, and as long as we keep Leno away from him, he'll stay that way. But it may give you some bargaining power, if the opportunity arises."

Kirk suddenly liked the way things were beginning to go. "Spock, keep an open channel to the ship as long as you can. Uhura, send a call to *Elizsen*. I want to talk to Captain Telris. *Now.*"

"Aye, sir." She steadied her headset with one hand. *"Enterprise* to Captain Telris." She glanced over her shoulder at Kirk, and her expression almost made him laugh. "Well, he's a rude individual, isn't he? Go ahead, Captain, but be prepared for the worst."

"Always, Lieutenant. Put him on-screen." The viewscreen image changed to the smoke-filled interior of the *Elizsen*'s bridge. Evidently the Romulans had been having as fine a time of it as the *Enterprise*. It did Kirk's heart good to see it.

Telris glared at him. "Are you ready to surrender, Kirk?"

Kirk snorted at the Romulan's bravado. "Hardly, Telris." He folded his arms challengingly. "I thought you should know that my people aboard the space station have taken a prisoner. A *Romulan* prisoner."

"Romulan!" Telris's meaty fingers clutched the arms of his chair. "There are no Romulans alive aboard *Reltah!* Our sensors showed as much!"

"Better check them again." Kirk was delighted to have caught the Romulan captain off-guard. "They have as prisoner the only survivor of your attempt at transportation."

"Prove it," the Romulan captain challenged, his chin held high in arrogance.

"Be my guest to contact the station, Telris. My first officer is waiting to hear from you."

Telris's response was a wordless growl. "Get me the space station!" he ordered someone behind him, and in a moment, Spock's voice came through for all to hear.

"This is Spock, first officer aboard the Federation starship *Enterprise*. How may I be of service, *Elizsen?*"

"Let me speak to my crewman!" Telris demanded.

"Certainly. One moment, please." There was a pause, and then an unfamiliar voice came over the link.

"Commander? This is Orrien."

"Then you *did* survive transportation."

249

"Yes, sir. Unfortunately, the same cannot be said for my comrades."

Telris's eyes flicked toward Kirk, and the *Enterprise*'s captain thought for a moment that the Romulan would begin to rail against the Federation and accuse them again of being murderers. He was surprised when Telris remained silent. Maybe the Romulan commander was beginning to believe that Kirk had had nothing to do with the death of his men.

"And you are a prisoner of the Federation?"

A short pause. "Yes, Commander."

If Telris had more to say on the matter, he let it slide. "Kirk tells me a story, Orrien, of a creature aboard the space station." His look was challenging across their staticky connection, and Kirk met it without flinching.

"It is no story, Commander. I have seen this creature."

Kirk would have liked a picture of Telris's face when he heard the news. "Is someone making you say these words, Orrien?"

"No, Commander. They could threaten me with death, and still I would tell you the truth. There is such a creature aboard this station. It is huge and takes up much of the engineering section. They tell me—" He broke off, and Kirk heard faint voices in the background, as though he conferred with Kirk's crew over some point of discussion. "Commander, I am told by the Vulcan that this creature feeds on energy, which is why the station and its crew were so affected. They warn that the same could happen to our ship."

"Rest assured, Orrien, that nothing adverse is going to happen to our ship."

Kirk shook his head. And he thought *he* had

chutzpah! Was Telris so blind that he would ignore the obvious?

"However," the Romulan commander continued, his eyes fastening on Kirk, "*if* this creature contributed to *Reltah*'s debilitation and is, indeed, so great a hazard to ships, then it must be destroyed before it can cause further damage."

"We can't do that, Telris." Kirk jumped into the conversation. "This creature is like nothing ever before encountered. We have reason to believe that it may be sentient."

"*May* be sentient? *May* be, Kirk?" Telris waved a hand, scoffing. "I don't have time for this. The creature is a threat and should be eradicated."

Spock's voice came over the connection. "Commander, one of your own scientists, a Doctor Rinagh, made note of the creature's intelligence and—"

"I have no time to listen to this. I don't care whether or not this creature is sentient! That means nothing to me. For all I care, it could be the central governing body of a planet. The point is that it is a danger to us and, as such, it must be exterminated."

"*No*," Kirk said forcefully, and Telris's eyes widened in surprise. When the Romulan laughed, Kirk pounded on the arm of his chair. "Dammit, Telris! I'm a starship captain and not a philosopher, but I know you can't change the universe just because it doesn't fit your personal view of things! That creature has as much right to live as do we. I'm not any more eager to die than the next man, but if there's a way to survive short of killing that creature, then we have to do it!"

"Is all of Starfleet so belly-soft?" the Romulan commander inquired softly. "The creature is drawing off your power, Kirk." Kirk chewed his lip in thought.

Despite his initial desire to kill the creature to rescue his crewmen, he knew that what he had just told Telris was right—the creature must survive, if a way could be found. There was so much the Federation could learn from such a being. And if it were *more* than rudimentarily sentient, the possibilities were endless. Maybe he and Telris could negotiate . . .

Negotiate with a Romulan?

Kirk took a deep breath. "Telris, I want to make a deal with you."

The Romulan looked askance. "What sort of deal, Kirk?"

"One of your crew is being held aboard the space station by my people. You can have him back in one piece, if I get your promise to leave the creature alone and unmolested."

"And the alternative?"

"You have no alternative."

"What about *Reltah?* You're a fool if you think I intend to leave her behind in Federation hands."

"She's in no hands but the creature's right now, Telris." Did the creature even *have* hands? "Let the creature go, and I'll guarantee that Federation and Romulan scientists can work together on this, and on getting *Reltah* back into its home territory." Well, he was stretching things a bit there, making that kind of promise, but Kirk didn't think Starfleet would hold it against him *too* much.

Telris abruptly nodded. "All right, Kirk. Agreed."

"Fine."

"Orrien?" Telris intoned.

"Yes, Commander Telris?"

"You will assist what needs doing."

"Yes, sir!"

Bones's voice came over the link. "Well, that's right neighborly of you."

Telris nodded to his helmsman. "Retreat to a safe distance."

"Aye, sir."

Kirk waited, watching Telris and wondering why the contact was still open. Then the word caught his attention. "Safe? What do you mean, a *safe* distance?"

Telris folded his arms across his chest and raised his chin. "The creature will be destroyed, Kirk, even if it means that *Reltah* is destroyed along with it."

Kirk stared at him. "I thought we just went through all that!" Over the link, he heard McCoy's muttered 'Uh-oh.' "Telris, you can't destroy a living being just because it doesn't fit in with your plans."

Telris had the oiliest smile Kirk had ever seen. "Watch me." He gestured to someone beyond range of the screen. "Even with systems affected, *Elizsen* does not need much power to activate the encoded self-destruct aboard the space station."

"What?!" Kirk leapt to his feet.

"Surely, you don't think I trust your assurances, Kirk, nor will I risk *Reltah*'s falling into Federation hands. As for the creature, its presence gives me all the more reason to destroy the station. The Romulan Empire has very specific rules about the takeover of our outposts."

"You can't detonate the station! There are people aboard!"

"So?" Telris couldn't have cared less had he tried. "Only one of them is mine, and I deem his life worth all of yours."

"What about *your* ship?" Kirk demanded. "What about your crew?"

Telris flipped a lazy hand. "We will not die, Kirk. *Elizsen* still has power to retreat to a safe distance outside the blast range. It's a pity you do not." He gestured over his shoulder. "Activate station self-destruct sequence."

"Station self-destruct sequence activated, Captain," replied helm.

Telris stared down his nose at Kirk. "I shall enjoy watching the annihilation of the Federation's prized flagship. It is a shame that the proconsul could not be here to enjoy it as well."

"Telris!" Kirk's hands clenched with rage.

The Romulan helmsman nervously cleared his throat. "Captain?"

Telris glared, loathe to leave off gloating. "What is it?"

"Engine systems failing, Captain." The helmsman looked as though he wished he was anywhere but within arm's reach of Telris. His hands flew over the board without result. "We're slowing down!"

"What?!" Telris's eyes were wild. "Deactivate station self-destruct!"

"We can't, Captain! It's encoded for twenty minutes!" He ducked as Telris's arm whistled by close over his head.

"Who's a sitting duck now, Telris?" Kirk fairly crowed. He didn't like the odds, but at least they were evening up. "Spock! You've got twenty minutes to get out of there! Are there any shuttlecraft you can gain access to?"

"Not according to the maps I've seen, Captain." There was a moment's hurried consultation, during which Kirk heard something faintly humming in the background, then Spock's voice returned. "Orrien says there *are* individual escape pods aboard. We may be able to jettison those by using the generator, but it is unlikely we will clear the blast range in time."

"Then somehow we'll make time! Go, go!" Kirk spun about. "Rand!"

"Rand here, Captain," came her voice over the speakers.

"Keep searching for the landing party's signal as power builds! Get them out of there the minute you see it!"

"Yes, sir!"

"Scotty, we need impulse power in twenty minutes or there won't be enough left of us to sweep together!"

"I'm on it, Captain!" the chief engineer yelled from deep within the ship. "I'm working as fast as I can!"

Kirk's brain roiled. But would it be fast enough?

Chapter Twenty

ORRIEN'S HANDS, cuffed with the binders, extended imploringly toward Spock as the Vulcan reached to hurriedly disconnect the generator from its conduit. *"Please,"* the Romulan begged. "There is a chance we may not be successful in our escape. Please give me a moment to say good-bye to my people."

"Spock, we don't have time for this," McCoy urged, already standing at the top of the stairs. He glanced down at the creature, marveling at it, and hoped that it wouldn't feel much pain when the end came. Twenty minutes could pass pretty quickly when you weren't paying attention.

Spock stared deeply into the younger Romulan's eyes. Something passed unspoken between them. Spock lifted his hands from the generator. "You have thirty seconds."

"Spock—"

"Thank you." Orrien bent over the mike. "Commander Telris, can you read me?"

The connection came through immediately, though somewhat brokenly now that *Elizsen's* systems were being depleted. "What is it, Orrien?" Telris sounded harried, as well he might.

Orrien began speaking rapidly in Romulan, his tongue flowing over the cadences of his native speech, so much more melodic than Klingon. It took him less than thirty seconds to say what he needed to say, and he stepped back from the generator, flushed with success, his eyes bright.

"What was all that about?" McCoy asked suspiciously, not liking the jubilant look in the young man's eyes.

Spock raised an eyebrow. "He has just told his commander how to modulate the output of the *Elizsen's* engines to counteract the creature's effect on his ship," he said calmly.

Orrien kept his gaze steady. "I have no more wish to see my shipmates destroyed than do you! Your ship has a chance. Does not mine also deserve the same?"

Leno sputtered. "If it weren't for you Romulans, we wouldn't be in this mess."

"Ensign," Spock admonished gently. "This avails us nothing. The damage, if there is any, has been done. We have little time to dispute the matter in any case." He quickly disconnected the generator, slid it into its sling, and pushed it across the countertop toward Leno. She slung the carry strap across her shoulders. Her eyes, on Orrien, were murderous.

Spock nodded to Chekov. "If you do not wish to carry our prisoner, Lieutenant, you must at least release his legs." His dark eyes fastened on Orrien's face as the Russian bent to untie the Romulan's bonds. "In truth, *do* you know the way to the escape pods?"

The Romulan nodded eagerly. "Yes! I've seen the

schematics for this station. They are right below this level."

"I wouldn't trust him if I were you," Leno warned. "Why should he tell the truth?"

"Because he wants to live as much as we do," McCoy said. "Or at least I hope he does." He waved an arm. "Let's get moving!"

He was halfway down the stairs with the others behind him, Orrien being carefully watched between Chekov and Leno, when he realized that Spock wasn't with them. McCoy pulled up short, nearly causing Chekov to stumble over him, and wheeled around. The first officer was still seated at the console. "Spock! What the hell do you think you're doing?"

The Vulcan sighed wearily. "Remaining here, Doctor. I no longer have the strength to—" He wavered. His eyes abruptly rolled up in his head, and Spock pitched forward onto the floor.

"Dammit to hell!" McCoy pushed past the others, taking the stairs two at a time, and skidded to a stop on his knees beside the prostrate Vulcan. "Spock!" He rolled him over and checked his pulse through the material of the e-suit. Still alive, though the beat was rapid and a mere thread. He checked the Vulcan's eyes.

"Can't you give him something?" Chekov called.

"I don't have anything left," McCoy explained angrily. "I didn't think we'd be setting up housekeeping here."

"Doctor!" Leno urged. "We have to get moving!"

"Tell me something I don't know, Ensign." Taking a deep breath, McCoy bent and, contorting wildly and convinced he would die from a burst artery, he hefted Spock's body across his shoulders in a fireman's carry. He bobbed his head at the others. "Go on! Get moving! I'm right behind you!" His knees felt as if they would crack wide open as he stood with Spock's full weight. "If I don't pass out first," he muttered to himself and started for the stairs.

Orrien and Chekov were two levels down already and moving fast. Leno was still there.

"What the hell are you waiting for?" he demanded.

"Here!" She thrust the generator at him by way of reply and, before McCoy could think to protest, eased Spock off the doctor's shoulders and onto her own.

"Leno—"

"Look, Doctor, we don't have time for an argument. I'm younger than you and I'm trained to do this kind of thing. I can run with someone in a full body carry. Can you say the same thing?"

"Not unless I have several drinks in me, Ensign, and feel like embellishing my life's story," McCoy admitted. He hefted the generator. "Lead on."

He was astounded by how quickly she could take the stairs with Spock's lean body draped across her shoulders like a weird version of a mink stole. He clattered along behind her, gained the floor at her heels, and crossed engineering at a run. McCoy spared one final, brief glance at the creature they'd discovered. It vibrated, colors rushing outward like the rings from a stone tossed into a pool of water. The humming it made had risen to a chiming sound, like what McCoy had always thought the stars should sound like.

There was no time to marvel. Following Leno, they raced for a lower-level door being held open by Chekov and dashed through into the outside corridor.

It was little more than a narrow stairwell, leading them upward. Orrien hurried ahead of them, running awkwardly with his bound hands behind him. Chekov ran hot on his heels should the Romulan try anything nasty. Behind them came Leno, her face flushed with exertion, Spock bouncing across her shoulders, and McCoy tagged along last, heart drumming in his ears.

"Up here!" the Romulan cried and held open another door. "The escape pods are at the top of these stairs!" He dashed through and they followed him down and around a corner.

Chekov skidded to a stop, his wail of dismay heralding news McCoy was certain he didn't want to hear. The security chief pounded his fist against the transparent wall separating them from the escape pod bay and didn't seem to care when it set his arm to bleeding again.

"What's the matter?" McCoy asked, panting. He wiped sweat out of his eyes and turned. "Oh, hell . . ."

The podbay doors were wide open to the universe, flooding the bay with vacuum. The pods were there, but inaccessible so long as those doors were open.

"Try the generator!" Leno gasped, shifting Spock's weight more evenly across her broad shoulders.

"We don't have time!"

"We don't have time *not* to try, Doctor!" Chekov rasped. He thrust the Romulan weapon into McCoy's hand and all but tore the generator off the doctor's shoulder, hurling the sling aside and pulling free the connecting wires, his eyes searching feverishly for a conduit. His hands were shaking so badly that McCoy wondered if he'd even be able to make the connections.

He couldn't watch. He turned his back and stared at the vastness of space beyond the open bay doors. The *Enterprise* was out there, somewhere, and the *Elizsen*. Who would successfully power up first? Would it be the *Enterprise* and would Jim bring them home in the nick of time? Or would it be the Romulan ship, homing in to destroy Kirk's beloved vessel at all costs?

* * *

Kirk knew his unceasing pacing wasn't doing any good to his ribs, but he couldn't sit still, not with so much hanging in the balance. "Power, Mr. Sulu?"

"No access to impulse power as yet, Captain, but systems are on the rise."

Too slowly, much too slowly. The Romulan helmsman had said detonation was encoded for twenty minutes. That was down to fifteen now, but would the creature's presence change that? Lessen it? Extend it? Kirk just didn't know and couldn't guess.

On the viewscreen, *Valgard* was being drawn in by the same tractor beam pulses with which they'd hoped to bring the *Enterprise* closer to *Reltah*. Even the little bit more power afforded the starship by Mr. Scott's work in Engineering allowed them to do that much, for all the good it would do. If they didn't get impulse power in less than fifteen minutes, the only consolation to Jaffe and Corey would be that they got to die among friends instead of alone in a shuttlecraft.

"Can you scan *Elizsen*, Sulu? Are they powering up?"

"Trying, Captain." The helmsman bent over his controls. "Hard to get a clear reading, sir. She's moving, but much too slowly to clear the blast range."

"But she's moving," he mused. "How did they manage that?"

"*They* don't have a shuttlecraft to worry about," Sulu reminded him. "Or people on the station. Not that they care about, anyway."

"And they had less ground to make up, sir," Estano added from the weapons console, where he could do absolutely nothing but stare at controls that wouldn't respond. He looked like he'd like to take a potshot at the *Elizsen* and, had they the power, Kirk might have let him. "But we have Mr. Scott and over four hundred Human crew. That ought to make some difference."

Kirk liked the younger man's enthusiasm. "Very true, Mr. Estano. Thank you for reminding me." The captain pulled at his lip. The pain in his side had dulled to a numbing ache. Evidently, he'd convinced it that he wasn't going to pay attention to it, so it had decided to go to sleep. Good. "Any sign of life pods from the station?"

"No, sir," Sulu responded heavily. He didn't need to tell Kirk that there was a good chance they wouldn't see any. Even if the landing party got to them on time, there was no guarantee they could jettison them, let alone get clear of the station before she blew. And without transporter capabilities, there was no way the *Enterprise* could aid in their escape.

"Any contact with the away team, Uhura?"

"Nothing, sir," she said tensely, a fine line sketched between her arched brows. "But it isn't likely we will, if they're trying to make their escape."

Kirk nodded brusquely. She was right, of course.

"Transporter room to bridge."

Kirk's heart skipped a beat. Was something finally going to go right after all? He crossed the bridge in two strides and hit the communications button on his chair. "Kirk here, Rand. What is it? Have you found them?"

Her voice had its usual clipped, precise tones, but she sounded shaken, nevertheless. "The signal is weak due to our low power, Captain, but I believe I've located the landing party's coordinates. But I can't beam them back, sir!" He had never heard her sound so desperate.

"You can't—" Kirk sank into his chair, unable to stand against this final blow. "Why not?"

"Interference from the buildup of detonation

aboard the space station is playing havoc with the signal," she explained bleakly. "I can't get a clear fix, so I don't dare attempt transport."

Kirk grasped at straws. "Is there any way to boost the signal?"

"Negative, Captain. Even if we were up to full power, we'd still need a clear signal from the source. If I can't get a fix, I can't bring them home." She sounded so defeated.

Kirk knew how she felt. He did not want to state the obvious, but he needed to hear it. "Rand—" He swallowed hard. "There's *no way* we can transport the away team back to the ship?"

"I'm afraid not, sir, not short of stopping the detonation."

And there's no way to do that. Rage poured through Kirk in a heady rush that nearly set his ears to ringing. "Scotty!" he barked.

"Aye, sir!" came the chief engineer's immediate response.

"Any estimate on how soon we'll have impulse power?"

"It's building, Captain," came the Scotsman's response. "I put it at fifteen minutes."

Kirk glanced at the clock. Ten minutes until detonation. There was only one thing left to do. "Mr. Sulu, is *Valgard* back aboard the ship?"

"They've just brought her in, Captain. Jaffe and Corey are suffering from the effects of exposure and are being taken to sickbay."

Kirk was sorrier than he could say that it wouldn't be worth the effort. "Put *Elizsen* on the screens, please." The view changed to that of the Romulan vessel, slowly pulling away *(away,* damn them!) from the *Enterprise.* Kirk took a deep breath, decided. "Mr. Sulu, divert all power to the tractor beam."

The helmsman turned in his chair and gifted his captain with a singularly confused expression. "Sir?"

"You heard me, Mr. Sulu," Kirk said calmly. He could not remember ever having felt so calm in his entire career. He crossed his arms over his chest and stared at the screen. "Direct the tractor beam on *Elizsen*." His mouth pursed, and he stared with hard eyes at the Romulan vessel.

Pleasure lit the Asian's dark eyes. "Aye, sir!" His head bobbed in a quick nod and his fingers danced across his board. "Power being diverted to tractor beam, Captain. Training on *Elizsen* . . . now!"

Watching, Kirk couldn't tell for certain if the bird of prey slowed in its flight, but it certainly looked that way. That suspicion was confirmed seconds later when Uhura turned toward him, a vindictive smile on her face. "Captain, Commander Telris would like to have a word with you."

"Visual only, Uhura."

The image of the *Elizsen* vanished, to be replaced by a silent interior view of her bridge. Telris looked as though he was about to have a seizure. His arms thrust in all directions, replete with rude gestures, and his face darkened as though he might go apoplectic any moment. He was screaming at the top of his lungs, or that's what Kirk supposed he was doing, anyway.

"Keep the tractor beam steady on, Mr. Sulu," Kirk ordered, and let the corner of his mouth rise in a slight smile that almost drove Telris to the breaking point, if looks were any indication.

"She's not going to get away, sir," the helmsman vowed darkly.

Kirk considered the viewscreen. Neither were they.

McCoy found himself watching Orrien and not liking what he saw. The Romulan didn't appear

particularly upset about the escape pod situation, certainly not as upset as he had every right to feel . . .
. . . if he really cared.

"You knew about this, didn't you?" McCoy asked quietly.

The Romulan turned toward him, features a blank, jaw swollen from Leno's attack. "What?"

"You knew about the podbay being open. You knew we couldn't reach the pods to escape. You sent us down here on a wild-goose chase."

Leno looked up from where she was watching Chekov furiously at work, Spock still slung like a sack of potatoes over her shoulders. "What's the matter, Doctor?"

McCoy nodded toward Orrien and his lip curled in disgust. "I think he knew about this. I think he knew that the pods were inaccessible."

Leno watched the Romulan, a speculative expression on her face. Chekov spoke without looking up. "How could he have known?"

"He was in a ship outside the station, wasn't he?" Leno challenged, following McCoy's line of reasoning. "He could have seen it from there."

Orrien spread his hands as wide as they would go in the binders, palms up in supplication. "I knew nothing! I have no more desire to die than do you! I—" He cut off when Chekov shoved the generator aside.

"Govno!" The Russian spat, shaking his head. "It's no good, any of it! The creature must have finally gotten a taste for the generator, because I can't get any power out of it at all." He looked back over his shoulder at the podbay and the open vista of space beyond. "We're not going out this way."

"There have to be other bays," Leno argued. "Probably on this level. If we just make a circuit—"

"That's providing we have the time," McCoy reminded her. "Detonation was encoded for twenty minutes." He glanced for the time. "We have ten minutes left."

"Then that's ten minutes we have left to try to stay alive!" Chekov vowed hotly. "Come on! Leno had a good idea. We'll circle around this level and—"

Orrien interrupted him. "There aren't any more bays on this level. I told you, I've seen the schematics. The next one is one level up, but a quarter around the station."

Chekov's eyes bore into his. "Can we make it in ten minutes?"

The Romulan's gaze was level, meeting the Russian's eyes unflinchingly. "We can make it in five if we run."

"Then let's go."

"I can't believe you're going to trust him again!" Leno was incredulous.

"What choice do we have, Ensign?" Chekov asked bitterly. He turned and held out his arms. "Let me take Mr. Spock."

She took a step backward. "Not on your life, Chief. I've already gotten acclimated to the weight. It'll throw you off your stride."

"Leno—"

"For God's sake, you two, we don't have time to argue about it!" McCoy chastened them. "We'll discuss this in committee when we get back aboard the ship. Now, will you come *on!*" He turned, gave Orrien a shove, and followed in the Romulan's wake. The security guards fell in at the doctor's heels.

A stitch of red-hot fire had worked its way up under McCoy's rib cage, flaring with every breath he took as he pounded along after Orrien. The run certainly felt a whole lot longer than five minutes, but McCoy knew that wasn't the case when he checked the time. Behind him, he heard Chekov's and Leno's ragged breathing. The woman must be exhausted from hauling Spock around, but she wouldn't admit it and wouldn't give up.

"This way!" Orrien urged from several yards ahead. "It's not much farther!" He skidded into a doorway. "In here!"

"Thank God," McCoy panted. But was it worth it? Would five minutes grant them enough time? He followed Orrien and stumbled to a stop just inside the door, catching himself on the jamb, his lung heaving white heat. He stared around him. "What the hell is this?"

It wasn't a podbay, or a shuttlebay, or anything remotely resembling any type of escape from the station. Orrien had led them into a small lounge fronted with wide windows affording a view of the galaxy and the two ships, which McCoy might have appreciated at another time, but not today. He turned and stared at the Romulan just as Leno and Chekov raced into the room and stopped dead.

Leno pulled up too short, and Spock slid from her shoulders into an untidy heap on the floor. "What the hell is *this?*"

"My question exactly, Ensign," McCoy growled. He rounded on Orrien. "What's the meaning of this?"

The Romulan laughed with malicious delight. "You Federation sheep are so easy to dupe! You didn't honestly think I'd let you escape from here, did you?"

"What are you talking about?" Chekov asked tensely.

"I promised my commander that I would do what needs doing. Did you really think that meant helping you escape?" He laughed, delighted. "You *did!*" He grinned openly at Leno. "You were right, little warrior woman. The other podbay *is* down below, just around the corner from where we were. Too bad you didn't have a schematic of the station to study."

Leno stepped over Spock and slowly advanced toward Orrien, fists coiled and ready to strike. The Romulan backed away from her and around toward the door. His eyes were watchful, but his delight at the upset was evident. "Only Federation worms would be so dishonorable as to strike a bound man."

Chekov moved in the other direction, sliding in behind the Romulan before he realized it. "No, Ensign," Chekov admonished Leno calmly, "this one's mine." He stepped into the punch, catching Orrien off-guard, and sent him flying against the wall where he sprawled, unconscious. *"That's* for the arm," the Russian muttered and sucked his bruised knuckles.

McCoy turned away from the fracas and stared out at the stars, at the distant images of the *Enterprise* and the bird of prey. This would be his last view of home, of friends. He lifted Spock onto a couch and sat down beside him, motioning for the others to join them. "We all may as well get comfortable." He watched the *Enterprise,* his eyes flicking back and forth between the ship and his clock.

"How much time do we have, Doctor?" Leno asked quietly, perched on the edge of one cushion.

"Two minutes, Christina."

"Oh." She chewed her lip. "What are we going to do?"

"That's the sixty-four-thousand-dollar question." And McCoy closed his eyes.

"Captain!" Mr. Scott's joyous voice interrupted Kirk's somewhat vindictive perusal of the Romulan vessel, startling the *Enterprise's* captain out of his reverie. "We have impulse power!"

Kirk could not have been more startled if God himself had appeared on the bridge to make the announcement. "Time, Sulu!" he barked, as the bridge lights came up to full.

"Two minutes, Captain!"

Not enough time, not damn near enough time . . .

"Rand!"

"Here, Captain!" her voice responded immediately.

"Any change in the signal output from the station?"

"None, sir."

That aced it, then. His friends would die. But if they were going to be forced to forfeit their lives, the Romulans would know the cost. "Status on *Elizsen.*"

"Sensors indicate she's still power-low, sir," Estano responded from his station. He grinned. "I guess all us Humans made the difference."

"I guess so," Kirk agreed. "Mr. Sulu, reverse tractor beam. I want to push *Elizsen* out of here."

"Sir?"

"You heard me. Uhura, get me Captain Telris."

"Yes, sir." She nodded. "Go ahead."

"On-screen." The viewscreen flared as Kirk stood and tugged his jacket into place, and stepped forward.

The bridge of the *Elizsen* looked like hell. Emergency lights were low and muddy-looking, the air smoky from burned circuitry. Telris wheeled around and glared at the screen. "Kirk! I demand you release my vessel at once!"

"Or you'll do what, Telris?" Kirk challenged. "You're in no position to make any threats." He folded his arms across his chest. "We're reversing the tractor beam and giving you a shove now." He nodded at Sulu to begin the process. "I want you out of blast range and out of here, preferably back over your own border."

"Or you'll do what?" Telris mimicked. "You have no power."

Kirk smiled lazily, one eye on the clock. "Move us out, Mr. Sulu," he ordered quietly before responding to Telris's jibe. "Don't we? Mr. Estano, give the good captain a warning shot over his bow, please."

"Gladly, Captain."

On the screen, Telris flinched as the *Elizsen* was narrowly missed by the phaser blast. "How do you have power?" he demanded.

"That's for us to know, Telris. And that was your only warning. You're going back home if I have to cart your carcass past the Neutral Zone by myself."

"So why not let us die?" Telris hissed.

"Why?" Kirk feigned surprise at the question. "Why, because I want you to be my emissary back to the proconsul."

"Your emissary?" Telris asked guardedly. "In what regard?"

Kirk's voice grew only slightly harder than his expression. "Send her a warning from me and from the Federation. Tell her that we are not sleeping—that we *are* watching. That we are *always* watching. Tell her your freedom was bought by the lives of my dearest friends. That's rare coinage, Telris, and I will exact a full due if our paths ever cross again."

The Romulan commander started to speak, then evidently thought better of it. "Power!" he snapped at his helmsman.

"Minimal rise, Commander, but not enough to escape blast range in time."

Telris seemed to be having trouble swallowing. "I'll deliver your message, Kirk. Beware the reply."

Kirk met the challenge. "I'll be waiting." At his nod, Uhura cut the connection. As the *Enterprise* accelerated, pushing the *Elizsen* ahead of her out of blast range and toward the Romulan border, Kirk turned to watch the final seconds count down on his friends' lives.

Five, four . . . McCoy kept his silent count. Three, two, one . . .

And then, nothing.

Time ran out. There was no explosion, but suddenly everything was full of light.

McCoy saw the patterns against his eyelids and opened them, astonished to find himself still alive. Chekov and Leno blinked at each other and stood to stare out the windows, their mouths gaping in astonishment.

"Doctor!" Leno called, and glanced at him quickly over her shoulder, loathe to give up the view. "Do you see it?"

He stood, amazed, and approached the windows. He couldn't see the *Enterprise* and wondered fleetingly where she might be, even as his eyes were caught by the view outside. Around the station flowed a riot of color, as though they'd all been caught inside some child's paintbox.

"Did the self-destruct fail?" Leno asked wonderingly.

"I don't know," McCoy mused, eyes rapt. He leaned forward to peer more closely at the patterns of light, and suddenly grinned. "Holy cow—"

"What is it, Doctor?" Chekov asked.

"Take a closer look out there and tell me if you see what I see."

They both leaned forward, and McCoy knew by their expression that they did.

Once, on vacation, the doctor had witnessed phosphorescent algae on the ocean. It had been a singularly gorgeous sight, and that was what this most reminded him of. Scintillas of light flashed in all directions, strobing from red to green to blue to other colors for which he couldn't supply a ready name.

"Is that . . . " Leno shook her head wonderingly. "Is that the creature?"

"Or what used to be the creature," Chekov amended. "Did we kill it, sir?"

"I don't think so, Lieutenant. I've been midwife to a lot of births, and I know babies when I see them."

Their faces brightened with delight. "You mean it was *pregnant?*" Chekov exclaimed.

McCoy shook his head. "Maybe, but I think it's asexual reproduction brought on by the intense consumption of energy from the detonation. We're damned fortunate that critter knows how to gorge itself."

"I'll say," Leno agreed, her wide eyes following the swirl of colors with all the avidity of a child at Christmas. "Maybe that's what it was looking for all along."

There was a sound deep in the bowels of the station, the sound of something kicking in, and suddenly the room was flooded with light as the station began to power up. For a moment, it was all disorientation, then McCoy suddenly heard a familiar voice. ". . . come in, please. *Reltah,* this is the *Enterprise.* Do you read us? Come in, please. *Reltah . . ."*

McCoy unhooked his communicator and flipped it open. "We read you loud and clear, *Enterprise,"* he drawled charmingly.

"BONES!"

He thought he'd never heard Kirk sound so happy. "Why, hello, Captain. Fancy talking to you again.

When I didn't see the ship, I thought you'd hightailed it for parts unknown."

Kirk was laughing with relief. "You old—What is all that out there?"

"It's a long story, Captain."

"I imagine it is. Is everyone all right?"

"Well, the Romulan's taking a snooze right now, courtesy of Lieutenant Chekov. Chekov and Leno and I are okay, but Spock needs sickbay right away. Do you have transporter capabilities?"

"We will in a few moments. Everything's coming back on-line. You just say the word, Doctor."

McCoy closed his eyes wearily. "I'm saying the word, Captain. It's time to come home."

Epilogue

CONTENT TO BE with his two closest friends again, Kirk followed McCoy and Spock toward the gymnasium and the anticipated game of Riseaway (and wouldn't McCoy have a surprise coming?). Spock had almost completely recovered, and the Romulans were gone on a receding tide of creative vilification, courtesy of Captain Telris. Two other starships had joined the *Enterprise,* to take over from here on, guarding the space station until Federation officials arrived to take over. A warning beacon had been placed in the area, and a report had gone out to Starfleet Command.

Let the big brass take care of it now. Kirk was glad to have it all be over.

The captain glanced over at McCoy as they walked. "It's hard to believe that creature just . . . *detonated* into all those babies."

"That is not precisely the case, Captain," Spock corrected from his other side. "It appears that the creature absorbed the shock of the blast, which should have caused the station to self-destruct, and overfed."

"So now there are more of them to worry about," Kirk mused. "Are we in any danger?"

"I postulate none at this time," Spock replied. "The residual energy from the blast consumption should be enough to sustain these creatures for some time. However, Starfleet Command will undoubtedly take precautions."

They started past the rec room, but McCoy paused in the doorway and shook his head. "Uh-oh."

Kirk backstepped to join him. "What's the matter, Bones?"

"Looks like a packed house, Jim." He smiled. "Scotty's holding court again."

"Oh, no." Kirk shouldered past his friend and stuck his head into the room. Couched comfortably in his usual chair, Montgomery Scott was once again holding forth.

Kirk cleared his throat loudly, and everyone in the room looked up. Scott smiled benignly. "Good evening, Captain!"

"Good evening, Mr. Scott, ladies and gentlemen." There were familiar faces in the crowd. Leno and Chekov sat near the front, sharing a bowl of finger food and ignoring Uhura's attempts to get them to try something on her plate that looked a little like jellied lint.

They had Kirk's sympathy. "What's this story about, Mr. Scott?" the captain inquired lightly.

"Oh, Martians, sir!" Scotty stressed. "Nice, safe, calm, normal Martians."

"Anyone who calls a Martian normal needs a vacation," McCoy said under his breath, and Kirk jabbed him with an elbow.

"Very good, Mr. Scott. Carry on." He backed out of

the room and ushered his friends down the corridor toward the gym. Kirk shook his head and chuckled.

"Now what?" McCoy asked.

"I don't know, Bones. Is a story about Martians any better than a story about ghosts?"

McCoy pursed his lips. "Well, Martians are certainly less scary than ghosts," he averred. "To my knowledge, no one's ever had nightmares about Martians."

"Tell that to anyone who heard 'War of the Worlds' the first time around." Kirk smiled. "At least in this day and age no one is likely to claim they've seen one."

"Oh, I don't know about that," McCoy singsonged. "He didn't have antennas and he wasn't little, but I do recall seeing *someone* with pointy ears and green skin in sickbay not all that long ago." He rolled his eyes toward Spock.

Spock glanced down at the doctor's impish face. "That is hardly surprising, Dr. McCoy, given your level of proficiency in the medical field."

Kirk couldn't suppress his laughter at the expression on Bones's face. It was good to have them home.

THE LONG-AWAITED FIRST ORIGINAL NOVEL BASED ON THE CRITICALLY ACCLAIMED TELEVISION SHOW

FAZ64W

#1 ALIEN NATION

THE DAY OF DESCENT

THE NEW NOVEL BY JUDITH AND GARFIELD REEVES-STEVENS

ALIEN NATION: a ground-breaking and thought-provoking television program that introduced the TENCTONESE, or NEW-COMERS, a race of aliens and former slaves who have landed on Earth and now comprise the world's newest and strangest group of immigrants.

THE DAY OF DESCENT is the incredible--never before seen--story of the Newcomers' first landing. The year is 1995 and a Tenctonese slave ship is headed for Earth and a landing in the California desert. As the Earth awaits its first encounter with an alien race, the Tenctonese are battling for their freedom. Suddenly, two men destined to be partners must work together for the first time--with the survival of both their peoples hanging in the balance.

POCKET
STAR
BOOKS

Coming in mid-February from Pocket Star Books